THE
HIDDEN
Diamond

CRYSTAL MM HUNTLEY

authorHOUSE®

AuthorHouse™
1663 Liberty Drive
Bloomington, IN 47403
www.authorhouse.com
Phone: 833-262-8899

This is a work of fiction. All of the characters, names, incidents, organizations, and dialogue in this novel are either the products of the author's imagination or are used fictitiously.

Published by AuthorHouse 10/31/2022

ISBN: 978-1-6655-7376-4 (sc)
ISBN: 978-1-6655-7446-4 (hc)
ISBN: 978-1-6655-7445-7 (e)

Library of Congress Control Number: 2022919980

Print information available on the last page.

Edited by Eric Rodammer

Cover image by Crystal MM Huntley

Scripture taken from The Living Bible copyright © 1971 by Tyndale House Foundation. Used by permission of Tyndale House Publishers Inc., Carol Stream, Illinois 60188. All rights reserved. The Living Bible, TLB, and the The Living Bible logo are registered trademarks of Tyndale House Publishers.

This book is printed on acid-free paper.

Acknowledgements

Dear Lord and Savior, Your abiding love lifted me from crippling wounds into healing and broke the harrowing chains of abuse. Your unfailing love has no bounds. You carried me through every grievous moment and taught my heart to forgive, transforming my deep scars into tools to reflect Your grace. Through You and You alone, all things are possible—all lives *can be* made anew. Only with the strength of Jesus Christ did I gain the courage and skills to write this book. I pray it is a blessing to all who read it.

I could not have written this story without the help of the many people my Lord and Savior has graciously placed in my life, including the multiple skilled therapists who spent countless hours guiding me out of dark spaces formed by wounds. I wish to give proper thanks to each one of you. But some, in particular, I desire to thank by name —

To my dearly beloved, Rich, I sincerely thank you. Your loving support and belief in me gave me the courage to take this leap and publish my works. Your selfless, patient, endless hours supported me while I remained engrossed in my computer to work on this project. Without you standing behind me every step of the way, this book would not exist. Through you, God showed me what true love is. And God graciously gave me you to gush all my true love into.

To my beautiful daughter Ella, my heart swells with gratitude. God gave me an angel the day He gave me you. I love you more than words could ever express. I will forever cherish those precious moments we spent brainstorming creative writing ideas. Through your youthful energy, we together fashioned the character of Dakota, which brought a much-needed entertaining lightness into a heavy topic.

I extend heartfelt thanks to my nephew Eric. I cherish the memory of the glint in your eye as you emphatically nodded in agreement to be my editor. Thank you for the many laborious hours you dedicated, between your intensive college studies, to proofread every typed word and punctuation within my manuscript. I am excited to watch you shine in a future career as an editor and fellow writer. I know you have what it takes.

To Trish, the mother-in-law of my eldest son, with warm appreciation, I give thanks. You saw my love of writing and selflessly gave your time and energy to teach me the skills you honed. I treasure those times we bonded a friendship over the written word, never, at the start, realizing our children would make us family.

And to Scott, the source of my first memory of the word "Awesome." Every time I hear that word, I think of you. Even though no other aspect of this story pertains to you, I injected your contribution each time my character, Dakota, used it. Thank you, dear Scott (1968 – 2021), for being a beloved brother. Rest in peace. I know you will dance the *awesomest* dance in Heaven.

Dedication

I dedicate *The Hidden Diamond* to each of you who have had families broken and dreams shattered by the hardened hearts of another's sins and those whose shining beauty has been buried deep beneath a lifetime of transgressions.

Light always swallows up the darkness. Let God's light shine into every dark crevice of your life so He can polish it into His brilliance and bring you back to the perfect, radiant diamond He created you to be. I pray that God's forgiveness restores you with the strength to heal. May my story inspire your own journey toward healing.

Reviews

What a beautifully written story of heartbreak and healing. Through faith, the healing begins within the heart. Crystal has a gift with her words . . . pulling at the heartstrings, she draws us in . . . with complex and moral questions. *Sandy Christensen*

Scripture Verse

"Hear them from heaven and forgive
And answer all who have made an honest confession;
For you know each heart."
1 Kings 8:39

Contents

Prologue...xv

Chapter 1..1
Chapter 2..7
Chapter 3..11
Chapter 4..19
Chapter 5..25
Chapter 6..29
Chapter 7..37
Chapter 8..43
Chapter 9..49
Chapter 10..59
Chapter 11..69
Chapter 12..77
Chapter 13..85
Chapter 14..93
Chapter 15..97
Chapter 16..103
Chapter 17..109
Chapter 18..115

Chapter 19..121

Chapter 20..127

Chapter 21..133

Chapter 22..139

Chapter 23..145

Chapter 24..153

Chapter 25..163

Chapter 26..167

Chapter 27..175

Chapter 28..183

Chapter 29..189

Chapter 30..193

Chapter 31..199

Chapter 32..207

Chapter 33..215

Chapter 34..221

Chapter 35..229

Chapter 36..235

Chapter 37..241

Chapter 38..251

Chapter 39..255

Chapter 40..261

Chapter 41..267

Chapter 42..271

Chapter 43..277

Chapter 44..285

Chapter 45..291

Chapter 46..297

Prologue

I know far too well the damage abuse inflicts on the soul. Forgiveness is crucial if one is to find peace once again. It is far easier to forgive a perpetrator who enters into a state of repentance, but sadly, that rarely happens. I wrote *The Hidden Diamond* with that in mind, giving the twist of a perpetrator who gains the courage to face his dark side and, with remorse, seeks forgiveness.

CHAPTER 1

ALDOUS

"OSCAR, WHAT DID YOU DO with my other slipper?" With the left one gripped in my hand, I searched this mutt's favorite places to stash things. "It has to be here somewhere."

Oscar cowered as he weaseled out from behind the couch. I shook the lone slipper in his face. "Where's the other one?"

He let out a squeaky bark and ran toward the kitchen. I followed behind, watching his short legs skid out from underneath him on the tile floor. His overgrown toenails scraped, sending a chill up my aching spine. The pug darted toward the basement door left ajar, then returned with my coveted item clenched firmly within his teeth.

Disregarding Oscar's mischief, I patted him on the head. "Good boy."

I slid my feet into the slippers. The painful balls of my big toes, along with my aching heals, rubbed smooth rawhide, polished to a dark caramel sheen—evidence of the many years of contact between my old, calloused feet and the inside of these slippers.

This very same pair had supported me well for many decades. No matter what obstacles life threw in my direction, I always depended on the sturdy build and excellent handiwork that had been poured into the construction of this footwear. Regardless of how horrible my day had been, this pair of slippers greeted me with warmth and comfort. Funny, that's more than I could say about most people who have entered my life.

I moved toward the front door. The little mutt bounded after me, his stump of a tail engaged in a perpetual spastic wag. That measly tail looked more like it belonged on the end of a shaved rabbit instead of a dog. Any canine would be insulted by such a scrawny appendage.

From the corner of my eye, I caught my reflection in the mirror Mariam had long ago hung next to the staircase. For some strange reason—I may never understand—I paused and stared into the reflective glass. The two eyes that gazed back, somewhere along the way, had lost their sheen, causing them to appear more like a dull gray instead of the attractive shade of blue Mariam fell in love with.

"Oscar, you stay here. I'll only be a minute. I'm going out to get the mail." The screen door slipped from my fingers and slammed shut behind me—an effective barrier between the animal and me.

Oscar whimpered as his nose pressed against the meshed wire.

"Mariam sure did a top-notch job at spoiling that beast," I mumbled as I shuffled down the steps toward the sidewalk. I drew in a deep breath of crisp autumn air, a refreshing change after the repressive temperatures of the long summer months. I've experienced many hot days in my time, but none seemed to melt the flesh from my bones quite as this past summer had.

I planted my feet firmly on the concrete and closed my eyes, allowing the cool, clear air to inflate my lungs. With my flimsy aluminum key in hand, I must have turned my body to the left, for the next thing I knew, my fist brushed up against something.

"Hey, that man scratched me."

I opened my eyes. A small boy, the size of an elf, stood beside me. His face scrunched up as if about to cry, giving me an instant reminder of that crazy, slipper-stealing mutt my wife had loved so much.

The lad turned away from me and wailed while a young woman, who must have been his mother, dashed toward him. She fell to her knees, drawing the distraught child into her arms. "Dakota, honey, what's the matter?"

"It's that man. He jabbed me with something right across my face. See, I think it left a scratch." The urchin child thrust an accusative finger in my direction.

"Oh, sweetheart, there's only a tiny red spot on your cheek. It'll go away before you know it. I'm sure it was an accident."

"Uh-uh, it was no accident. He did it on purpose."

I stuck my key in its designated slot and pulled out a bundle of envelopes and unwanted advertisements. "I didn't jab anybody. That hooligan child ran into me. The incident would never have happened if we were allowed to keep our own individual mailboxes in our own front yards. But nooo, this fiend called *progress* had to invade everything, even our postal delivery system. Now we're left with this crazy contraption that looks like a miniature steal apartment complex." My empty hand thumped the hard side of the undesired device.

"Excuse me? I didn't catch what you were saying." The mother stepped closer as she stared directly at me. Green specks floated within her blue eyes, illuminated by the afternoon sunlight.

"Don't worry. It was nothing." Since my Mariam had passed, I developed the bad habit of talking to myself. Consequently, this practice had become so ingrained that I no longer realized when I did it. "I'd advise you to keep a closer eye on your child in the future before he causes some real damage."

I peered down at the boy. Blotched freckles dotted his nose like a splattering of mud. "Next time, young man, if you happen to run into someone, you need to say, '*excuse me.*'"

"Well, I wish to apologize for my son's behavior. He didn't mean to bump into you. I'm sure you know how rambunctious a little boy can be. My name is Alexandra, and this here is Dakota." She stretched forth her hand with long sleek nails painted a pale peach, the same shade as Mariam's favorite mums.

Each fall, my wife searched every garden shop in the city to find the best-looking batch of premium peach-colored blossoms. Why can't I seem to get my thoughts off of my deceased wife? I placed her in the ground almost three years ago. By now, I should be over her and ready to move on like one of those swinging singles. But then autumn returns, and it's as if she passed away all over again.

The puny lad glared up at me. His wide eyes glimmered, so pale one would think he had stolen a piece of blue from the sky.

"You want *me* to say, 'excuse me?' *You're* the one who rammed into me." The child spun around and faced his mother. "You can't *polly jive* for me. I didn't do anything wrong. I ran to the mailbox and stood still beside that man when *he* spun around and jabbed *me* with his key. It was him, not me."

What was it with this breed of kids these days? Can't a parent do their job right and control them? In no way would Lacey have gotten away with speaking to me in such an unacceptable manner. And if she had tried, I would have delivered a firm smack right across her buttock. Strict parenting was expected back then, but today's society would peg you with child abuse. It's no wonder so many kids are out of control.

"Dakota, that's enough. And the word is, apologize, not *polly jive.*"

As I watched this young woman and her little nuisance, no desire to befriend them soaked in. I nodded my head and then turned back toward my house. Another subconscious grunt slipped out as I walked away.

"Dakota, it doesn't matter how it happened. No harm was done. Remember to use your manners next time when you talk with adults."

"Why should I? He wasn't very nice to me."

"We may never know why someone reacts how they do, but God made everyone special, just like He made you special. And when we honor God's creation, we honor our Lord."

"Well, in that case, God did a real good job at making that cranky old man an extra *special* grouch."

I heard every word this mother and her son spoke as I headed down the sidewalk toward my house. In the future, I might want to choose a different time to collect my mail, anything to avoid bumping into them again.

As I stepped back into the house, Oscar leaped about my feet, acting as if I'd been gone an entire year instead of ten minutes at the most. I never could understand Mariam's attraction to this ugly pug.

I pulled the rocking chair closer to the front window and eased into it. While alive, Mariam had spent countless hours in this same chair as she watched the comings and goings of the neighborhood.

Oh, she wasn't a busybody like that nosy Gladys Kravitz on the *Bewitched* TV series my wife and daughter had watched when Lacey was young. Mariam merely enjoyed seeing the people, as if viewing their whereabouts had been her favorite social hour activity. Also, unlike Mrs. Kravitz, any action Mariam reported always painted the picture of the ideal situation. In my dear wife's eyes, nothing evil existed. If only I, too, could share that sentiment.

Sometimes Mariam even dragged this rocking chair outside onto the front porch. Never would I be so bold as to do such an action. I preferred to observe from behind the glass pane, concealed with its lace sheers.

Oscar hopped onto my lap. Regardless of how bothersome this mangy beast could be, I did draw a bit of comfort every time I stroked his short felt-like fur.

I watched as the young mother—I think she said her name was Alexandra—took the boy by the hand. Together they crossed back to their side of the street. Less than a month ago, my nose pressed against the window as I observed this family move in. I shouldn't have a problem remembering the boy's name, Dakota. What's with this generation and the unusual names they brand their children with? Are they all so desperate to be different from their parents that they name their children after states instead of the honor of distant relatives?

DAKOTA

$\mathcal{M}$OMMY SQUEEZED MY HAND SO tight I imagined this must be how it felt to have your fingers clamped in one of those vice grips that Daddy used whenever I brought him some broken toy to glue back together. I tugged to wiggle free from her grasp, but it did no good.

"Dakota, you will hold my hand when we walk across streets."

"What does it matter? There are no cars."

"It matters. You never know when one will speed through the neighborhood. I wouldn't want you to get hurt."

A wrinkle split the usually smooth space between her eyebrows. It only showed up when my mom meant business. So, even though I didn't want to, I let my hand relax in hers, and we continued to walk home.

Mommy opened the side door to our house and stepped in first. I stomped my foot on what she called a threshold, 'cause I suppose that's what that piece of metal's there for, to stomp on. I couldn't think of any other reason. I never did like that nasty threshold, especially after the day it tripped me up when I tried to glide out of the house on my roller skates. My knee still hurts, but now it's got an awesome huge scab. I should have shown that crabby old man my scuffed-up knee. He might have thought it looked just as neat as I did. Then maybe he would have been nicer to my mom and me.

"Dakota, I wasn't very pleased with the way you conducted yourself just now."

What's with Mom and her big words? *Conducked?* What's a duck got to do with it anyway?

Mommy paced through the entry and turned into the kitchen. She must have dropped the pile of mail onto the table because before I finished climbing the stairs, she appeared again with empty hands and headed down the hall.

I meant to follow her after I finished stomping my foot hard on each step. I liked the buzz that vibrated up my leg whenever I slammed my foot down extra hard. It worked especially good this time with my new sneakers—the ones Mommy had bought me now that I was a big boy in kindergarten. Mom usually ignored it when I did this kind of thing. Sometimes she shook her head, but that's about all.

"Koty, come with me. I want to read you a story." She sat down on the couch. Mommy always called me Koty when she wanted me to do something extra sweet with her.

I climbed onto her lap.

"I recently bought us a new book. Now might be the perfect time to read it."

I loved it when Mommy or Daddy read to me. So, I snuggled in and sucked on my sleeve, ready to listen. Mommy really must have wanted me to hear this new story, for she didn't say a word about me making my sleeve all soggy or even removing it from my mouth.

"I recently heard of this book and thought it would be a good one for you. It is about a little angel who tells God that she wants to learn forgiveness, so God sent her to Earth to grant her wish." Mommy opened the hard cover and flipped to the first page.

As my ears listened while she read, my eyes focused on large, brightly painted pictures. I forgot all about the crabby man who had jabbed me with his mailbox key. That was until Mom had to bring it back up again. She went on and on about how I had to be like that angel in the story and forgive so I could be nice to people, even ones like that mean old man. I don't know how she did it, but *somehow*, she turned a nice and cozy storytime into a lesson on not being mean to cranky people, even if *they* were mean first!

DAKOTA

STIFF COILED SPRINGS POKED THROUGH the icky brown covering of the school bus seat, but that didn't matter much to me because it made a great springboard each time the bus drove over a bump.

Me and Traven—a cool boy who happened to live just down the street from my house—had a great time bouncing extra high with each bump the bus drove over. Our fun lasted until the driver yelled at us, saying we had better "remain in our seats." It shows how little he knows. Just because our bodies hovered over the cushion from time to time, not once did we leave the general area.

Oh well, it seemed adults always need to boss over us kids. I guess that helped them feel important or something. Anyhow, I decided it wouldn't be a good idea to get in trouble this early in the school year. Mommy and Daddy sure wouldn't like that very much. So, I squeezed my lips into a perfect pout and hugged my arms across my chest as I sat still in my seat—in spite of all the super bounces I missed.

I stared straight ahead. I didn't want to give Charlie, the bus driver, any reason to think I misbehaved. From the corner of my eye, I spied on Traven as he continued to bounce. "You better cut that out." I clenched my teeth as I spoke. I didn't want to get called out because *he* refused to obey. It's bad enough to get into trouble when *I* don't follow the rules, but completely unfair when it happens because of somebody else.

Traven shot his best glair back at me. "You're not being a very nice friend." At that moment, I felt the same about him.

Ignoring him, I reached into my backpack and found the big fat envelope Mrs. Miceli, my teacher, had handed out just before the bell blared, telling us it was time to go home. She had said it was some form of fun-raiser. I didn't understand why we needed something to raise our fun. As long as all these adults didn't keep over-bossing us kids, we do a pretty good job raising enough fun on our own.

I opened the packet and started to inspect what was inside, but before I got a good look, the screech of brakes stopped me. The bus jerked as it slowed down. Charlie hollered out that we had come to our stop, so I stuffed everything back into the envelope, grabbed my backpack, and rushed off the bus. However, I slowed down a bit when I came to the big black steps—to be careful not to trip.

Traven followed me off. "See you tomorrow." He waved as if he forgot all about being mad, then turned in the opposite direction and headed toward his home.

I watched him for a few seconds as he marched up the sidewalk, glad I now had a new friend. Then I turned around and found my mommy standing at the end of our driveway, just as always. I wondered if she thought I might forget which house was mine if not stationed as a guard to mark that exact spot each day.

She waved at me as I ran to her.

"Hey, Dakota, did you have a great day?"

"Mostly, till the bus driver yelled at me. He said I needed to stay in my seat. The weird thing was I never did leave my seat, not once." I felt okay telling Mommy that, for I knew this had to be true. Because if I actually had left my seat, that would have meant I either moved into the aisle or to a different seat, and I didn't do either one.

"If you never left your seat, why did he yell at you?" Mommy's nose crinkled as she led the way up the drive toward our house.

"Yeah, pretty weird, isn't it?"

She held the door open, and I marched inside. My nose sniffed the air—fresh baked cookies. I dropped my things and darted toward the kitchen. My stomach grumbled so loud we both could hear.

Mommy chuckled. "Sounds like I chose the perfect day to bake. Want a cookie? A cup of milk is waiting for you on the table, poured just before your bus arrived."

"You bet. Can I have more than one?"

"Yes, you may. But first, head to the bathroom and scrub those grubby hands."

I stared at my palms and could not find a single speck of dirt, so I held them out to let Mommy inspect them. "They're clean, see? I don't need to wash."

"Oh yes, you do. Now march."

It wasn't worth arguing. If I did, it would only take longer to eat those yummy cookies. So, I headed straight to the tiny bathroom that faced the entryway and turned on the faucet.

For a moment, my brain thought of letting the water run a short bit and then joining Mommy in the kitchen. She might think I actually washed them. But then I remembered how she had caught onto that trick and started to sniff my hands for soap before I was allowed at the table. I pressed down on the pump a couple times and let actual bubbles—instead of just that imaginary kind—form between my fingers. Bubbles rose, tempting me to play in the foam, but then I caught another whiff of chocolate chip cookie and, as fast as possible, rinsed off the soap, dried my hands, and hurried back to the kitchen.

Good thing I did the job the way Mommy wanted because the first thing she did was sniff my hands. I passed inspection, then sat down and stuffed my mouth with large bites of warm cookie oozing with melted chocolate chips, followed by big gulps of ice-cold milk.

Mommy leaned both elbows on the table and propped her chin in the cup formed by her hands. "So, tell me more about your day."

She's good at asking questions right as I take big bites. I gulped down my mouthful and wiped my mouth on my sleeve. Mommy flashed me one of those looks that meant I did something she wasn't pleased with and handed me a napkin.

"It went pretty great. Jonny got sent to the corner for pulling Savanna's hair. He made her cry. I saw the whole thing—oh yeah, I almost forgot—"

I leaped from my chair and ran back to the entry where I had dropped my backpack. On top laid the envelope Mrs. Miceli had passed out. When I came back to the table, Mommy had one of those amused smiles on her face as if my actions entertained her. It felt good inside to know how easily I made her happy, and I usually didn't even have to think about it. This kind of thing just came naturally.

I plopped the packet down on the table in front of her. "Mrs. Miceli says we need to do a fun-raiser. What's a fun-raiser? She said to be sure we don't knock on any stranger's door unless an adult is with us. I don't get it. How does knocking on someone's door raise fun?"

Mommy's look said I did it again. See what I mean? I didn't even try. I asked a simple question, and somehow, she found it funny.

"Sweetheart, the word is 'fund-raiser.'" She placed extra emphasis on the *D* sound. "It means to raise money. They want to raise extra *funds* for your school."

"Well, Mrs. Miceli could have explained *that* to the class. I wonder how many other kids are confused."

Could you believe it? Mommy laughed. She often told me I was her gift from God, sent straight from Heaven. I guess God thought she needed some serious cheering up.

"Let me see that." Mommy opened the packet and began sifting through the many pages. Most were those shiny papers covered with all sorts of colorful pictures. Items like candles and stuff, the type of thing that when in stores, Mommy would say, "Keep your hands to yourself. This is a no-touch store." I always hated it when we went into one of those shops. What's the use of tempting people to buy nifty items if we couldn't even touch them? Didn't store owners know we need to test the merchandise to see if it's good enough to purchase?

"Oh yeah . . . at this past PTA meeting, they mentioned extra fundraisers to earn money to purchase new playground equipment for your school. That must be what this is all about."

"Playground equipment? Then I was right. It is a fu*n-n-n* raiser." I drew out the *N* sound to make sure Mommy heard it. Feeling extra proud of myself, I gave her one of my really big grins.

Mommy continued to look through the papers. I caught a glance at a page with toys on it. "Hey, let me see that." I grabbed the sheet before she could answer. Usually, she would have given me a talking-to if I did such a thing, but not this time. Mommy remained so engrossed in all the pictured sale items that she hardly seemed to notice.

My eyes glued onto the neatest thing I had ever seen—Super-Bat accessories for a bike. Man, I sure did want that prize. "Mommy, look. Can we purchase these, pleeease?" I shoved the page under her nose.

"Dakota, none of those items on that page are for sale."

"Then why are they here?" I scrunched up my nose real well.

"They are rewards. You have to sell a certain amount of orders to earn them as prizes."

"Really, how much do I have to sell to get the Super-Bat bike package?" It had a water bottle, hanging bag, bell, side mirror, and lots more nifty items, each made to attach to your bike. Altogether, it would turn my bike into the slickest one in the neighborhood.

Mommy pointed to a number near the cool Super-Bat prize collection. "To earn that package, you must sell at least one-hundred-and-fifty dollars worth of merchandise."

Wow, that sounded like a huge amount. "Can we sell that much, please? I *really* want my bike to look like Super-Bat's."

"We'll see, honey."

"Well, let's get going." I hopped to my feet and tugged on her sleeve.

"Not right now. We need to wait for people to return home from work. Why don't you go upstairs and play for a few hours, and then we will see about going out."

A hollow feeling entered my stomach, even though I had just filled up on cookies and milk. This type of thing happened whenever I got disappointed. Definitely not one of my favorite feelings.

Mommy must have known because as she looked at me, somehow, her face seemed softer than before. "There are enough leftovers in the fridge, so I shouldn't have to cook tonight. The food will spoil if we don't eat it up anyway. So how about we use the time I usually spend to prepare our meal, and instead we go through the neighborhood to get some orders?"

Yuck, I hate leftover nights, but I wasn't about to tell Mommy that. She was big on not wasting food. I didn't see why. Every time we went to the grocery store, the shelves were always full of more than enough food for everyone, but Mommy acted as if the whole world would run out if we wasted.

But none of that mattered now. I would gladly put up with leftovers if that meant we could go out and make enough sales to earn me that Super-Bat bike package. "Can't we, please, go out now?" I tried real hard to give her my wide-eye look, which she found hard to resist.

"You heard me. We will wait a couple of hours, or else not enough people will be home to make it worth our effort. No one home to answer the door means no sales." The wrinkle between her eyebrows returned.

Rats, my effort didn't work. Even though I didn't want to admit it, what Mommy said made sense, but it was so hard to be patient.

I let out a sigh and made certain a sound came with the air as it left my chest. "Okay, call me down when it's time to go."

I stared at the carpet and watched my feet drag lines into the fibers as I moved down the hallway and upstairs into my room.

"Koty, grab your jacket. Let's go do that fundraiser." Mommy's voice hollered up from the first floor.

I left the pile of blocks and my army men in the middle of the play rug in my bedroom and then thundered down the stairs. I loved it when my feet made booming sounds. When I came to the last three steps, I leaped over them and spun around the banister like the real-life superhero, Super-Bat, would do. Mommy stood by the side entry, waiting for me. I dashed in front of her, taking the four steps in one giant leap, grabbed my red jacket with the stripes down the sleeve, and sped out the door.

We had hiked down sidewalks for what seemed like years and must have knocked on a thousand doors. Even though we waited so late into the evening, many people still were not home. We already had turned around and began to head back down the opposite side of the road.

"Mommy, do you think we did it? Did we earn enough money so I can get the Super-Bat bike accessory set?"

Mommy studied the sheet held in her hand. "Not yet, honey, but don't worry. We can always go out again another day. The order form does not have to be turned in for another week and a half."

Disappointment ran all the way to my toes. I shuffled my new sneakers as we strode down the sidewalk, kicking up dry leaves along the way. The crunch of the colored leaves took my mind off the gloom of having not yet sold enough items.

"This should be the last house for tonight. It's getting late, and I don't know about you, but I'm hungry." Mommy gathered her light-brown hair and flipped it over her shoulder. She always looked pretty whenever she did that.

I glanced up and noticed that we stood in front of the house directly across the street from ours. Mommy paused at the end of its driveway, just like she did at the last five homes we had approached.

At the first house she had done this, she said I spoke so well to the people that I was ready to talk to them on my own. When I told her that sounded scary, Mommy said not to worry. She would remain close enough the entire time to hear and see everything. Her one big rule remained—under no circumstance was I to step into a home. Mommy kept her promise. Each time she stayed near enough that everything seemed okay.

So, I marched up the steps, all brave like Super-Bat—a much better feeling than that disappointed one I had earlier. I balled my hand into a fist and knocked on the door.

CHAPTER

4

ALDOUS

"OSCAR, GET OFF THAT BENCH." I shooed the pug back onto the floor where he belonged. The disobedient animal barked once, spun in circles, then hopped back onto the piano bench. With a bit more force, I shoved him off a second time. "What are you doing? Those sharp toenails will mar the woodwork!"

Thankfully, the mutt sped out of the dining room and toward the front door. With a catch in my left hip—*I hate arthritis, the curse of Adam!*— I followed after him. "Where do you think you're going now?"

Oscar stopped in front of the door. His squat body bounced up and down as he maintained a continuous, obnoxious yip. "No, we're not going for a walk. Not now." Under normal circumstances, this proclamation would have ceased Oscar's insufferable behavior, but the sound of the knock egged on the animal's overzealous excitement.

"You stay." I shoved him back with my foot, then opened the door. The same small boy, who had run into me at the mailboxes the other day, stood on my porch. A streak of mud smeared beneath his right eye. His unappealing cavern-like mouth dropped open, highlighting the gaping hole of a missing tooth.

"What do *you* want?"

Instead of answering, the boy spun around and darted down the porch steps. His short legs didn't stop until he reached his mother, who stood at the edge of my driveway. Whoever taught this kid his manners sure failed at that job.

With no idea what the kid was up to, I stepped onto the porch. Oscar weaseled out between my leg and the doorframe.

"Dakota, what do you think you are doing? That was very rude." A pinch between her eyebrows sharpened her smooth facial features I remembered the other day.

Glad to see his mother put effort into directing the young boy in proper behavior, I felt my upper lip curl into a sneer. I could not help but hear their conversation from my position on my top porch step.

"I don't want to sell to that man. He's mean. He's mean, and he's old, and he's nasty."

The mother glanced up at me and then back at her child. "Dakota, you are not acting very nice. Am I to understand that you have decided to be mean and nasty right back at him? Now go. Get back to that house right now."

The boy stomped his foot. His mother jutted her pointer finger in my direction. The child turned around and, dragging his shoes, plodded toward me.

Darn it! I wished she had given in to her child's wishes. I would have much preferred to see them head straight back toward their own house.

The boy trudged back up my painted wooden steps. "Hi, mister, would you like to buy something from me? It's to earn money so my school can build us a new playground." He hung his head, addressing my bare toes. The boy obviously boasted no more desire in having to deal with me than I held toward him.

"My eyes are up here, son, and the name is Aldous. That would be Mr. Aldous to you." Forced to converse with this lad, I at least could drill some manners into him.

He lifted his freckled face. Two round, sky-blue eyes shined up at me. "Well, Mr. Aldous, would you, *please,* buy something?" He held out a colorful brochure.

"Since you said 'please,' I'll take a look." I grasped the item from this insufferable child.

"Ahh, look, Mommy, a puppy! What's his name?" The boy knelt on the porch and petted my trader of a mutt that lapped at this child's face.

"Oscar," I groaned, then glanced over the pictured objects on the front of the multi-paged advertisement. I wouldn't know what to do with any of those items offered, all candles, knickknacks, and such—the type of thing Mariam would have liked, but she's—"I don't think I'd find a use for anything like that." I thrust the brochure back at the child.

"But wait, mister, you didn't even really look."

"There you go calling me *mister* again. How would you like it if I called you *kid?*"

"I wouldn't like that very much." The boy pursed his lips into a pout.

"The other day, your mom said your name was Dakota, didn't she?"

"Yes, sir, that's my name."

"Well, now it's sir. I guess there is some hope for manners from you after all."

Freckled cheeks puffed out like a chipmunk's as the boy laughed. "Mr. Aldous, please take a closer look. If you don't want anything, maybe, you could find a nice gift for someone else."

Despite my desire for this child to go away, something about him appealed to me, so I held out my hand. "All right, I'll take a second look." This time I did more than just glance. I flipped pages and examined each item pictured.

On the second page, my sight froze onto the image of a vase etched with hummingbirds. Mariam loved hummingbirds. When we were first married, I built a set of shelves on our bedroom wall to hold her collection. Back then, her assortment contained less than a dozen items. By the time she passed away, her treasured hummingbirds had grown in number to take over the top of both dressers along with the five-shelved wall unit.

A sickening hollow sensation churned my stomach. I shoved the advertisement back at the boy. "Here, kid, I told you I didn't want to buy anything."

A look of shock filled his pale-blue eyes. "It's Dakota, remember? And you're not 'mister,' you're Mr. Aldous." The child spun toward his mother. She flashed him a sharp look of disapproval.

He turned back toward me with a softened expression. The lad bent over and tugged up a pant leg. "You want to see my scab? I've got an awesome huge one right here on my knee."

His action threw me like a lasso. I didn't quite know what to think of it. "My feet are cold. I left my slippers in the house. I'm going back inside. Come, Oscar."

Before the boy could spit out another word, I grabbed Oscar by the collar, slipped into my house, flung the door shut, and turned the deadbolt. Although the house felt warm that day, I slid my feet into the familiar comfort of my slippers—happy Oscar had not removed them from the entry mat—then climbed the stairs to my bedroom.

A thousand tiny hummingbirds drilled their beady eyes into my heart as I stood in the doorway to my room. I diverted my sight from their imploring glares.

"You don't need another. You already own more than enough." I glanced out my bedroom window and watched this young mother and her son enter their house through the side door. Why they don't ever use the front, I may never know."

DAKOTA

"**I** DON'T LIKE THAT OLD MAN! Mommy, I tried. I gave it everything I had! I even showed him my scraped-up knee. You saw how he acted. I'll never understand how someone could turn up their nose at a neat-o' scab like this one, right here." I jabbed my pointer finger at my knee, shoved up my pant leg, and admired the awesome wound. All boggled and frustrated, I turned back toward my mommy. "Yet that is what he did! I don't want to talk to that nasty old geezer again."

I pressed my lips tightly together and stomped my foot hard on the kitchen floor. My pant leg slid back down toward my ankle. I folded my arms so tight across my chest that a puff of air squeezed out. Of course, because of how I was behaving, Mommy would be real angry with me, but I had had enough of that hook-nosed man. I held that position and used my stare to dare Mommy to make me change my mind.

A bit nervous she would be upset with me—especially since I had called Mr. Aldous an old geezer, I held my stance. Most of the time, she would have said something about that kind of talk. I also thought

Mommy would be angry with me after the way Mr. Aldous had stormed into his house and slammed the door shut when I tugged up my pant leg. I wondered if I should back down some but decided not to. I had a message to get out, so I stayed put and let my body action speak the words for me, loud and clear.

I thought of the scab on my knee and didn't get it. Traven and the other boys on the playground were impressed when I showed it to them. One would think Mr. Aldous should have been interested in something as cool as that. But he wasn't? It just proved nothing would work on someone as cranky as that man. No matter what I might try, that nasty old Mr. Aldous would remain "bound and determined"—as Mommy would say—to stay just as mean and nasty as always. That's just who he was, a fact not even God could change.

But as strange as it seemed, instead of getting angry with me, Mommy gazed into my eyes and stroked her hand over my hair. Her face looked soft and gentle, just like it did when she tucked me into bed at night.

"Koty, I know this is a hard concept to understand. This type of thing is difficult for even grownups to comprehend, let alone a five-year-old boy." She pulled a chair out from the table, then drew out another, turning it to face her as she sat down. Her hand tapped the empty seat. I plopped down onto it.

"Remember on your first day of kindergarten when that boy, Jacob, gave you so much trouble, and how much he bullied you those first few weeks? Yet you didn't let him get to you. Instead, you held your own and remained firm."

When Mommy mentioned Jacob Downing, pride bubbled up inside of my chest. If you haven't ever had that feeling, make sure and do so someday. It's real cool.

"You told me how other kids ran off in tears when Jacob approached them. Or worse yet, they did some mean and nasty action right back. Yet not once did you react negatively to his bullying. Mrs. Miceli confirmed that fact."

"No way will I ever let Jacob get to me. I want to have fun at school, and he keeps trying to suck away all our fun. I can't speak for the other kids, but I won't let him do that to me."

"You found a way to stand up for yourself without harming Jacob. That's a pretty special ability, Dakota. Many adults have spent their entire lifetime trying to do exactly that. And you, at only five years old, have succeeded."

As I listened to Mommy's words, that pride inside me seemed like it was about to burst out. "And he doesn't bother me anymore. Anytime he acts as if he's about to do something mean, I give him one of my firm stares, like this"—I squeezed my eyebrows tightly together and gave my best glare—"and he backs off."

Mommy laughed. I must have humored her again. "Sort of like the stare you gave me when we started this talk?" She winked.

"Yeah, something like that." This time I laughed, then Mommy mussed up my hair.

"Your teacher called the other day and told me how impressed she was at the way you had been handling the Jacob situation." She tipped her head and gave me one of those smiles—the small, closed-lip kind that meant she was pleased with me. A piece of light-brown hair fell across her forehead, almost into her eye.

Then I remembered that nasty Mr. Aldous. I felt all glowy inside about my success with Jacob Downing, and Mr. Aldous had to ruin everything. And he wasn't even here. "But I even showed him my scabbed-up knee. When he looked down at me, all angry like, I could see hairs growing in his nostrils, yuck!"

Mommy hiccupped back something. I supposed it could have been another laugh. I didn't think there was anything funny about what I had said.

"Honey, I don't believe he intended to be unkind. He has lived a long life, and I'm certain many things have occurred that have caused him great pain—things which for one reason or another he has not yet healed from." She placed her hand on my arm. The warmth of her touch soaked through my sleeve.

With her hand, Mommy brushed away the stray hairs. "Probably many Jacob Downings—or even people far worse—have entered his life. And for some reason, Mr. Aldous could not stand up to them. When we don't heal from our wounds, we pass that pain on to those around us in other ways."

"By being mean and cranky?"

"Yes, sometimes by being mean and cranky." Mommy's teeth sparkled as she grinned. My mommy had the prettiest smile.

She glanced up at the clock above the kitchen table. "Your daddy should be home in half an hour. Go wash up, then help me set the table for dinner."

"Okay, but first, I have one more question."

"What's that, Dakota?"

"What kind of flower is a *kinder*, and where is the garden?" This question had been burning a hole in me ever since my first day of *kindergarden*. I knew what dandelions, daisies, and even sunflowers looked like, and Mommy loved it whenever Daddy brought her home roses, but I had never heard of a kinder flower. I had been going to this school now for at least five weeks, and not once had I seen a garden anywhere on that school's property, and I looked!

Can you believe it? Instead of answering my question, Mommy burst into a full-blown, tummy-rolling laugh.

ALDOUS

HE FRONT WHEEL OF THE shopping cart pulled to the left as it wobbled. My attention remained distracted by its inept craftmanship. Why this store keeps such an ample supply of ill-equipped carts? I would never know. If I weren't so dog-tired, deep down to the center of my worn-out bones, I'd bring this matter up to the manager. How was it that, more often than not, I grabbed a cart that limped? Every time it happened, I'd threaten, through gritted teeth, to report the issue. But just like those irresponsible young'uns of today, I've yet to follow through. In my younger years, such a thing would have never been a challenge for me. One wobbly cart would have been all it took for me to march up and have a word with whoever might be in charge—proof that I had gotten soft in my older years, either that or just cynical. The truth was, no one cared these days, and I'm not sure even I did anymore.

Now, what do I need to get next? I stared at the over-stocked shelves, bogged down with colorfully labeled cans and boxes of food that never should have been allowed to be called instant, like potatoes, for example. Until my dying days, I will never understand how people could call this mess progress. The multitude of products in front of my weak eyes blurred, like colorful candy melted in a bowl of warm ice cream. My memory blanked out on me, a direct betrayal. It shouldn't be this difficult to buy groceries. Mariam did it every week, and she even enjoyed the chore. If she were alive today, before we left the house, she would have insisted on us drawing up a list. That habit of hers always seemed to be a silly waste of time. To be free to shop empty-handed from written instructions became a luxury I enjoyed since my dear Mariam had passed away. Yet there I stood in an oblivious stupor, leaning against this defective shopping cart while my vacant brain threatened to concede to reason with Mariam's maddening method. I wouldn't give in.

"Mommy, we need Pasta-O's."

I turned in the direction of that far-too-familiar, high-pitched voice. Near the end of the aisle, Dakota hopped off the back end of a cart pushed by his mother and then snatched two cans off the shelf.

Grabbing a box of cheesy potatoes, I dropped them into my cart, then sped from the aisle, making sure to keep my back toward Alexandra and her son. As I executed my stealth exit, I clung to high hopes that the dysfunctional wheel's rattle would not betray my presence.

Containers of various juices lined the shelves of the next aisle. As much as I hated to admit it, I missed those days when whatever item I wanted would appear as if magically in our kitchen cupboards—the labors of Mariam. I imagined I would never get used to this grocery shopping nonsense, especially now that I must do it alone.

I gazed over the assortment of juices, twisting my brain to remember which flavor I favored. When Mariam had poured it in a tumbler with shaved ice, it took on a much different appearance than the disguise of a labeled jar stashed on a laden shelf, hidden among a hundred other brands of similar beverages.

"There he is, Mom! I knew I saw him."

Oh, good grief, will that kid *ever* go away? I grabbed a mixed berry juice and zipped around the corner, pretending I hadn't noticed them.

Finding myself in the refrigerated meat department, a bit of glee seeped into my rickety old bones. A nice juicy steak with sautéed onions and mushrooms sounded fantastic. Could I cook the dish as mouthwatering as Mariam had done so many times? I moved close to the display and hovered over the assortment of fresh cuts.

"Mommy, do we have to go over to him? If we ignore him, he may not even know we are here."

"Chances are he already saw us. It would be impolite to ignore him. It won't hurt to say hi."

Go ahead and ignore me. I'll go along with the game and pretend we hadn't noticed each other. Trust me, that would be far more pleasant. It won't hurt my feelings in the least. I picked up a package of ribeye and continued to stare straight ahead, as if I had not heard their conversation, yet peered from the corner of my eye in the direction of their voices.

Sure enough, a heaped shopping cart with a far too familiar boy, who hung off its side like a monkey clinging to a tree, inched toward me.

I turned to my right and scanned the environment for an effective escape route but detected none. Too exposed to succeed at another swift getaway, I took a deep breath and braced for the inevitable.

The unwelcomed cart came to a stop not four feet away. Dakota hopped off and stood beside me. My chance to pretend I did not notice them came to an abrupt halt.

"Hello, Mr. Aldous."

Surprised to hear Alexandra's soft voice speak first, I turned toward her and nodded. "Alexandra, Dakota."

Her eyes flashed toward the meat cutlets in front of me. "Does this mean you enjoy steak? We've intended to invite you over for dinner one of these days if you'd care to join us. I would love to cook you up one."

I gazed down at the boy who fidgeted between his mother and me. A stray piece of sandy-blond hair fell between his watchful eyes that seemed to bulge clear out of their sockets. The unruly child scrunched up his nose and stared back. For some strange reason, it appeared he gazed up my nose.

It seemed I had developed a new mission in life—to avoid this child who so tactfully disrupted my quiet life of solitude. Accepting Alexandra's offer would defeat the purpose of this newfound goal. "Don't bother. I prefer to eat alone."

A cold sensation from the packaged meat held in my hand seeped into my arthritic fingers, making them quite uncomfortable. I dropped the chilled item into my shopping cart and headed toward the bakery department.

There were days I wished my hearing had aged along with the rest of my decrepit old body, but for some unknown reason, these ears had escaped that fate. They retained complete ability to remain as sharp as when I, too, was a small lad. With my back turned toward them, I pushed my cart along the polished floor. As the distance between us increased, I focused on the clatter of the ill-aligned wheel. Even that obnoxious racket could not drown out the unsolicited voices of Dakota and his mother.

"How rude. . . . See what I mean, Mommy? He's just a mean old man. I didn't want him to come to our house, anyway."

"Dakota, that's enough. You are not to talk offensively of others like that."

"But, Mommy—"

"You heard me, Dakota. Listen, sweetie, it's just like with Jacob

Downing. Neither Jacob nor Mr. Aldous is a bad person. They both are just wounded."

For some reason I may never understand, my feet froze in place while my ears sharply tuned into the exchange of words between this mother and child duel.

"Remember that big white dog, with the patch of black fur over one eye . . . the one who roamed our old neighborhood?"

"Uh-huh."

"Do you recall when we found him lying by the side of the road after a car hit him?"

"Yeah, he was hurt real bad. I wanted to go up to him and give him a big hug like you do whenever I get hurt, but you wouldn't let me."

"Do you understand why?"

"You said he might bite me, but that made no sense because I knew that dog. I had petted him many times, and he never once bit me. He always acted real friendly."

"But when he got injured by the car, that made things much different than all those times he ran the neighborhood, happy and free. It is very important to use caution while approaching a wounded animal. They would be in a survival state. Even though under normal circumstances he may be friendly, while injured, he could easily bite, even the people whom he trusts."

I tipped my head toward the left and pretended to be interested in a loaf of French bread. Every word they spoke seared into my mind. Sweat formed on the palms of my hands as they gripped the handle of the shopping cart.

"People are not much different than animals. When someone is seriously hurt, it is often hard for them to remain friendly. Not that they intend to be mean, but their wounds rob them of the capacity to reach out. When a person's injuries become that immense, they turn within and allow time to heal. Often while doing so, they lose the ability to be kind toward others. That is when it becomes our job to reach out to them with extended love, understanding, and forgiveness, even when they bite."

The buzzing of a fly sliced into my consciousness like a minute irritant off in the distance. It landed on my cheek, so I swatted it away, yet even that distraction did not break my concentration on Alexandra and Dakota's conversation. I stole a glance in their direction. They hadn't moved from that spot in front of the ribeye steaks.

Dakota stood beside the shopping cart, facing his mother. Alexandra knelt before him with her hands placed over his upper arms. Memories of the gentle way Mariam spoke with Lacey conjured within my mind.

"Just like last month when you were sick. All you wanted to do was cuddle under your blankets to watch TV or sleep. If I had asked you to pick up your room, would you have done the job without getting cranky at me?"

"No way, I felt awful. If I moved to put my toys away, I would have thrown up."

"Well, it's the same with Mr. Aldous."

"You mean Mr. Aldous feels all queasy in his stomach?"

Something about Alexandra's pleasant laugh at that moment chiseled an opening clear through to my heart.

"Probably not in his stomach, but I bet he does in his heart."

I maneuvered again, a bit to the left toward the sweet rolls. Alexandra combed her hand through Dakota's bangs, brushing them out of his eyes. Even though I remained too far away to see clearly, I imagined they still shone bright, like two shooter marbles carved from a section of clear blue sky.

"What I mean is that inside he is badly hurt. We don't know how it happened or from whom, but the fact remains that he is severely wounded. People don't become mean and cranky without any reason. It's like this, sweetheart, hurt people hurt people."

Alexandra stood up and reclaimed her shopping cart. As she pushed it to a side aisle, Dakota hopped back onto the rear of its wire frame. Their words faded from earshot.

My feet froze in place. The silence of the broken wheel had served me well. I swallowed a lump that gnawed at the inside of my throat. No doubt Alexandra had assumed I remained far enough away to have not overheard their conversation, yet every word they spoke stuck, uninvited, to the inside of my gut like a burr trapped in a shoe.

CHAPTER

7

ALDOUS

𝓘 REMOVED EACH PURCHASE FROM ITS bag, lined everything on top of the butcher's block in the center of my kitchen, then neatly folded the grocery bags and stashed them beside the sink. Common logic would tell me to throw them away, but Mariam had always stockpiled every paper bag that came into our house for reuse at a later date. Whatever that use might be, I never did find out. Funny how when she was alive, I did whatever I wanted, never considering how it might affect those around me. Yet, with Mariam gone, I now contemplate what her needs would have been far more often than I ever had before that dreaded day she died.

I stood back and stared at the assortment of mismatched items, a jar of red juice, cheesy potatoes, some ribeye steaks, a can of diced meat—whatever type I'm not sure—and a few other cans and boxes that contained some odd form of food. *Darn, I forgot to pick up an onion and some mushrooms to sauté with the steaks.*

How someone could transform such a hodgepodge as this into

a palatable meal, I may never know. Somehow Mariam, with ease, collected usable produce and compiled the most delectable meals. While alive, I never realized how exceptional that talent of hers was. Too often, I took it for granted and seldom extended proper appreciation for her abilities. I wondered if she could look down at me from her place in Heaven and see how much I missed the loving ways she had cared for me.

An eruption of unexpected rage stormed through my veins. I grabbed the box of instant potatoes. My fingers crumpled thin cardboard as I hurled it at the sink. The unsuspecting container smacked against old copper fixtures, splitting open a corner of the box. A shower of dry flakes scattered over the countertop and sink like a miniature blizzard had sliced through the wall and poured its fury into what once had been my beloved Mariam's kitchen.

I leaned against the center island, my elbows propped on its surface and my head buried in the cup of my hands as I bawled an ocean of hot tears. A hoard of suppressed feelings hidden deep within marched forth from the far recesses of my soul like an invasive army set on overtaking a foreign land. How many times had I begged for the luxury of solitude while Mariam still lived? Well, I guess God does answer our prayers. I now cursed every thought that forged my sadistic desire.

The ache slashed my heart like a butcher knife slicing flesh from a dead cow. Only unlike that cow, I remained very much alive. What would it take to make such intense pain go away? I did not solicit to recollect Alexandra's words as she spoke to her son. Nonetheless, her gentle voice echoed loud and clear in my mind. *"Hurt people hurt people."*

In Mariam's final years, she had begun to lose tolerance for my selfish antics. No longer silent, she built up a new level of courage—one I had no leniency for—and stood up for things that, before then, she had never dared complain about.

I hated her newfound gall. Why couldn't things remain as always? Our tried-and-true method had served us well for over half a century. After all those years of keeping silent, why did she have to rock the boat and disturb our clear sailing?

She complained more and more about how she missed our daughter and hated that Lacey refused to come around our house. That was Lacey's problem, not ours. Mariam and I had formed a method that functioned well for us. Why rewrite the script this late into our relationship?

Mucus seeped through the fingers of my soggy cupped hands. I straightened up and edged toward the counter, ripping off a paper towel. The coarse material felt as abrasive as sandpaper against my nose. I should have picked up a box of tissues at the grocery store. Maybe a list would have been a good idea after all.

I knew how to take charge. While Mariam and I had raised our daughter, I became a brilliant master of control. So why now did my body fold inward, as if in complete surrender to twin enemies named helplessness and vulnerability? I loathed the knowledge that these longtime rivals had overtaken my soul. Nothing could be worse than to lose command of my helm.

A faint whisper snaked into my mind, like an unwanted vixen that ran naked in an open courtyard. *That which you now experience is how your wife and child had felt all those long years.* The uninvited voice hissed loud and clear. It came from the overloaded stockpile, deep within my head, where I had stashed innumerable thoughts and memories I never wanted to recall.

"Shut up!" The harsh words roared from within, startling me as they erupted from my chapped lips.

Oscar yelped a sharp bark in response.

"No, bud, I wasn't talking to you." A wave of regret washed over me as if an attempt to cleanse my soul. I bent down and scooped the animal up into my arms. "I didn't mean to alarm you, little guy." I stroked his short, silky fur.

From where had this newfound compassion originated? I never before even liked this pug-faced beast Mariam had so greatly cherished.

For some mind-boggling reason I would never understand, I carried the furry fellow into the dining room and sat him beside me on the piano bench. The same one I had forbidden him from being on the other day for fear that his sharp toenails would scratch the well-polished wood. Now, none of that mattered.

Oscar remained alert and still on the bench as if he anticipated something of high interest to transpire. Then to further shake up my nice, neat, carefully fashioned world, I looked into his pleading eyes and became overtaken with the need to accommodate his silent request.

I shuffled through a basket of music that sat on the floor, untouched beside the piano for over three years. My sight latched onto an old piece of sheet music, held together by yellowed tape: "Valse-Arabesque" by Theodore Lack. Mariam had been an accomplished musician. This piece was one of her favorites and most challenging numbers, yet, in no time, she had mastered its complicated cords and memorized every stanza. I closed my eyes and remembered how her long, slender fingers dusted over the ivory keyboard, creating magnificent music with such ease only a true musician could achieve.

Mariam had always exercised great patience—one of her most noble talents—yet, at times, I'd wondered if it also might have been her major downfall. Could a person be too patient and, in so doing, enable those around them? Now was not the first time that question had weaseled into my troubled mind. And like always, as it crowded the forefront of my brain, I adamantly shoved it back to ignore its persistence.

My thick, shaky fingers—not the tools of a musician—opened the sheet music and placed worn pages on the narrow shelf above the keyboard. I positioned my hands over the supposed accurate notes and struck a chord. Instead of a pleasant multi-keyed blend, a sour noise reverberated to my eardrums.

My hands jerked from this pose and hovered above the black and white keys. My eyes squinted, attempting to calculate the placement of flats G, B, and E, indicating the key of this cumbersome piece.

Oscar lingered motionless beside me. His round beady eyes stared straight ahead at the sheet music. If I hadn't known better, I would have sworn that he, too, attempted to decipher the intricate selection before us.

"So, you think I can do this?" Mariam had spent many painstaking attempts to teach me how to play—a superb test of her patience. I knew with certainty that, countless times, she swallowed back great gulps of frustration, yet her angelic mannerism never revealed it.

Oscar yelped. His curled-up stump-of-a-tail wiggled—the best attempt he could achieve at an official wag with his puny appendage.

Deciding to give it a second try, I again placed my arthritic fingers over what I hoped were the correct keys. A harmonious chord rewarded my ears. I pressed down on the floor pedal to let the vibration echo. A touch more confident, my sight advanced across the weathered page. With slow, careful calculations, I hammered out the first one-and-a-half measures of the piece, then my hands froze in place as I stared at the run that followed.

Oscar again yelped.

"Go on? Are you kidding? There's no way I can play that run."

The piano had not come easy to me, despite the many weary hours Mariam had sacrificed to teach me her gifted passion. Still, I did succeed in mastering some much easier numbers. We even together played a few simple duets.

Refusing to let up on his request, Oscar nudged his flattened nose at my arm.

"Okay, okay, I'll give it a try." My clumsy fingers ran over sour keys—a feeble attempt to plunk out the intricate run. Who was I fooling? To think that my old, wrinkled, untalented hands could mimic Mariam's masterpiece was a ridiculous notion.

In frustration, I slammed down the keyboard cover, then stashed the sheet music deep in the basket, hidden under a horde of other arrangements. There it would remain buried for another multitude of years.

"Come on, Oscar, I'm hungry. Let's go make us some supper."

The furry fellow barked, adding more creases to his overtly crinkled nose. Toenails scraped as he hopped off the bench, then followed me into the kitchen.

I marched toward the sink, took in the potato flake mess, and froze. A deep sigh exhaled from my lungs. "Well, bud, I might as well clean this up. There's nobody else around this place to do the job."

My fingers flinched under the cold water while I wrung out a rag and then wiped off the counter and rinsed scattered flakes down the drain. From the mounding pile of clean dishes I had neglected to put away, I grabbed a pan and placed it on the stovetop, then read aloud the instructions on the side of the instant potato box. "'Heat two-thirds of a cup of water.' Sounds easy enough. I can do that."

I measured the proper amount, poured it into the pan, then turned on the burner. "'Add a quarter cup of milk and a tablespoon of butter.'"

Opening the icebox, I peered inside and grasped the carton of milk. I shook the drizzle within. Setting the almost empty carton aside, I sifted through the sparse assortment of items and discovered no butter.

Three years—this day marked three years to the day when my Mariam had died, and I still couldn't even whip myself up a decent meal.

DAKOTA

*M*RS. MICELI'S VOICE RAN ON and on in my head. It buzzed in the background like an annoying bee I wanted to swat.

I knew what annoying was because every-so-often someone would use that name on me. They said I pestered them too much with never-ending questions. Mommy and Daddy never talked about me that way, unlike some other big people, like that one babysitter who I did not like very much. I was happy my mommy did not make me stay with her again after that first time.

I stopped listening to Mrs. Miceli's words, yet her voice continued to hum as I focused on the long hand on the big clock in our classroom. When I watched closely enough, I could see it jerk forward slightly. As soon as the hand tapped the edge of the number ten, the bell for recess would ring.

Only two swings hung outside on what we called the giant swing set. Whatever lucky kids got to those swings first could soar up so high they could be sure to touch a passing cloud. These were nothing like the ordinary swings over by the tetherball court. These were special. If I could get to the front of the line, I could claim one of those giant swings before anyone else.

Since my first day of kindergarten, I watched other kids fly through the sky. But, I haven't yet had that awesome experience. Today was going to be different. Today would be *my* day.

I worked real hard to figure out how to be the first kid to reach one of those prized swings. The secret must exist in that long hand on the wall clock. The one I stared up at now.

My focus glued onto its shiny black surface against a white background. *It's moving—almost there—one more second—*Pow! *We have contact.* I punched the air with my fist—a small victory dance. Both my hands gripped the edge of my chair, ready to push away from my desk the instant the recess bell rang.

Finally, the loud ring drowned out my teacher's never-ending voice. Chair legs scraped the floor as I shoved it back and darted toward the door.

Success, I did it! Yes! The first leg of my mission achieved! Why did they call it a leg, anyway? Wasn't it more of a step? And if it were a leg, wouldn't that mean there'd be a foot somewhere? Anyhow, I firmly planted my feet on the floor to claim my spot as first in the boy's line.

Roberta came up beside me, as a human marker to start the girl's line, and glared at me. For some reason, this girl almost always had a snarl on her face. Even when she did smile, it came out as more of a sneer than a grin. I wondered if she kept a slice of lemon tucked in her cheek to suck on whenever she wanted.

I ignored every attempt she made for eye contact and stared straight ahead toward the empty hallway. Neither Roberta nor any other kid would distract me from my mission.

The rest of the class lined up, girls behind Roberta and boys behind me, then Mrs. Miceli marched us down the hallway and out the big double doors toward the playground. The instant my shoe hit the concrete, I darted off toward the giant swing set.

All the other kids scattered off in different directions. I didn't care which way they went, just as long as no one raced in front of me, and no one did. *Hooray, Astronaut Dakota is free to execute his mission!* I could taste the sweet flavor of success on my tongue. I bet if I stuck it out, someone would see excitement marked across it like a half-sucked gumdrop.

Victory! I reached my destination. I grabbed the two extra-long linked chains and slid onto the swing. *Three . . . two . . . one . . . blast off!*

I used all my strength to get going, pumping my legs harder than they ever had on one of those ordinary swings. My muscles burned as if on fire. With all my willpower, I pulled on the chains each time my legs straightened out to slice through the air. Then I extended my arms and leaned back while curling my feet underneath me.

Before I knew it, I soared far above the playground. *Astronaut Dakota reached orbiting level.* I flew far into the sky. If it were nighttime, I could have snatched a star. The seat of my swing hung nearly level with the top crossbar and then swooped back down again. My guts tumbled to the pit of my stomach. *This is success!*

At the top of each sway for a swift instant, I hovered above the earth in my own spaceship. Surprised at how small everything below appeared, I spied Jacob Downing.

Frozen in his footsteps, Jacob's glassy eyes glued toward me as he gazed into the outer space—my space—the outer space Astronaut Dakota's rocket soared through. Jacob didn't shout, get in my way, or force me to stop as he would normally. He didn't do a thing.

My brain got to thinking real hard. I could not remember Jacob ever having had a turn. I knew how tough it was, day after day, to watch other kids have fun on this giant swing while, all the time, I, too, wanted my chance to fly.

By now, our recess period would be half over. I stopped pumping and dragged my feet through the woodchips each time I swooped near the ground. My rocket slowed down. My fist stayed gripped on one of the chains when I hit the eject button and leaped off.

The pile of woodchips did little to soften my landing. I fell hard, right on my already busted-up knee. Good thing that great big scab had almost completely healed by now, or that bad landing would have caused far more pain. Still, it stung, so I rubbed my knee and straightened up. I then hobbled over to Jacob and handed him the swing. "Here, you can have this for the rest of recess."

Jacob stared at me. His mouth hung wide open, yet not a word fell out.

I rattled the chain in his stunned face. "Really, I mean it. You can have the swing."

Jacob gawked at me. A confused gaze filled his eyes. Finally, a grin broke through, and he yanked the chain out of my grip.

I spun around and headed toward the tetherball court, kicking up stones on my way. Roberta ran to my side and socked me right in the arm.

Shocked, I stared at her. She had hit real hard and with no reason. I didn't do a thing to her.

"How could you do that, you stupid head? How could you give Jacob Downing your swing? If you were finished with your turn, you could have handed it over to anyone you wanted, but nooo, you chose Jacob Downing." Spit squirted through her teeth as she shouted.

"So, I gave Jacob Downing the swing, big deal. He wasn't doing anything mean to anyone. And no one else was near enough to give me the idea that they wanted it."

"But . . . you . . . dumb head! Jacob always gets anything he wants, and you just *hand* it over to him—the best swing on the playground!"

Seeing no reason to stay and argue, I scrunched up my nose and stomped away. Glancing back, I watched Roberta take off in the other direction. I rubbed the spot on my arm where she had slugged me. I didn't want her to see—it hurt real bad.

DAKOTA

*C*AREFUL NOT TO SHAKE UP the treasure within, I set my worn-out shoebox down on the bottom step, well out of the way against the edge of the wall. It would be safe there until later when I take it to my room.

Yesterday Mommy said that since the weather was getting cool, we would soon want to build a fire, so she cleaned out the fireplace to prepare it for winter. I don't know why she had to do that. The fireplace would just get dirty all over again. After watching Daddy build more than a thousand fires, from what I saw, Mommy only needed to put together some sticks and wadded up pieces of paper, then strike a match. But for some reason, Mommy again made something simple far more complicated. It probably had to do with some form of cleaning. Mommy is constantly cleaning something.

And this time, it's a good thing she did because when she peered up the chimney, she found a dead frog right near the opening, all flat and stiff. Daddy said it looked as if it had been mummified. I didn't know what that meant, but the frog sure did look cool. So I placed this flattened, dried-out frog in the shoebox my new sneakers had come in and had brought it to school for show-n-tell. All the boys thought my treasure was nifty, but some girls screamed, which made no sense. They act squeamish around the neatest things. Something must be wrong with them.

Once I knew my frog was secure beside the wall on the bottom step, I raced into the living room, where my mommy sat on the couch. "See, Mommy, take a look. I bet my arm is all swollen and bruised." I pushed my sleeve way up past my elbow, into the part of the arm Daddy called the bicep, and then I told Mommy everything about that day at recess time—my successful space launch on the giant swing, Jacob Downing's odd reaction, and then how Roberta had slugged me. "See, it's black and blue, isn't it?"

I'm sure Mommy saw where I had been punched because as I stood in front of her, Mommy's eyebrows pinched together and made that little crinkle that appeared whenever she saw something she didn't like.

Warmth poured from her finger as she ran it over my arm. "There is a bit of redness here. Did you tell your teacher?"

"No way! I didn't want her to know I got hurt by a *girl*."

"A girl can deliver just as painful a blow as any boy."

I rubbed the sore spot on my arm and pulled my sleeve back over it. "Yeah, you can say that again."

Mommy blinked as she sat silent and stared in the direction of my arm. She must have been thinking real hard about what had happened to me.

I climbed up on the couch beside her. "Are you going to call my teacher?"

"I am considering it." A ring of green crowded out the blue in her eyes—another hint that she was concentrating on something.

My cheeks felt hot, so I covered them with my hands and wished she wouldn't tell Mrs. Miceli, but I didn't say a word. Arguing with Mommy was never a good idea. She always won. "Mommy, why did Roberta hit me? I didn't do anything to her. When I asked if she had wanted the swing for herself, she told me '*No.*'"

"Well, it sounds as if her action had nothing to do with the swing and maybe everything to do with Jacob Downing."

"Because I gave him the swing? She called me a stupid head for that." I spun sideways on the couch to better face Mommy.

"Now that name-calling wasn't very nice, right along with the sock in the arm. Roberta must have felt very angry about what you had done and did not have a more effective way to express her rage."

It never occurred to me that when kids punch and kick, their behavior might be their way of saying they were mad. I always thought it just proved that they were bullies. What Mommy said got me thinking. "Maybe Roberta's parents don't help her put words into feelings as you and Daddy do for me. And since she doesn't know how to speak her feelings, she punches?"

Mommy brushed her finger across my forehead, moving straggly hairs out of my face. "Something like that. However, her action suggests she must have been quite angry that the class bully had received something special."

"I thought he *should* have my swing. I can't say he was nice at that moment, but he sure wasn't mean, like usual."

"That was very kind of you to reward him with your swing. Your incentive proves you don't hold past actions against him. It took forgiveness to do what you did. However, some people resent it when a person with a bullying reputation receives any reward, regardless of how nice they may have been at the time."

"Why would Roberta not want Jacob to get a reward?"

"Maybe she has been on the receiving end of bullies far too often.

As a result, she might carry intense anger toward anyone who torments another."

I felt all confused inside. None of what Mommy said made sense. Out of frustration, I pinched my lips together and stared real hard at her.

Mommy must have understood my message because she gave me one of her closed-lip smiles. She often did this just before better explaining something that had me all mixed up. "It's like this, sweetheart. It is common for someone who hurts too badly to lose their ability to feel happiness for others, particularly toward those who have caused much pain. We don't know anything about Roberta's life. She may have a good reason for resentment when someone like Jacob gets a reward. If she has been tormented by bullies too often, it would be easy for her to feel angry when she saw you reward Jacob with the swing."

Mommy poked at my chest with her long pointer finger. "Wounds in here are the most difficult type to heal. A large wound can cause a person to react instead of act. It sounds as if that's what Roberta did. She *reacted* to your show of compassion toward Jacob."

Sometimes Mommy could be *real* confusing. I think she knew I did not understand because, this time, a sigh followed her closed smile.

"Remember the day you put your skates on in the house? And a wheel got caught on the threshold as you tried to get through the doorway."

Finally, she talked about something that made sense. I stuck my legs straight out and pressed my back against the couch cushions. "You bet I do." I tugged up my pant leg. Only a red spot now hinted toward the mega scab that used to be there. And *that* mark probably came from when I landed on the woodchips. "See, it's almost healed now. And a good thing, too, for I fell on it again today when I jumped off that giant swing. It only hurt a little bit, though. By the time I handed Jacob the swing, the pain had gone away, well, almost."

"Imagine how much your knee would have hurt if it had not recovered from that first accident. One fall on top of the other could cause one majorly busted-up knee."

"Yeah, when I landed on those woodchips, I thought of that very thing and felt happy my knee was almost completely healed-up." I gazed at my banged-up knee with the pride of an honored soldier wounded in battle.

"It mended well because you took proper care of it. You did not continue to pick open the scab and impede your body's natural healing process. If you had kept messing with it, like at first, that knee may still, today, hurt too much to roller-skate."

The couch's springs bounced as I pulled both knees beneath me. "That would be awful. I would hate to not skate for that long."

"That would be pretty bad, Dakota." Mommy tickled me on the stomach through my shirt, and we giggled.

But then Mommy got all serious again. "Not everyone has the proper tools to care for their wounds or the ability to leave open sores alone and allow time to heal. That may be how it is with Roberta and even Jacob. It sounds as if they each have a whole bunch of injuries deep down inside that need mending."

My eyes dried out as I watched Mommy's mouth move. No matter how hard I tried, my brain would not soak in any meaning to her words.

"Open sores are vulnerable to further injuries. You know that from your knee." Mommy patted my leg. "Roberta's and Jacob's need to protect their own wounds ends up harming others." Not only was Mommy right back to being serious, but she also continued to talk in her hard-to-understand manner.

"By proper tools, do you mean bandages, ointment, and a mommy to make things all better?"

"Yes, that could be part of it. You never know what type of injury a person may be nursing that would cause them to react inappropriately."

My eyesight bounced up and down on the shiny white buttons that looked like pearls attached to Mommy's yellow sweater. "So, Mommy, do *you* have any unhealed wounds?"

"Everyone does."

"What are yours?"

Mommy pulled her sweater tight as if she wrapped herself up. "Well, you know how I encourage you to reach out and be friendly toward Mr. Aldous? I have a personal reason for you to do so."

"Yeah, you tell me we need to be kind toward everyone, even those who are not always nice. That is one of the reasons I gave Jacob my giant swing."

"You did very well, my dear. However, my reason with regards to Mr. Aldous is somewhat different."

Mommy's eyes glazed over as if she stared at something not there. Just in case someone came into the room, I turned toward the big double doors that led into the hallway, but no one else was there. That weird expression in her eyes somewhat scared me.

"Koty, remember when I explained how I had lived with my grandparents as a child?"

"Yeah, your mommy and daddy died in a car wreck, so your grandparents raised you. I sure am glad you and Daddy never died. I'd have no one to stay with since I have no grandparents."

My words must have made Mommy all emotional because she pulled me into her arms and hugged me so tight I could hardly breathe. When she let go again, tears sparkled in her eyes.

"Have you ever wondered why I don't speak much about my grandfather?"

"Uh-huh, you tell lots of stories about your grandmother, but not many of him."

"There's a good reason for that. I was only seven the day my parents died. Losing them and then moving in with my grandparents was difficult for all of us. Grandmother handled it well. She always treated me with kindness like I were her own child. However, I can't say the same about my grandfather."

Just then, I had one of those light bulb moments. I bounded up higher on my knees. "Was your grandpa mean and crabby, just like that nasty old Mr. Aldous?"

Mommy laughed. It sounded good to hear her laugh. This talk had been far too serious. "Yes, my grandpa was mean and crabby, much like Mr. Aldous."

"Do you think Mr. Aldous is so cranky because he has unhealed wounds inside of him, just like Roberta and Jacob?" This time *I* poked at my chest.

"Possibly so. I do believe my grandfather had many unhealed wounds. Most people do. I may never know what his all were. One day, when I was a teenager, my grandfather became ill, and my grandmother wanted me to take his dinner to him on a tray as he rested in bed. I didn't want to enter his room because I knew he'd yell at me. So, I held my ground and told Grandmother, 'No, I won't do it.' That day, she sat me down and gave me some insight about my grandfather."

Mommy disobeyed? My eyes must have bugged clear out of my head. I often had fun as I watched the faces of other kids at school when they looked bug-eyed and surprised. Boy, was I surprised now.

"When my mother was a teen, she had gone through quite a rebellious state. As a result, her father, my grandfather, held a grudge long after my mother had matured beyond that phase. Too many scars on a person's heart make it difficult to forgive. Grandfather died an angry, bitter man." The outline of Mommy's nose formed a perfect triangle as she gazed straight ahead.

"Grandmother told me that when my mother had passed, Grandfather accumulated even more anger from his pain. He never figured out how to heal and release that rage."

Mommy started to cry again. She even got up from the couch and grabbed a tissue. When she sat back down, she took my hand in hers. "My grandmother told me that I hauntingly resembled my mother at that same age. One day, Grandmother got out an old photo album, one I had never seen, with pictures of my mother as a teenager. Every snapshot confirmed her strong likeness to me. Grandmother explained that was why Grandfather persisted in snapping at me. Whenever Grandfather looked at me, he saw my mother, his daughter, instead. For some reason, he lacked the courage to grow beyond all that pain created by his bitterness."

Mommy looked so sad—I ached inside for her. Whenever I felt sad, Mommy did something to make me feel better. I wanted to help her feel better, so I put my other hand on top of hers.

"Every time I tried to break through Grandfather's hardened crust, I never succeeded. He passed away a few years later. Even though I had lived with him for twelve years, we never bonded." Mommy's chest rose as she sucked in a long breath and patted my hand with her free one. "We all carry wounds. Most bury their injuries so deep within they long forget how those wounds originated and never connect the dots that their current problems result from a long-ago repressed infliction.

"Photos and stories are your only opportunity to get to know your grandparents. I want you to experience their love. Whenever I see Mr. Aldous, a whisper inside tells me that this is my chance to make up for what I could not achieve with my grandfather and, at the same time, provide you with a grandparent's love."

I bounced on the couch. "Who whispers to you? Is it God?" I felt that same pull on my eyebrows. I had asked Mommy once what that was. She said it came whenever I stretched my eyes and made them big. Could it be similar to the bug-eyed look?

"It's hard to tell whether the whisper is from God or my own self-conscious."

I swore a rock fell into my gut. "Whichever voice gave you the whisper, now I don't have a choice, do I? I have to be nice to Mr. Aldous."

DAKOTA

"GET UP, DAKOTA. IT'S NICE and sunny outside, perfect weather for making repairs on the car."

Daddy's voice startled me awake. Today was Saturday, so I didn't have to get up early to catch the bus. I buried my head beneath my fluffy blue quilt, the one with the picture of a puppy dog on it. Mommy and Daddy promised that someday we would get a real dog, but for now, I had this puppy dog pattern on my bedding as a reminder.

Daddy pulled back my covers. Cool air met my nose. Along with it came a whiff of bacon frying on a pan from below. I took in a long sniff. Boy, did that smell good. "Can I see if Traven can come over?"

"I don't see why not, but first, get dressed and eat some breakfast."

I hopped out of bed and ran to the window.

"What's the matter, Dakota? Did you forget what sunshine looks like?"

"Just about." I wanted to see for myself that the rain had stopped. Bright bolts of lightning woke me up more than once during the night.

The continuous claps of thunder and pounding rain these last few days made me think giants might have moved into our attic.

Sure enough, as I drew back the heavy curtains, which Mommy called insulated, blinding sunlight streamed in through the glass.

Daddy moved toward my doorway, "Hurry up and get dressed. Mom has breakfast ready and waiting."

I couldn't wait to get outside and play. After being stuck in the house for such a long time, I grew so antsy that if Jacob Downing asked me to play, I would tell him yes.

Luckily, Jacob did not have my phone number. He didn't even know where I lived, so there was no chance he'd ever ask. And even more, luckily, Traven said he could come over.

Traven showed up at my door right as I started to eat breakfast. I swallowed my food so fast it could have been a plate of dirt instead of crisp bacon and yummy pancakes smothered with syrup, and I wouldn't have known the difference. Mommy told me to slow down and chew, but I gulped every bite, then ran outside to join my friend.

While Daddy tinkered with the car, Traven and I transformed our backyard into a baseball diamond.

"What's taking you so long? Throw the ball." Traven stood at home plate and swung the wooden bat through the air as if he swatted flies.

Stomping my feet into the soggy ground, I claimed my position at the pitcher's mound—a piece of scrap wood found in the garage. As I glanced at the odd collection of junk we used to mark each base, that cool sensation of pride bubbled up inside me again.

I secured the baseball between my knees, then spat in my hands and rubbed them together. Professional players do this, so spit must be their secret to a fastball.

I opened my hands and stared at brown-streaked palms. Dirt mixed with spittle settled into the cracks, creating what looked like a nifty piece of artwork—body art, cool. If Mommy saw this, she wouldn't appreciate these awesome designs painted on my hands. Mommy had this thing about hands having to be clean, but she didn't have to see.

All set to pitch a strikeout, I clutched the baseball between my thumb and knuckles the way Daddy had shown me, then, with all my might, flung it at Traven. The ball zipped through the air in a straight line, faster than the last time we had played. Wow, maybe that spit trick worked!

The ball traveled halfway toward Traven when, looking like an ostrich about to lose his balance, he stretched out his arms and upper body over home plate and swung. A faint crack sounded as the tip of his bat nicked the softball. Traven toppled forward. Before wiping out in the mud, at the last minute, he caught his footing. If he hadn't, Traven would have landed right on his nose.

The ball flew toward the edge of the driveway, bounced once, then rolled off toward my dad.

His old, worn-out work boots stuck out, the only part of Daddy I could see as he laid under the car on something called a creeper. It looked more like a giant skateboard, large enough for an adult to take a nap on. The baseball rolled up to this low-riding stretcher and wedged itself by a wheel near Daddy's feet.

Traven threw the bat and dashed toward first base, marked by a trashcan lid. The sound of crumpling aluminum caught my ears as Traven jumped up and down on the lid, wagging his arms and legs in the air in some goofy victory dance.

I couldn't take my eyes off this nutcase. "What are you doing?"

"What do you think? I'm running bases." He leaped over a puddle and headed toward second.

I stayed put at the pitcher's mound and shook my head. "You can't run bases. You have to get a hit first."

"I did get a hit. What's the matter? Are you blind or something? Didn't you see?"

"Yeah, I saw. Whatever that was, it sure wasn't a hit."

The goofball rounded second and continued running. "I sure did. I hit that ball square on. Aren't you going to get the ball and tag me out? Go ahead and try!" His words puffed out in short breaths as he dashed toward the next base.

Traven slowed his pace as if daring me to stop his home run. His foot tapped third base, marked by a tray Mommy had used under her large planted pots in the springtime. She said it caught water overflow. I don't know why she doesn't just use less water in the first place. That would be a much easier solution.

Skipping down the baseline toward home, Traven made it obvious he intended to make a home run out of his foul ball.

I deserted my post on the pitcher's mound and dashed through a soggy patch in the yard. Mud splattered up my pant leg—a nice touch to go with the nifty dirt pattern on the inside of my hands. Determined that Traven got the point, I was not about to let him reach home plate. I cut him off, grabbed him by the sleeve of his jacket, then tackled him to the ground.

"Get off me! You can't tag me out. You don't even have the ball."

"Can too. That was a foul ball. Can't run bases on a foul ball."

"Was not! I hit that ball fair and straight. Let go of me!" Traven shoved his hand in my face and pushed.

If I let him succeed, I knew he'd jump right back up, continue toward home plate, then claim a run. It'd be easier to stop him right here and now.

We rolled over each other in the muddiest part of the yard. Traven wrestled to get free. I refused to let him go. Somehow, I found my face shoved into the ground. I spat out a mouthful of dirt.

A large hand rested on my back and yanked me to my feet. At the same time, Traven got pulled off the ground and propped upright beside me. Having been peeled apart, I found myself staring up into the face of my dad.

He didn't look very happy—funny how his chin sticks out when he's mad— "What do you two think you are doing?"

The grimace on his face led me to believe he wasn't interested at all in what had happened. He just wanted our wrestling match to stop. But still, Traven and I blurted answers over each other's frantic words.

After Daddy allowed us time to calm down, he explained the difference between a foul ball and a good one. I had been right the whole time, but I knew Daddy wouldn't want me to make a big deal about it, so I tried real hard to hold my tongue and not say a thing. I guess "hold your tongue" must be one of those sayings Mommy used that didn't actually mean what it said, for I was not about to stick my dirty fingers in my mouth and grab my tongue. However, I could bet that my chest puffed out, and no matter how tight I pinched my lips together, I could not stop a grin from forming.

"The two of you are filthy. You better get inside and clean up." Daddy pointed us toward the house.

As I opened the back door, the smell of chocolate chip cookies met my nostrils. Mommy once explained that those two little holes at the end of our nose are called nostrils. I decided I liked that word, *nostrils*. It seemed extra fun to say.

Mommy stood in front of the kitchen counter, scraped cookies off a tray, then placed them on a wire rack to cool. The amazing smell of fresh-baked cookies caused me to forget about my dirty hands, not to mention the rest of me. As fast as a camera's flash, I stood at her side, my fingers outstretched, ready to grab one.

With the spatula gripped in her fist, Mommy smacked my hand

away. "Don't you dare. My goodness, the two of you are filthy. Now go. Get yourselves to that bathroom, and clean up, then we shall see about cookies."

One of my least favorite feelings was the one called disappointment, which I thought of as my enemy. This time, an extra huge amount of that disappointment walloped me. "Come on, Traven, we better do what Mommy says."

Finally, all scrubbed clean, Traven and I sat at the table and dunked cookies so warm that the melted chips pulled apart into a chocolaty drizzle when we broke them in half.

Once Traven had gone home, Mommy sent me upstairs to take a bath. I didn't understand why she wouldn't just let me get into a pair of pajamas. We had already eaten dinner, but, for some reason, she made me put on a clean shirt and some nice pants. Slouching, I puttered down the stair, dressed as if ready to go to church, and reentered the kitchen.

Not a single dirty dish cluttered the table or counters. Hurray, I wouldn't have to help out with that chore tonight. Mommy stood in front of the counter, stashing a bunch of our favorite chocolate chip cookies inside a plastic container, the kind used whenever we took food out of the house and didn't care whether or not the dish would be returned.

I watched her lay yet another cookie inside. Since the beginning of the school year, Mommy had been teaching me all about feelings. She helped me identify which ones I had at different times. At that moment, a huge feeling definitely spread clear through my entire insides. I believed it was the one Mommy labeled *concern*.

Desperate for help, I glanced back at Daddy. He sat at the table, his nose buried in the newspaper as he completely ignored the fact that Mommy, at that very moment, stashed our cookies in a "go-away" container.

My sight glued back onto Mommy's hands as they placed one cookie after another into that plastic tub—the one I knew would not remain in our house.

"Why are you doing that? The cookie jar is right here." I lifted the lid and peered inside. Only a few freshly baked cookies rested within.

"I thought it would be nice to take a batch across the street to Mr. Aldous." Mommy rearranged the top layer, then added yet another highly desired treat.

I took a second look in the almost empty cookie jar and counted. "One, two, three, four . . . I don't think it'd be all that nice. There aren't that many left."

"We can always bake more another day." Mommy ran her finger around the outer edge of the plastic lid. It popped, securing the seal. She turned toward me with a toothy grin spread across her face. "You look very handsome, Dakota."

Usually, it felt good to see Mommy's smile, but not this time. I stared, at her and the plastic tub with all our yummy cookies stashed inside, so hard without blinking that my eyes dried out and began to itch.

Hoping for a bit of help, I again glanced back at Daddy. How could he remain so calm, as if nothing important was happening? These chocolate chip cookies were his favorite also. But just like before, without a word, Daddy nodded at me and continued to read the paper.

Panic bubbled up inside. *Doesn't anyone see how unfair Mommy is being?* "How about, instead, we keep these cookies. Then we can go to the store tomorrow and buy some other treats for Mr. Aldous? That would still be nice." Feeling certain Mommy would love my brilliant idea and release the captive cookies, I reached my hand out toward them.

"Well, maybe . . . but it wouldn't be very special, now, would it?" Green specks in Mommy's eyes sparkled like the emerald jewelry she wore whenever she dressed up extra fancy. Mommy gazed down at me with the hint of a grin on her closed lips.

My stomach sunk. As hard as I tried to, I could not take my eyes off Mommy. And I was growing angry enough that I wanted to. "Are you *really* going to give away all our cookies?"

"Not all. A few are left." Mom nodded toward the cookie jar, then winked at me.

That wasn't very funny.

"Or, for that matter, we could always go to the store and buy ourselves a box of cookies after we give Mr. Aldous all these fresh-baked ones." Her smile opened wide but not close to as pretty as usual.

"Hey, that's not fair." I shot around toward the table. "Daddy, aren't you going to help me out here? Mom's home-baked cookies taste far better than any store-bought ones."

"Well, buddy, don't you think that right there is a good enough reason to give them away?"

I couldn't believe my ears. They both had turned against me! "But . . . I . . ."

Mommy laid her hand on my shoulder. "Don't worry, Dakota. We can always bake more another day."

"But these are so good, the best cookies in the world. Why does no other kind taste nearly as yummy as these?"

"They're made from our family's secret recipe. These chocolate chip cookies taste extra delicious, a result of the special love our relatives have passed down throughout the generations, all poured into the creation of these cookies. Doesn't that sound like the perfect gift to give to an elderly man who could use a bit of joy in his lonely life?"

"I don't know. It still doesn't sound all that fun to me." With all my might, I puffed my lips into the best pout I could muster.

It didn't work—Mommy just laughed.

"Mr. Aldous would enjoy a bit of this special kind of love. And that is why we are going to share our cookies with him. So keep your hands out of this container. As soon as possible, you and I will go to visit our across-the-street neighbor and deliver these cookies while they're still warm."

CHAPTER

11

ALDOUS

I MAY NEVER KNOW WHAT SADISTIC fiend possessed me, but for some absurd reason, this wild notion that I must master the initial run to Theodore Lack's "Valse-Arabesque" refused to release its grip on me. After the last time I attempted this complicated composition, I buried it deep in the bottom of the sheet music basket. Yet, it persisted in pecking at my thoughts in the same unyielding fashion that a vulture would peck flesh from the bones of a fallen gazelle.

For what felt like the hundredth time, I shoved Oscar's scrunched-up face out of my own as I knelt beside the piano and dug through the contents of this disdained basket. The animal's spastic persistence mirrored the hold that this favored piece of Mariam's obtained on me, clenching so tight one could assume it attached itself to my mind with the aid of a carpenter's vice clamp.

"Would you cut that out!" I prodded the beast back again, then wiped my hand across my left cheek—a feeble attempt to remove his slobber. The animal seemed to have an infinite supply. We never did succeed much at training this mutt.

Mariam's voice rang clear in my mind as if she stood beside me in this very room. "Don't call him a mutt. A mutt is a mixed breed. Oscar is not a mixed breed. He is a purebred pug. A pug is a very noble dog you should be honored to own."

For some ridiculous reason, pride had always shined in her rich brown eyes whenever she declared the breed of this animal. They had sparkled like a beam of light dancing in a cup of espresso as she spoke of this crazy dog. Almost as if this beast had become Mariam's baby, taking the place of Lacey. I would never understand what difference it made. A mutt's a mutt, and this animal would always remain a mutt in my eyes.

"I said, 'stop it.'" This time, I picked the *mutt* up and moved him to my other side so that my body, along with the leg of the piano and its matching bench, could block his access.

Finally, I came across the sought-after piece of music near the very bottom of the stack, of course. I removed it from the basket and spread it on the rack above the keyboard. When I sat on the bench, Oscar took this as an invitation to join me as he hopped up at my side and settled into place.

A sharp pain invaded my head as I squinted to scrutinize the multitude of confusing notes scattered across each stanza. They lined up like tiny bugs, ready to embark on an intimidating march. Why did I ever imagine I could decipher such gibberish?

My stiff hands found their position on the ivory keys. In a clumsy attempt to work together, one by one in a painfully slow fashion, I plunked out the notes.

My achy fingers persisted until I successfully completed this first section of Theodore Lack's lengthy arrangement. If I had wanted to master this instrument, there were many other, much easier melodies I could have chosen to work on to sharpen my musical skills. But this particular composition had been Mariam's favorite and, for some peculiar reason, the only one that gnawed for my attention.

Satisfied, I glanced down at Oscar. "So, what do you think, boy? I did it. Well, somewhat. That noise I made was certainly nothing to brag about."

Oscar yelped back, then nudged his flattened nose on the edge of the keyboard. Sometimes I wondered how much he really did understand.

"What . . . you want me to try again?"

My eyes wandered back up to the sheet of music. The tangled maze of black dots taunted me. I waited for this mess of notes to come into focus and marveled at how the insane notion had led me to believe that *I* could accomplish something by persisting forward. "Oh, what will it take to make this crazy mutt content?" Foolishly, I mumbled the question under my breath.

Oscar heard and possibly even understood, for he nudged my elbow as if attempting to force my hands back onto the keyboard.

Simply to appease the little fellow, my stiff fingers plowed through the complicated run a second time, then a third, and yet again until a bit of smoothness accompanied the perplexing collage of notes.

I removed my hands from the ivory keys and flexed my fingers. Strange, a bit of their stiffness had faded. I scanned the notes I had just played and considered my progress. A touch of pride weaseled into my decrepit bones.

Oscar again prodded his schnozzle at the keyboard. His shiny eyes, like two polished black buttons, sparkled at me. Who knows, maybe this beast was onto something. So, I started again from the beginning and played "Valse-Arabesque" clear through until the end of the first run. Yet this time, instead of stopping, I attempted further on from that point.

Oscar hopped off the bench and ran toward the door. His stubby legs pranced onto the welcome mat in a double-time beat with the sound of a knock.

"Now, who could that be?" My knees creaked as I unfolded from the bench and followed after the little guy.

He barked and twirled like a gyroscope.

I shoved him aside to get to the door. As I held it halfway open, Dakota, the small pesky boy from across the street, pushed through.

Aghast by his audacious behavior, I turned toward his mother, who remained beyond the doorway—her mouth gaped open with a look of shock. I swore this young woman couldn't control her two-legged beast any better than I managed my four-legged one.

"I heard music, beautiful music. What were you playing?"

I spun my body toward the child's voice. He stood in the center of my living room as Oscar hopped about his legs. The kid glanced in every direction, indicating that his search would not end until he found the answer to some noble quest.

Alexandra stepped inside, and I closed the door behind her. "Dakota, get back here." Faint creases, like a crescent moon, molded onto the corners of her mouth. She angled back toward my direction. Rosy streaks inched her cheeks as if an invisible paintbrush delivered a fresh application of blush. "I am so sorry, Mr. Aldous. I don't know what has gotten into that boy. He usually doesn't behave like this." Horror reflected in the mother's aqua eyes.

For some odd reason, her mortified expression, combined with Dakota's determined stance as he searched my living room for this phantom source of music, struck me with great humor. It had been years since the last time I had laughed—I mean powerfully roared from amusement. As I soaked in their actions, a massive guffaw I could not control howled out from somewhere deep within. I had not hooted so hard for such a long time that it surprised me I remembered how.

I doubled over, gasping for breath. Alexandra dropped an item she had carried in on the doormat, then grasped my arm as if to stabilize my trembling body. Her powerless effort to support my much larger physique caused yet another wave of full-fledged hoots to burst from within me.

An expression of terror streaked across this young woman's face. Dakota bounded to my other side and latched onto my right arm. The two of them shouted repeated phrases, "Breath, Mr. Aldous. Are you okay? Should we call 911?"

The more they inquired, the more I became struck with humor, and the louder I roared. Finally, I inched over to the rocking chair beside my front window and sat down. Bent over, I clutched my cramped belly.

"Mommy, he must be having a heart attack!"

The child's desperate declaration invoked additional waves of snorting spasms.

"I'm not sure, Dakota. He may just be laughing. Go, sit on the couch. I'll fetch him a cup of water." Alexandra left the room.

I turned toward Dakota and strained through tear-streaked vision, aiming to focus on the child's rigid posture. His wide eyes—as round as Oscar's feed dish—glued in my direction.

Every bit of inner tenacity united together in an attempt to tamper the tremors invoked by this intense laughter. Finally, I gathered a speck of control and settled down.

Alexandra rounded the corner and held a tumbler of ice water out toward me. "Here, take a sip. It might help."

I gulped a few breaths of air to further steady my diaphragm, then reached for the cup. "Thanks." The cool drink soothed my throat, providing strength to gather a bit more much-needed self-control.

"Mr. Aldous, are you okay now?" With a probing gaze, Alexandra scrutinized the situation. A wisp of blonde hair fell over her eyes. Green specks swam within deep pools of blue. She swiped the strand aside, allowing a kaleidoscope of color to shine through. *Which hue was her dominant shade?* Mesmerized by those vivid orbs, I stared.

"Mr. Aldous, sir," Dakota pleaded. "Since you are calm now, could you please tell me where that amazing music came from? It must have been the most beautiful music I've heard in all my life."

My full attention drew to this small boy. The reality of his short-lived existence forced me to bite the insides of my cheeks to keep from resuming my laughter. Perched on my sofa in creased pants and a pressed, button-down shirt, he resembled a miniature grownup. I would never have guessed he had it in him to act so politely. "What do you mean?" I couldn't imagine what music he inquired about, certainly not my awkward attempt at the piano.

"When we came up to your porch, we heard music."

I rose from the rocking chair and approached the antique piano in the next room. "Do you mean this?" I tickled my clumsy fingers over a few keys.

"That's it!" The child bounded from the couch and landed in the same spot Oscar had occupied earlier. "Do it again."

My goodness, this child was just as nutty as my mutt. Oscar hopped up on the bench on my opposite side. Trapped by two conspiring pests, I repositioned my fingers on the keyboard. Slowly, with many blunders, I again ran through the first couple pages of Theodore Lack's thirteen-paged composition, not to mention all the repeat sections that, if added on, would increase the page count to fifteen.

"Mommy, did you hear that? Wasn't it beautiful?"

"Yes, darling, it sounded very nice." Alexandra moved closer until she stood just inches behind me. She gazed over my shoulder, similar to how Lacey did when she was young.

Dakota's stubby fingers inched toward the brittle, dog-eared sheet music that Mariam had treasured. Panic, combined with a touch of rage, rose within like an unleashed storm. "Don't touch that!" My voice roared out, far more intense than intended.

Dakota flinched. His rosy freckled face paled. "I'm sorry, I didn't mean to . . ." The child's voice wavered with suppressed tears as he slid off the bench.

"Well, we've taken up far too much of your time." Alexandra swept toward the front door, with Dakota keeping pace close behind. She picked up a plastic food container—the item dropped on the entry rug shortly after their arrival.

I stood and moved out to the living room. Alexandra popped open the lid. The delicious scent of freshly baked cookies escaped. "We made these earlier today and thought you would like to have some."

"They were baked from scratch, from our family's secret recipe." A bit of pink flushed over Dakota's plump cheeks as a backdrop to copper-colored freckles.

She handed me the container. A strange and undesirable sensation—one that, for many years, I exerted great effort to avoid—zigzagged through my bones. Mariam had often referred to the abundant amount of shame that overwhelmed her. Whenever she brought up that unsolicited topic, I ignored her. My deceased wife no longer remained at my side, yet, at that moment, the shame she spoke of flooded my insides.

"Thank you." My voice quivered as the words slunk out.

"Well, we better go now. Thank you for sharing your music. And don't worry about the container." Alexandra grasped Dakota's hand, and the two slipped through the door, shutting it behind them.

I stood alone in my living room, the gift of cookies in my hand. Oscar nudged my pant leg, a bold reminder that I wasn't entirely alone. "What is it, boy?"

His knotted tail, like a bun pasted to his rump, remained motionless as he released a single bark.

"I know, I know. I shouldn't have yelled at Dakota."

Two more yips escaped Oscar's flattened muzzle.

DAKOTA

NOTHING UNUSUAL HAPPENED AT SCHOOL today, just the same old thing, causing time to tick by extra slow. After school, I wanted our special cookies for a snack. But they were all gone because we had to give so many away to Mr. Aldous. Then Mommy got dinner going, and Daddy arrived home from work.

Even though Mommy had cooked one of my favorite meals, shepherd's pie, for some strange reason, I didn't feel much like eating. I scraped off the mound of mashed potatoes from the top of my portion and scooched the glob to the edge of my plate. Then a brilliant idea struck.

Mommy usually did not like it when I played with my food. But this evening, she and Daddy paid no attention. They sat deeply involved in some conversation on the other side of the table while my dinner begged me to join in on a top-notch adventure. Of course, I had to accept, so I took my fork and piled the potatoes up high into the form of a white, squishy mountain.

Daddy had once told me a story about the Matterhorn, a mountain in the Alps in a far-off place called Switzerland. He said that every year, people climbed to the top of this mountain, even though, way up there, it got so cold a person could freeze into a living ice pop in no time at all. But, if they froze to death, they wouldn't be a *living* ice pop—they'd be a dead one. Anyway, I decided to turn this mound of potatoes into my own model of that famous mountain.

I concentrated hard and placed each glob of mush in the perfect position. Then I leaned back and squinted until my eyes ached as I examined my project. Yeah, it looked pretty great if I did say so myself.

Wanting to show off my awesome sculpture, I glanced up at Mommy and Daddy but then remembered that they might not feel as pleased as I did about my project. So instead, I bit my tongue and kept quiet.

If not for the mess—not to mention the smell—this sculpture would make the perfect add-on for one of those miniature train sets that Daddy and I saw a couple of months ago at the train show.

I glanced back up at my parents. They showed no sign of noticing what I'd been doing. Or maybe, for some strange reason, they didn't care. Mommy and Daddy acted as if they had no idea I just created the next most-wanted addition to some person's model train set. I laid my fork down and listened in on their discussion. From the tone of their voices, it sounded very important, but before I figured out what they were talking about, I got bored.

Since no one seemed to mind what I was doing, I dug my fork back into my dinner and pulled out each green pea and carrot slice, one at a time. I positioned these on either side of my mushy mountain. Now I had the Green Coats and the Orange Coats as two separate armies to fight over ownership of the Masherhorn. That was the name I chose for my mountain. Cool, huh? Whichever team got to the top of Mount Masherhon first would plant their flag and own the mountain. So, the excitement continued. Would the flag be made of mushed-up green peas or squashed carrots?

Before I discovered which team would be Champion Mashed Potato Mountain Climber, Daddy glanced across the table at me. And I was about to turn the meat and crust from my shepherd's pie into a base camp.

His eyes squinted into that look that meant, "I know what you are doing, and you better cut it out." Mommy joined in with her equally silent yet just as powerful glair.

Rats, why couldn't they have remained focused on their conversation a few minutes longer? I was about to have a champion Masherhorn team claim their prize. And I had looked forward to mushing a bunch of peas or carrots into the shape of a flag. But instead, I answered their silent warning with a big sigh, puffing it out with an extra big breath of air to make it a loud one, then, with my fork, sliced off the top of Masherhorn Mountain and ate it.

Well, that one bite I swallowed must have satisfied my parents because they turned back toward each other and continued their talk as if nothing had happened.

Funny, that first mouthful landed in my belly, and, all of a sudden, I felt hungry. So now something huge like a natural disaster had to interrupt this race. With the top of my mountain destroyed, all team players screamed and yelled as I scooped them up, stuffed them into my mouth, and gulped them down.

Would Mommy and Daddy ever know that their son had become the monster who ate the green and the orange teams? I shoveled another extra-large bite into my mouth. A few more monster-sized swallows, and the mountain transformed into flatland while my tummy filled up. Wow, it took a lot of mountain, base camp, and team players to fill up my giant-sized stomach.

Mommy's and Daddy's plates were almost empty.

"Can I go watch some TV?"

"After you pick up your dishes." Mommy nodded toward my plate. Mashed potatoes skimmed its surface—a last reminder of the legendary Masherhorn.

I stacked my silverware and cup onto my plate, carried the load to the sink, then marched off into the den. Grabbing the remote, I punched buttons and flicked through channels until one of my favorite cartoons flashed across the screen. I dropped the remote in front of the TV and backed up toward the couch. My body sank into soft cushions while I curled up and watched my show, tugging my sleeve halfway over my hand to suck on the fabric.

The heavy wooden door to the room creaked open. Daddy stepped in, picked up the remote, and lowered the volume.

I no longer could hear my show. Scrunching up my face to look as angry as possible, I stared at Daddy, but he showed no effect. *Not fair. Both of my parents' silent looks worked great. And they even got to use them during dinner time. Why didn't my glares work?*

"Hey, little buddy." Daddy dropped the remote onto an end table. "It took quite a while for you to start eating. That's not normal for you. So, what's up?"

Wow, he must have paid more attention than I thought. I glanced down at my soggy sleeve and scrunched up my shoulders. "I just didn't feel hungry, that's all."

Daddy plopped beside me on the couch, then placed his open hand over my forehead. He must have thought I ran a fever. "Why not? Are you feeling all right?"

"Oh, I feel fine. There's just a lot of stuff on my mind."

"I see." Daddy's lips pinched together as he nodded. "Did something happen at school today? Was there more trouble with Jacob Downing?"

"Nah, since I gave him the swing last week, he pretty much has left me alone."

"So . . . do you want to share all this stuff that's on your mind?"

I didn't realize it until Daddy asked the question, but I did want to share everything that boggled up inside my head. Here comes the confusing part. I couldn't figure out what all that stuff was. Again I bit onto the edge of my sleeve, then yanked it loose from my teeth. Since he asked, I guess I'd give it a try.

"Remember last night when Mommy and I took the cookies to Mr. Aldous?"

"Yes, I sure do. I also remember you weren't too keen on the idea."

"I don't like Mr. Aldous very much. Every time we bump into him, he acts mean and cranky. It makes no sense why we had to give away our special cookies, especially to him. But Mommy insisted." I rambled on and on about that cranky Mr. Aldous. The words and feelings rushed into each other as they dumped out of me.

Daddy sat silent and listened. Every so often, his thin mustache twitched. He had the niftiest mustache, skinny as a pencil—not the big bushy kind like some people. This one made him look like Zorro.

"It was strange, Daddy. When we walked up the steps to Mr. Aldous's front porch, I heard the most beautiful music coming from inside. For a moment, I forgot all about how nasty Mr. Aldous was. By the time he had opened his door, all my yucky feelings toward him had vanished like a magic trick." I waved my hand as if I held a magician's wand.

"All I could think of was where did that music come from? Then Mr. Aldous and I sat on his piano bench and—oh, his cute puppy, Oscar." I couldn't forget about Oscar. "Then Mr. Aldous played that same music I had heard. Daddy, it sounded amazing."

I got so excited I bounced on the couch cushions. "I want to make music just like that. I want to learn to play the piano. Daddy, do you think *I* can?"

Before my daddy could answer, my brain sped forward like a racecar, and words spat out with each drive of the piston. "He *actually* acted nice. He *really* did. Daddy, he even laughed. He laughed so hard that Mommy and I thought something terrible was wrong, and we were about to call an ambulance. But we didn't have to, for he calmed down on his own, and that was when he and I sat at his piano, and he played." Words flung off my tongue as fast as flipping pancakes. "For a tiny moment there, I thought we might be friends. Then suddenly, all the fun vanished. Everything changed. Like a peapod had snapped open and mean Mr. Aldous popped out." That's one pea I'd never eat, no matter how hungry I might be. "Mommy handed him the cookies, and we left."

With both of my hands, I grabbed Daddy's gray striped shirt. "Why did he do that, Daddy? How could a person be so friendly one minute, then go back to 'Mr. Mean' the next?"

Daddy unclasped my fingers and held my hands. "It's hard to tell why anyone would act that way. When someone doesn't have a safe place to share their feelings, they sometimes stuff them inside, but nothing can remain buried forever. After a while, those feelings burst forth."

The bump, which Mommy called an Adam's Apple—I've wondered if somewhere along the way Daddy ate a crab apple and it stuck in his throat—anyway, the apple bobbed as he talked. I sometimes got so interested in watching it move up and down that I'd forget to listen, but not this time. "So . . . maybe he never had a Mommy or Daddy or someone else to talk to, the way you talk with me?"

"Maybe, but not always, Mr. Aldous might have people in his life willing to listen and be there for him, but for some reason, he may push them all away. Often a person will close up for reasons that have nothing to do with their current situation. Mr. Aldous's actions may be related to some long unresolved issue. When a person does not heal old wounds, in time, they take the pain of those wounds out on others."

Oh boy, now Daddy was getting all serious. *What is it with adults and their need to have serious talks?* "That all sounds very confusing."

"It can be, Dakota."

"Sooo, you think Mr. Aldous yelled at Mommy and me and pushed us away because old wounds told him to?"

"Something like that," Daddy tipped his head side to side.

Now I felt more puzzled than ever. "How do we deal with that? Mommy seems dead set on us making friends with Mr. Aldous, regardless of how nasty he gets."

"You ask a difficult question, Dakota, with no easy answer. I suppose that is where we pray for God's guidance."

My mind rolled fast again and filled with excitement. "While we're praying for Mr. Aldous, can we also pray for a piano? I want to learn to play like Mr. Aldous."

ALDOUS

$\mathcal{A}$LARMED BY A COOL NIP in the morning air, I groaned and drew the covers up over my head. My aged body had lost all motivation to rise and start a new day. Autumn's crisp air did little to inspire me.

Oscar bounded on top of my covered-up legs, startling me half out of my wrinkled skin.

"Get off me, you crazy mutt. I'm still sleeping. You'll have to wait until I'm ready to get up before I take you outside."

This spastic animal had different plans. Oscar continued to pounce on top of my weary body concealed by a hoard of bedding until I kicked at him with my foot, bopping the furry fellow back onto the floor.

He's the most persistent mutt I have ever known. My efforts did little to deter him as he spun in circles, his toenails grating the Persian rug, while he let out a string of barks. A distinct line scraped among colored threads by the beast's sharp claws. My blood boiled. I never understood how Mariam could let such occurrences slide.

"You are not going to shut up until you get what you want, are you?" He answered with three high-pitched barks.

Once again, I had been done in by a dog. I threw back the blankets and hovered on the edge of the bed. Every bone in my body ached. I had no desire to move any further toward this ridiculous goal to arise for the morning. So I lingered as if frozen on the edge of the mattress while Oscar remained planted by my feet. Determined to defeat the animal, we stared each other down.

The drawn-out screech of hydraulic brakes disrupted my glower and drew me to the bedroom window. Once again, this pesky mutt won.

My movement sent Oscar into yet another barking spasm. I ignored him and parted the curtains to peer outside.

A thin layer of condensation covered the glass pane, distorting my view—a reminder that these old windows had lost their seal many years ago—yet I could still make out the obscured shape of a bright yellow bus as it pulled up the street.

Dakota would be inside that bus. That thought, for some reason beyond comprehension, caused a boulder-sized wadded lump of guilt to thump in the pit of my stomach. My left hand clutched the striped fabric of my pajamas over the belly region. I could not let that child, or anyone else, get to me.

With my other hand, I wiped the moisture off the chilled glass to clear up my view. Alexandra stood at the base of her driveway and waved after the bus that carried away her only child. I pressed my fingers onto the poorly insulated window. A bitter cold seeped through my flesh and into my bones.

Oscar's bark jarred my thoughts, returning me to the present space and time. My hand flinched from the frigid glass. If I cared enough, I would replace every window in this ancient house, but the time and expense required didn't seem worth the effort.

"Come on, boy. I might as well take you outside." I grabbed my robe from the bedpost and draped it over my shoulders, then ambled downstairs toward the front door as Oscar scampered at my heels. The instant I unbolted the lock and pushed open the screen, he bounded outside toward a row of bushes.

Alexandra still stood at the base of her driveway. She folded her arms across her chest, appearing to shield herself from the morning's chilled air. Her fingertips on her outer hand wiggled a wave in my direction while a closed grin spread across her lips.

Wishing I had waited until after she'd gone indoors, I returned her greeting with a nod while grumbling complaints under my breath. Heat radiated from my cheeks regardless of the cool air. This sudden fire sensation from within myself unsettled me. Throughout my adult life, I've held a firm grasp on my carefully constructed façade. No one, not even my beloved Mariam, could break through. *So why now are this neighbor and her pesky child chiseling cracks into my strategically fashioned blockade?*

Oscar's short hind legs kicked up a patch of grass among soggy leaves—remnants from last night's thunderstorm—his signal that he had completed his business. "Oscar, come on . . . back inside, boy."

He angled his pugged nose in my direction, then scampered up the porch steps and back into the house, leaving a trail of muddy paw prints in his path. I closed the door behind him and glared down at the relentless animal. His curled stump, which Mariam had called a tail, wiggled in spastic rhythms like a metronome set on high.

"Well, thanks to you, I'm up now. Look at that mess you made." I let out an exaggerated sigh. Mariam had done all the cleaning when she was alive. I never had to worry about such trivial chores. I stared at the grime. My only choice now was to mop it up or leave it to spread out and multiply. Usually, I settled with the latter since, throughout the day, more mud would eventually be tracked in regardless. A clean entry floor did not seem worth my effort.

"I might as well get dressed." The words tumbled from my mouth like lyrics to the creaking sound of the bottom step as I headed back upstairs. Instead of shadowing close behind, this senseless mutt, almost always under my feet, remained stationary beside the door. "Well, are you coming?" Oscar let out his telltale bark, scampered toward the steps, then trailed behind me.

As I reentered my bedroom, my eyes fixated on the multitude of figurines overcrowding both dressers and every shelf. Oh, how my dear wife had loved her collection. Hundreds of tiny hummingbirds each sat stagnant as they caught an endless supply of dust. I may never understand how anyone could draw joy from such a hoard of useless objects like this, yet Mariam had done just that. A random thought stole into my mind—*Do hummingbirds exist in Heaven? Wouldn't Mariam love it if they did?*

Some days dragged on at an extra slow pace, and today counted as one of them. I could find nothing better to do than sit in the old rocker and stare out the living room window. Too often, lately, I fought with the wretched belief that the only purpose left in my life was to watch time inch away, minute by agonizingly slow minute—a sadistic form of hell on earth.

Since Mariam's death, I had done very little to maintain the flowerbeds she had taken great pride in. Even though this fall marked the third year since any new plants have been placed within the decorative stones that edged the garden, a lone chrysanthemum bloomed on the end of one scraggly green stem. Mesmerized, I gawked at a multitude of brilliant orange petals. How, after all this stagnant time, could a plant find its way toward glory?

Frozen in my stance, I stared. A flicker of movement caught my eye, shaking me from my stupor. *No! It couldn't be.* I rose from the rocking chair for a better look. *There, I saw it again, a hummingbird.* But it's too late in the season for hummingbirds. All of them would have flown south weeks ago. Not to mention, I've never known of one to draw nectar from a chrysanthemum blossom. I closed my eyes and rubbed aching knuckles over tender skin, hoping to clear the blur from my vision. After blinking a couple of times, I reexamined my view. Sure as my favorite pair of slippers that covered my feet, my eyes squinted at the metallic green flash of a tiny hummingbird.

A streak of excitement rushed through my veins. "Oscar, do you remember where Mariam kept the feeders? And where is her nectar recipe?" I sped inside toward the kitchen and then entered through the cellar door. Displaying more agility than I had expelled in a long time, I ran down creaking stairs. Oscar panted beside me as I hunted through a horde of discarded items stashed on utility shelves. Finally, inside a dusty old paper bag, I located a feeder.

The heavy thump of my feet as I thundered back up the basement stairs echoed in my ears. Oscar kept a close pace behind me with each step. I tore open every drawer in the kitchen and shuffled through cupboards, searching for that sought-after recipe. Finally, in the back of an upper cabinet, I came across a half-empty carton of sugar. A piece of paper taped to its side contained the information for the correct sugar-to-water ratio for nectar. A pull on my lips gave away my inner relief as I cradled this container in my shaky old hands. Mariam had left instructions on how to nourish her most treasured friends.

I set a saucepan on the stove. A much-needed renewed sense of purpose sifted into my cells as each grain of pure white sugar dissolved into the heated water. Once the mixture cooled, I poured it into the feeder. Grabbing my jacket, I proceeded outside to hang this feast in the neglected garden, among the solitary chrysanthemum blossoms.

Oscar and I retreated to the porch. I relaxed on the swing and waited for our little friend. Oscar hopped on my lap, curled into a ball, and fell asleep.

To the melodic drone of Oscar's snores, my vision roved like a dance over the front yard in search of Mariam's hummingbird. An irresistible heaviness pulled on my eyelids. I gave in and leaned onto the wooden slats of the swing, then drifted into a deep sleep.

The loud screech of hydraulic brakes jarred me awake. Oscar let out a string of barks and leaped from my lap. Through blurry, half-asleep eyes, I stared toward the street at Dakota's yellow school bus parked in front of his driveway. The small, unforgettable boy strolled off the large bus and then sprinted toward his awaiting mother. Together they walked into their house.

How could I have napped half the day away? My knees groaned as I stood up, the left leg numb from Oscar's body pressing a nerve for far too long. With a half-limp gait, I ambled indoors to confirm the time. Relief eased into my cells as I gawked at the hands of the old grandfather clock that pointed to just after noon. School must have let out early.

A rumble in my stomach signified a reminder that I had missed lunch, so I smeared a bit of peanut butter onto a slice of rye bread and took a bite as I leaned against the butcher's block. My mouth dried up the instant it made contact with the gooey spread. The wad of food I had bitten off stuck to the inside of my cheek like glue. Oh, how much I would have rather instead enjoyed one of Mariam's mouthwatering lunches, made to my liking.

She had always prepared my food with great care, yet, I took her efforts for granted. I couldn't remember thanking her even once. Yet every day, she labored on with a permanent smile on her sweet face, as if unaware of my gruff unappreciative attitude.

With each step, Oscar affixed himself to my heels. "What's the matter, boy? If you don't watch out, you'll get stepped on." The mutt's persistence irritated me.

"Oh, goodness, I never fed you today. I bet you also are starved." I set down my partially eaten sandwich, then poured a heap of dry dog food into his empty dish. His sharp canine teeth loudly crunched as I gulped the remainder of my measly meal, then brushed stray crumbs onto the floor. *Good thing Mariam couldn't see. She would have had a fit.* "Come on, boy. Let's go back outside and find that hummingbird."

Oscar chomped one more mouthful, then followed me out the front door. Like a loyal sentry, the irritating mutt hopped up at my side, joining me as I eased back onto the porch swing. I stared at this mangy beast. *How could I, at the same time, both detest and gain comfort from this crazed animal?*

A high-pitched shriek grabbed my attention. Across the street, Dakota stumbled out the side door to his house with a clunky pair of roller skates strapped to his feet.

Distracted by a glint of metallic green that flashed at the corner of my eye, I spotted the hummingbird. It fluttered to the feeder, took a long draw of nectar, then hovered above its food station. This tiny bird continued its perfectly designed choreographic dance like an elegant ballet.

Dakota's squeal again met my ears. I would have cursed my sharp hearing with wishes to tune out his obnoxious noise, but the boy's joyous cries sparked my interest.

"Hey, Dakota, want to come and watch a hummingbird with me?" The shout of my voice startled me. The action had burst from my being with the un-expectancy of a hiccup.

Pausing in the center of his driveway, the boy gazed in my direction. *Darn it, he heard. Now I have to follow through.*

"What did you say, Mr. Aldous?" The child cupped an ear and slowly glided toward where the road met his driveway.

"I'm watching a hummingbird. Come see." *Dear God, what was wrong with me? I did it again.* I clamped my mouth, hoping no more treacherous phrases could burst out.

Dakota's chin dropped as his mouth hung half-open in confusion.

I'm in luck. Dakota hadn't understood my invitation. "This little guy is fun to watch. You might find it fascinating." *What the—another betrayal?* I recognized the voice as my own, but the words could not have come from me.

Dakota glanced behind him toward his house, then back in my direction. "Just a minute!" He spun around and bolted up his drive. The screen door slammed shut as he fled inside.

What did I say? You would have thought I had warned him of a grizzly bear in the area.

The hummingbird continued to flit from the feeder to the branch of a nearby tree and back again. Finally, it perched like a tiny green dot among yellowed leaves. "Come on, Oscar. The show's over. We might as well venture back inside."

CHAPTER

14

ALDOUS

I RESTED MY HAND ON THE small of my achy back. All this rain we've had has caused my arthritis to act up. The sharp pain in my spine informed me that I had held the same position on my sagging mattress for far too long. Yet I could not peel myself away. I had wasted the entire afternoon upstairs on my bed, gazing from one hummingbird figurine to the next. I studied each of the one-hundred and thirty-seven useless items collected over the years and wondered if Mariam even knew how many she had accumulated. What an absurd misuse of money, yet for some ridiculous reason, she had loved them, why I will never know.

Oscar lay sound asleep on the floor beside my bed. An infrequent snore buzzed from beneath his flappy upper lip. The irrational idea that I might sneak past this mutt without him knowing tugged at my brain.

I slipped from my bedcovers, cautious not to evoke squeaks from worn-out springs, then crept downstairs and out the front door. A sense of relief seeped into my tormented soul as the screen door swung shut behind me. I paced down the porch steps while my attention fell on the vacant feeder. A dark shadow from the low evening's sun cloaked it like bedclothes, causing a lonely sensation to bite into my soul. I wondered where our little friend had gone for the night. Wishing to bury myself deep within the fabric of the nylon jacket I had grabbed on my way out, I pulled the collar up toward my ears and then sped across the vacant street.

What was I doing? Nothing logical could result from this. I hesitated, then knocked on the side door of Dakota's house. Common sense told me to turn away and run before anyone could answer, yet, for some unknown reason, my feet refused to comply.

The door eased open, revealing the five-year-old boy I dreaded to see. His round blue eyes stared up at me as he chewed the edge of his left sleeve, stretching the striped fabric.

I peered down at the child. The smell of sweaty boy met my nostrils. For a fleeting instant, that acrid aroma flashed me back many decades. I rubbed my hazy eyes and then focused on the child's mussed-up hair. Perspiration plastered straggly blond strands to his forehead. It looked as if he hadn't seen a comb in the better part of a year. I gulped back my reluctance and took a breath. "Are you still selling fundraiser items for your school?"

The boy relaxed his clenched jaw and dropped his soggy sleeve, revealing the gap from his missing front tooth. He then spun away. "Daddy, Mr. Aldous is here!"

His screechy voice sent chills up my crooked spine. Heavy footsteps announced the arrival of a man.

"Daddy, he's that neighbor I told you about. You know, the one we gave all our cookies away to."

"Dakota, that's not polite." The solid bridge of the man's nose—an exact replica of his son's—canceled any question of him being the boy's father. He held a steady hand out toward mine.

Fighting a burning desire to turn around and disappear without a word, I planted my feet firmly on the ground and accepted his greeting.

"I'm Randy. You've already met my wife and son."

I quickly yanked my hand back, careful to conceal my disdain toward this ludicrous notion of venturing into this neighbor's home.

With his mouth hung half-open, Dakota's sight appeared glued to my worn-out slippers. Before I had left my house, I saw no logical reason to switch to shoes. I cleared my throat, motivated to complete this business transaction as promptly as possible. It achieved my desired effect, for the child's gaze rose from my feet and met mine. I glared at the boy. "Dakota, I'd like to take another look at your fundraiser sheet."

"Sure thing, Mr. Aldous." The child sped up the entry stairs and disappeared. An instant later, he thundered back down toward me. His small feet moved with such haste I feared he might plow right into my aching body. "Here you go, mister. Are you going to buy something?" Grinning like a jack-o-lantern, he shook the tattered pamphlet in my face.

"I might." Irritated by the actions that had led me to this moment, I grabbed the pamphlet and glanced over many pictures of needless junk. As I turned to page two, I spied what I sought after, a brown glazed vase encircled with hummingbird etchings. Mariam would have loved this. "That . . . here . . . this is what I want." My finger shook as I pointed out the coveted item.

A grin from ear to ear overtook Dakota's face. He snatched the brochure and handed it to his father. "Daddy, how much does he owe me?" The child's eyes illuminated like the tips of lit sparklers.

"Fourteen ninety-five."

"So, did I do it? Did I sell enough to earn my Super-Bat bike kit?" The child bounced as if he had springs affixed to the bottom of his stocking-covered feet.

I pulled out my wallet and handed him three five-dollar bills.

Randy glanced over the order form. Fingers fell beneath sandy-blond hair as his hand tapped his temple. "Yes, Koty, you did it. Mr. Aldous's purchase takes the total just above the required amount. You reached your goal. From now on, I'll have to call you Batkid." He mussed his son's hair, a shade lighter than his own.

"Yippee! I need to tell Mommy." Dakota poised to flee.

Randy grabbed the edge of his son's untucked shirt. "Just a minute, young man, you're not finished here. Thank your customer, take his money, and give him his change."

I shook the bills toward the excited lad, his cheeks a pinker tint than previously. He grabbed the money out of my hand and stuffed it in a pouch.

"Aren't you forgetting something?" Randy's eyebrows raised in sync with a mustache twitch.

"Oh yeah, thank you, Mr. Aldous."

"Dakota, you owe him change."

"I do?"

"Five cents."

I gritted my teeth and held back impatience while, with painstaking deliberation, this child sifted through coins within the money pouch until he concluded which one was a nickel. I'll never know how his father could stand there and wait as he did. If Dakota were my son, I would have snatched the money from him and completed the task myself, anything to get out of there as quickly as possible.

DAKOTA

ALMOST EVERY NIGHT SINCE THE first day of school, I had fallen asleep to the sound of thunderstorms. So much rain poured from the clouds it had no place to go, so all that water ran down the sidewalks and turned them into fast-flowing streams. Splashing through this new river was awesome enough, yet the pile of dirt and gravel left behind once all that rain had dried up made it even more so. I had the best fun zooming over all that built-up gravel with my roller skates.

As soon as the weekend got here, I knew Daddy would sweep off the sidewalk and take away all my fun. For some reason, he seemed to think that making the outside look presentable was important.

I never understood why it was such a big deal. To me, only the fun we got from that very cool gift God left behind after His excellent rainstorms mattered. Anyway, with the weekend still a couple of days away, I planned to spend as much time as possible enjoying my bumpety skate ride.

Traven came to my house right after school. I tried to talk him into joining me in this adventure, but he didn't want to. He mumbled something about his mom not being happy with all the guck caught in his wheels, which he had brought home the last time we did this.

His excuse made no more sense than Daddy's desire to clear the sidewalk. Didn't Traven realize that any mom would get mad if their kid brought dirt into the house? Moms get hung up about stuff like that the same way dads do about keeping their lawns cut. Why couldn't Traven rinse off his wheels with a garden hose? I always did before I took my skates back into the house.

I'll never get why so many people waste time worrying about silly things that don't matter. They need to ease up and have fun. I don't ever want to be like that when I grow up.

No matter what everyone else thought, I was determined to have as much fun as possible with God's fantastic present while it lasted. Part of the way up my drive, I stuck out a foot to stop myself, tested my balance, then skated back toward the sidewalk, gaining as much speed as possible. As I neared the edge of our driveway, I leaned to one side and splattered through the wet, dirt-covered walkway. I hollered out while my skates bumped over muddy gravel. My whole body juddered as my voice shook. I got to our next-door neighbor's drive and spun around, then started again over the same bumpety trail.

Mr. Aldous sat with that dog of his outside on his porch swing. He seemed to be watching me. Lately, Mr. Aldous did that an awful lot. The other day, he tried to call me over. He hollered something about a hummingbird, but I refused to go. Mommy had made it clear that I was never to leave the yard. Anyway, something about that Mr. Aldous, I didn't like. Mommy often told me to be nice to people, and I made sure not to act mean toward him, but that didn't change the fact that he gave me the creeps.

I ignored Mr. Aldous as he stared in my direction. Maybe he wished to play also. Many grownups appear to have forgotten how to have fun. I bet Mr. Aldous was one of them.

I sped down the sidewalk over the loose gravel, then up toward my driveway, making sure to whoop louder than before.

Mr. Aldous shook his head and yelled something at me, but I couldn't make out his words. I stuck my foot out and stopped my skates, right in the middle of the best bumps. "Excuse me, Mr. Aldous. What did you say?"

He shook his head. "I said, you sure are obnoxious."

Wow, he *had* been watching me the whole time. Maybe he liked the way I skated. I felt that tight pull on my cheeks again. I had practiced my biggest smile in a mirror, and every time I did, my cheeks felt a tug like they did now. That was how I knew I had just flashed Mr. Aldous a doozy grin.

"Kids these days . . . I swear that boy is proud to be obnoxious. Come on, Oscar. Let's get inside." Mr. Aldous scooped up his dog in his arms and carried him into the house.

I kept the smile on my face until his door slammed closed. I wanted to make certain he understood that his compliment filled me with pride.

My stomach gurgled—a reminder that it must be about dinnertime, so I should clean up and go inside. I skated over to our garden hose, turned on the faucet, and sprayed my wheels down extra well. Mommy would be pretty mad if I traipsed mud into the house, so angry she may not let me skate over muddy areas again, which would be terrible.

Positive my wheels were clean, I marched, balancing on the tiptoes of my skates, into the house.

"Oh good, there you are. Dakota, wash your hands and help me set the table. Your dad will be home any minute." A strange glint shone in Mommy's eyes as if she was up to something.

I scrunched my mouth to one side and gave her a look of suspicion. *It worked for those detective guys on TV.*

The "I-mean-business" crinkle between her eyebrows returned. "You heard me, Dakota. Now go."

Rats, why didn't it work for me?

"So, honey, I've been thinking." Mommy set her knife and fork down on the table. "Remember when we saw Mr. Aldous at the grocery store the other day? I mentioned I'd be happy to cook him a steak dinner. What do you say we invite him over this weekend?" Mommy stared right at me. She should have asked Daddy this question, not me.

"Well, Dakota, what's your answer?" Daddy's green eyes drilled into mine.

I glanced from Mommy to Daddy so fast I got dizzy. *What's with those two?* I *knew* Mommy was up to something.

Frustrated, I threw my hands into the air. "Why are you guys asking me?" And I *had been* enjoying the fried chicken Mommy cooked. What a way to ruin a perfectly good dinner.

Daddy laid his silverware beside his plate. He and Mommy had to be scheming up something. "Okay, Dakota, we asked because you, too, are a part of this family. Your mother and I want to reach out to our neighbor, yet we do not want to make you uncomfortable. You should have a say in the matter."

I swallowed the wad of meat that balled up inside my mouth and stared down at my plate. I didn't want that cranky man over to ruin one of our meals. Even though he complimented me today by calling me obnoxious, and the other day he played the piano really well, I still couldn't imagine him being very fun. "Do we have to?"

"No, Koty dear, we don't have to, but it would be nice, don't you think?" Mommy had that solid tone to her voice—the one that implied I *should* do the right thing, whether I wanted to or not.

No, I didn't think so. I had a feeling it was going to happen anyway. "So, what's with this guy and the two of you wanting to be all nice to him anyway?" If I wanted any of that butterscotch pudding Mommy made, I knew I first had to clear my plate, but at that moment, I didn't care. I decided to go on an eating strike.

"Every day, he sits on his porch, all by himself for hours. It's obvious he is lonely." Mommy brushed her hand across the hair on my forehead. Sometimes I think she is far too nice to others.

"Dakota, this is important to your mother."

"Then why doesn't she go and eat lunch with him while I'm at school?"

Daddy's brows slanted inward at a sharp angle. I could tell he wasn't very pleased with me at that moment.

It didn't matter what I thought. Mr. Aldous would be coming to dinner whether I wanted it or not. "Can I, *please,* have my pudding now?"

DAKOTA

"AH, COME ON, DAKOTA, I want to see." Traven lunged toward my backpack.

I had wedged it between me and the side of the bus so he no longer could get to my stuff. "No! I already told you. I don't want to dig out my order form. Not until we get to school."

Traven crossed his arms and scrunched his face into a pout. "Well, I don't believe you. I think you made the whole thing up."

"Go ahead, don't believe me. See if I care. That won't do a thing to change the truth." Some friend he was to think I'd lie, especially about something as important as the number of sales I got. After Traven's last comment, I didn't want to talk to him anymore, so I gripped my backpack tighter and stared straight ahead so as not to look at him. I focused on the squeaking sound of the tires and each bump we drove over as we sped down familiar streets. The rest of the ride seemed horribly long, but finally, I spied our school up ahead.

The bus pulled into the schoolyard and came to a stop. Traven stood up beside our seat, towering over me. "Well, are you going to get off or not?" For being my friend, he sure acted mean this morning.

The rest of the kids swarmed into the center aisle. I had no desire to get pushed about by that crazy mob, so I decided to stay put until everyone had cleared out. I glared at Traven and shot him my best attempt at a firm-looking face that made it clear I meant business. "I'll get off when I'm good and ready."

"Man, you sure are a loser." Traven shoved into a girl as he sped past, causing her to drop an armload of papers. They landed all over the seat across from us before he darted off the bus.

That last comment he made hurt. I bit onto the insides of my cheeks to keep from crying. If the other kids saw me in tears, it would make things much worse.

The last kid slipped past our driver, then out the folding double doors. Only that girl, who had dropped her things—thanks to Traven—and I were left. An urge deep inside my gut screamed at me to be like Super-Bat and make right all the wrongs caused by mean people. I fought to hold back tears, yet this internal command filled me with courage. I straightened my back and stood as tall as possible, then went up to this unfamiliar girl and helped her collect the scattered papers.

"Thanks." Her head tipped downward as she spoke. She nodded in my direction just before stepping off the bus. Her blue eyes glistened as if she were about to cry.

I grabbed my things and scuffed my shoes on the floor mat as I marched toward the front row. "So long, Charlie." I swiped the air, forming a broad wave.

Once confirmed that everyone had run off toward the playground, a sense of relief splashed over me—everyone except for that new girl. She hovered by the side of the building. Maybe all the rest of the kids would leave me alone. I hopped down the steps and leaped out the door.

"Have a good day, Dakota." Charlie pulled the lever that shut the door, then drove off in the direction of where they parked the busses.

I wished I had not bragged to Traven about how many sales I had made, but how could I have known he only sold one measly candle, and it went to his mom? I figured everyone would have gone out and knocked on doors to sell as much as possible, just like I did. They all had talked as excited as I did about earning one of those awfully cool prizes.

We had lots of time before recess ended, but I didn't feel much like playing, so I plopped down on the concrete and leaned against the brick wall. The cold ground sliced through my pants, but I didn't care much. I had no desire to get up and play with the rest of the kids. I peeked over at that girl. She glanced away as if pretending not to have noticed. I never saw her before and wondered who she was.

"No way, I don't believe you." Roberta challenged Traven with both hands propped on her hips as if she tried to look important. I had seen her use that sassy expression so often that even though her back turned toward me, I could imagine her far too familiar snotty look taking over her face.

"Yes way, Dakota told me himself." Traven stomped his foot.

Wow, maybe he did believe me after all?

"Well, did you see it?"

"No, but why should I? If Dakota said so, it must be true."

I grabbed my backpack and dashed toward Traven. If he was going to defend me, the least I could do was help. "Traven's right. I did *so* sell enough to earn that Super-Bat bike kit."

"Prove it!" Roberta shifted her body in a sassy twist that caused her straight, jet-black hair to bounce off her shoulders.

"All right, I will!" No girl was going to prove my buddy and me a fibber. I yanked out the order form, then dropped my bag at my feet.

"Let me see!" Roberta grasped the sheet and tried to snatch it out of my hands, but I held on tight. The very important order form got ripped in two.

"Now, look what you did!" My cheeks burned with anger.

Roberta shut her eyes and raised her brows while she shook her head. "I didn't do it. That wasn't my fault." Her bossy attitude glared through her every action.

"Did too! You tried to rip it from my hands." I had no idea where she came across acting all innocent-like.

Traven backed up a few steps. His mouth hung wide open.

"Well, are you going to show us your sales or not?" Roberta folded her arms tight across her chest.

I couldn't believe her gall. She ripped my order form in half and refused to say she was sorry, yet still had the nerve to not believe us.

"Fine then, I'll show you." A mob began to gather around us. I set the form on the pavement and opened it. Carefully placing the two ripped halves together, I pointed out all the filled-in lines, each with a different scribbled handwriting.

Kids crowed in and gasped as they gawked at the full page-and-a-half of orders. Roberta stared at the multitude of names. Her eyes rounded. "Humph, that's not such a big deal." She tipped her head, pointed her nose toward the sky, and stomped away.

I proved her wrong, yet she still refused to recognize the achievement I had made! "What do you mean this is not a big deal? It's a huge deal, so much so that one of my customers called me obnoxious." I had to say something to impress her.

I expected everyone to be amazed by what I had just said, but, for some reason, the entire crowd grew stone quiet.

Roberta snorted a huge chuckle. Then everyone broke into laughter.

"What? What's so funny?" I glanced from one kid to another, each hooting and hollering.

Traven slapped his knee with one hand and covered his mouth with the other. A string of snickers spilled out, despite his efforts to contain them. "Dakota . . . that was a great one. I can't believe you said that. You have got to be the funniest kid at this school."

"What? What's so funny? I don't get it?" Completely confused, I spun around as the crowd scattered.

The new girl had stepped away from the wall and stared in my direction. A gust of wind blew her light-brown hair into her face. She pushed it behind her ear and caught my eye. A shy grin formed on her face, then she turned and headed toward the school entrance.

A loud buzz filled the air. All the kids ran toward the big double doors. Roberta slapped me on the back. "He called you *obnoxious* . . . Good one, Dakota. Even *I* wouldn't have thought up one as great as that."

ALDOUS

A CRISP AFTERNOON BREEZE CUT THROUGH the thin layers of the jacket that I, in haste, had thrown on earlier that morning. I wrapped it tighter across my frail body, which seemed to grow leaner with each passing day. I should take better care to feed myself a proper meal now and then. Maybe that way, I could regain some weight. If Mariam were alive, she would be frantic with worry at how gaunt my five-foot ten-inch frame had become.

A shiver ran through my cells like an electrical current. This unorthodox method to block out the cold would be much more efficient if I zipped up my coat. But I didn't care.

I didn't care much about anything lately. All I seemed to do, day after day, was plant myself on this rickety old swing and waste the hours away. First, I'd watch this silly hummingbird drink his fill and then scrutinize Dakota as he entertained himself on those crazy skates. I kept with this daily regiment until the sun ceremoniously danced in the western sky, signaling the passing of yet another drawn-out, purposeless day.

Across the street, Dakota spun on his skates at the top of the driveway, then sped toward the road, picking up speed. Everything about that boy rubbed my nerves raw like exposed wires. So, why didn't I retreat indoors where it would be easy to ignore that child? For some unexplained reason, it felt far worse to bear the multitude of neglected chores awaiting me inside. Have I become so desperate to distract my stagnant mind that I now depend on this pesky child for entertainment?

As if answering, Oscar nudged his flattened nose against my thigh.

I glared at the animal and shook my head. "You're right, my friend. I'm pathetic." The sound of my words made me chuckle. "Listen to me—I'm talking to a mutt. I even call you 'friend.' If that's not desperate, I don't know what is."

The speed of his wagging coiled tail, which resembled a jiggling cinnamon bun, increased, confirming my comment.

A voice inside my brain grumbled. Despite promptings, my body remained glued to this swing, as if paralyzed, with no other option. Dakota had gotten off the bus well over an hour ago. I peered at my watch and struggled to interpret those digital numbers. *Had I done nothing but observe this child for one more drawn-out evening?*

Before that monumental day when I bumped into this obnoxious boy and his mother at the mailbox, I had busied myself well and kept the place reasonably clean. Mariam would have had little reason to complain. But lately, that well-oiled routine had screeched to an abrupt halt. What was it about this child and his ability to mess with my proficient, systematical mind?

For many years, I stashed countless boxes of files within the dark confinements of my brain. Innumerable, ominous thoughts and memories I never wanted remain hidden deep within its crevices. With the skill of a tightrope artist, I balanced a load of useless information near the surface. That way, there would never be a need to filter further down within that menacing pile. But then this insufferable boy came along and, in one big swoop, messed up my well-controlled system and, with it, my entire carefully orchestrated life.

"Augh." The unsuspected groan roared from somewhere deep within my gut as if an attempt to purge many years' worth of frustration.

Dakota skated to a dead halt mid-stride and turned in my direction.

"Why my eyes insisted on following after this obnoxious child, I may never know." Again, without thinking, that thought had escaped my lips at an alarming volume.

A toothless grin beamed across the lad's face. He stretched his scrawny arm into a wave.

I sucked in a deep breath of crisp autumn air, then slowly blew it out through my nostrils. The pile of dirty dishes that filled my kitchen sink would grow for yet another day. This evening proved no different than many before it.

Dakota spun circles on his driveway, sped down the sidewalk, and glided back up again. He repeated this pattern in a similar consistency to the sway of a clock's pendulum.

My eyes refused to perceive the freckled-faced boy before me. Instead, I observed a dark-haired Aldous, far younger than the old geezer, who gazed back at me whenever I stood in front of a mirror. That adolescent self had become a person I long ago strove to forget. I blinked until the juvenile me faded, and Dakota returned to full view. No wonder I detested that boy—he resurrected the child within me.

Dakota pierced my ears with a shrill warrior's cry and halted in the middle of the sidewalk. He raked his hand through sweaty bangs, forming spikes at his hairline. The child turned in my direction and stared.

Even from this distance, I deciphered the pale blue hue of his round eyes. How could they suddenly dull to a shade of gray? At the same time, the child's build morphed into someone with a slightly taller and leaner stature. Why had young Aldous again surfaced to haunt me? And why did I, day after day, return to this same God-forsaken spot where such treacherous apparitions torment my soul? Would I ever gain enough wisdom to avoid such perilous situations? Where had all my good sense gone? I lost hold of the key to my past. It now lay, the lock jimmied open, in Dakota's small hands.

My body cringed as this child-aged Aldous flashed before my mind's eye. Maybe it wasn't Dakota whom I loathed, but instead, this boyhood version of me. Why did I detest my past self with such vigor?

I shut my eyes. My temples throbbed. Dakota's high-pitched voice rang in my ears, blending with an even clearer image from my past. Once I, too, had basked uninhibited as a carefree child, then all was lost. The age of innocents ripped forever from my grasp, like an irreplaceable document torn into fragments so tiny even strips of tape would fail to piece it back together again. *How could someone do such a thing to an innocent child?* The question scorched holes through my heart while pointed teeth of rage devoured my soul.

Alexandra's sweet voice rang in chorus with the poisoned words she had declared while at the grocery store, "hurt people hurt people."

Young Aldous had become one of those unfortunate "hurt people." *But I rose above that. That one man's unforgivable actions wounded him,* not *me.* I'm *better than that!* I'm *stronger than that! I overcame every atrocity and grew far beyond every single effect. So much so that now I'm a totally different person.*

"Hurt people hurt people." *If I once had been one of those hurt people, how have I hurt others?* A wave of shame flooded my soul while images of sins I've committed invaded my memory, as vivid as a movie flashing across a screen.

"No!" How dare I entertain such a question! Complete betrayal of the self. *I am stronger than that! In no way would I have ever wounded another, simply because of the selfish actions someone else had inflicted on my child-self. I carried on with dignity and taught those around me to hold their heads up with pride. They never had reason to darken our household with such shame. I refused to allow such disgrace to exist within the walls of our home.*

I bent forward and placed my pounding head within the palms of my trembling hands. Pain shot through my skull like a fractured bone. "Pull yourself together, man. Regain control." What ability did this harmless child across the street have on me to crumble my carefully composed self-restraint? I had held it together now for nearly sixty years. Maybe my father had filched away my manhood, but I stole it back. I rose above every malevolent action. He may have been a weasel, not worthy of existence, and "I'm no better than him."

My eyes popped open. Blood pulsated through the veins at such an intense pace it felt as if they bulged clear out of their sockets. "What did I say? 'I'm no better than him?'"

I gripped my skull and shook my head, attempting to jar the thought from my mind. "That was wrong. I misspoke. A mistake, that's all it was." *I'm nothing like my father. I'm much better than he ever was. There's no comparison, and could never be any. It was just a reckless mistake, that's all, nothing more.*

My heart pounded with such intensity I feared its beat could be seen through my jacket. I closed my eyes in an attempt to diminish its rhythm.

Wet slime latched onto the side of my face—the disgusting yet far too familiar sensation of this pesky mutt as he licked my cheek.

It jarred my senses like a bucket of ice dumped over my head. "Come on, mutt. We might as well get inside."

I took one final glimpse across the street. Dakota must have received his dinner call, for the child spun around to the back of his house and disappeared. I knew if I continued to observe, he soon would reemerge, walking with tenacity on the toes of his skates before entering the side door. But tonight, I possessed no desire to witness this well-rehearsed routine.

Ready to retreat inside, I hitched a squirmy Oscar under my arm and carried him into the house. He leaped from my grasp and skirted into the kitchen. I guess he, too, announced dinner time.

CHAPTER

18

ALDOUS

*M*Y BRAIN ACTIVITY PLOWED FORWARD with the untamed energy of a runaway horse-drawn carriage. No matter how hard I tried, I could not slow it down. Every notion revealed yet another betrayal. Why did my thoughts continue to torment me? Perpetual memories, chosen long ago to forget, flashed as an unwelcomed backdrop in the recesses of my mind. Distressful faces emerged, escorting voices I never again wished to hear, yet they buzzed unceasingly in my ears. It had to end *now*, or I would lose this battle I had fought my entire life. Up until this moment, I believed I had conquered that pivotal war.

Oscar scampered to the piano bench and spun in circles in front of the basket of sheet music. Maybe the little fellow was on to something. Allowing my fingers to mindlessly tickle ivory keys might be just what I needed to regain control of the reins to my rampant thoughts.

I scooched the bench out and sat down. Oscar hopped up beside me. My fingers hovered above the keyboard, similar to how that silly hummingbird hovered above his feeder. *Now what?*

A pile of stacked hymnals sat on top of the piano. Mariam had collected music books with almost as much passion as her cherished figurines. How odd the fashion in which these two components now met. I pulled down the top hymnal and blew dust from its hardbound cover. Mariam would never have allowed dust to collect like this, yet to expel energy on such a tedious task seemed an absurd waste of time.

I opened the book and thumbed through it. Multiple blue tabs protruded from its pages. I turned to the first tab. It marked the well-known children's hymn, "Jesus Loves Me." My sight riveted to its words. Vivid memories of me as a small lad emerged as I learned this song. My parents had worshiped nearby in a larger building while other children and I gathered in the children's chapel. A warm sensation melted over me, catching me completely by surprise. Black-printed notes blurred before my eyes from unexpected moisture.

It had been decades since I last conjured up thoughts of God and church. Mariam had pleaded with me for years. *"Please, Aldous, pick a church. Anyone will do. It doesn't matter. I want our daughter brought up in a Christian home."*

The more she nagged, the greater my resolve to have nothing to do with organized religion. Finally, by the time Lacey turned seven, my defiance had worn Mariam down, and she stopped her incessant harassment.

I placed shaky hands over the correct keys and hesitated as a strange sensation took residence within the pit of my stomach. Slowly my clumsy fingers plunked out the notes. A few chords resonated in perfect tune. Others rang sour as words resounded clear within my mind. *"Jesus loves me! This I know, for the Bible tells me so. Little ones to Him belong; they are weak, but He is strong."*

"They are weak . . . I'll say . . ." Horror rippled through my veins from the extreme vulnerability that wrapped around me. My mind lost grip of all control. I panicked as weakness infested my being.

I detested this repulsive emotion above all others. My mind raged out of control, racing with thoughts that weak people are never acceptable! These pathetic beings provide others an open invitation to attack boundaries. Once invaded, any number of harmful elements can inflict. Long ago, I mastered the art of alertness. I kept my guard solid as steel. No one could get close. Never again would I be harmed.

A spasm cramped my stomach as if a cord twanged within me, accompanied by an uninvited voice that spoke loud and clear within the back of my mind. *"You succeeded well, Aldous. You kept your guard solid, and all those years, not a soul broke through your barricade—not your wife, your daughter, nor even your Lord. You achieved your mission and never again fell vulnerable. As a result, you kept everyone at a safe distance, even those dear to your heart. Your life's dedicated charge became your idol,* your god. *So, tell me, Aldous, did that false god serve you well?"*

Those troublesome words faded. My heart flooded with loneliness. An intense notion that my existence had long ago worn out all sense of purpose hit with the velocity of a cannonball thrust through a flimsy blockade. Was that my reward for a lifetime of devotion to a counterfeit savior?

Tears stung my eyes. I blinked them away and stared at the words in the second half of the stanza. *". . . but He is strong."*

So what if God is strong? I know strength. I survived all those years, and not once had I needed Him, nor anyone. Sure as anything, I would not crumble now.

Throughout those arduous decades, I handled everything that came my way all by myself. Life had proven that to submit and trust meant to be let down. Far too many callused people have entered, uninvited, into my life. And each one sliced their hand-forged sword deep into my flesh, etching multiple scars into my soul.

Never again will I allow another human being admittance to my heart. No one will ever gain vital knowledge of how I tick. I will never again be sliced open!

An uncomfortable pull within my stomach grasped my attention like a greedy unrelenting child. I sucked in a deep breath and forced myself to focus.

After all, I had not even permitted Mariam close enough access to gain insight into my behaviors. *I did not need a fantasy god to pretend to be strong on my accord. I am strong enough for myself. I always have been and always will be. I* don't *need anyone!*

Oscar nudged his flattened nose against my thigh. Closed in by the animal, I pushed back his furry body. Instead of getting the hint, he hopped onto my leg, stretched up on his hind quarters, and licked my face.

With the palm of my hand, I wiped off the appalling slobber and swiped it across my pant leg. If Mariam had witnessed this action during the beginning of our marriage, she would have let me have it. However, after a few years, I had her confined to her proper place. There she understood who was in charge and kept her silence.

My glance returned to the hymnal splayed open in front of me. *"Yes, Jesus loves me! Yes, Jesus loves me! Yes, Jesus loves me!"*

Startled by a knock on the door, my shaky hands sprang from the keyboard. Oscar gave a high-pitched yelp, hopped off the bench, and darted toward the front door. "What now?" I shuffled my tired feet after this spastic mutt. "Would you move aside so I can open it?"

The insufferable pooch scampered to the edge of the doormat as if he understood my every gruffly uttered word. I pulled the door open. My sight fell onto the profile of Alexandra's symmetrical nose, unlike the slightly pugged-shaped freckled one of her son's. My lips pressed tight as I stared at this uninvited guest. *What had I told myself earlier about not letting others close enough to enter my life?*

"I hoped you would still be up, Mr. Aldous. Sorry to disturb you, but I wondered if you would like to join my family for dinner tomorrow. I'll grill you a steak with sautéed onions and mushrooms on the side."

As if my lips had been glued together, I found it nearly impossible to pry open my mouth. I must have looked like an opossum caught in headlights.

A partial smile rippled across Alexandra's mouth. "Did you hear what I said?"

Embarrassment shocked my system. "Yes, I heard you. What time do you want me over?" *Darn it, my own words once again betrayed me.*

"Would six o-clock work?"

"Yeah, that'd be fine." A flash of heat radiated from my head. *There I go again. My own audible words crossed onto the enemy's battlefield.* Rage, aimed at my inner weakness, flamed.

She twittered her fingers at me, turned around, and strolled off toward her house.

I stepped back inside and twisted the lock as I shut the door. Oscar gazed up at me. A pleading look glistened in his glassy, marble-shaped eyes.

"What the heck was I thinking? Of course, I didn't want to go over to their house. Why would I ever want to give up an evening and be social, especially knowing that obnoxious kid of theirs would pester the life right out of me before the night would end?"

Oscar barked once, then rubbed his head against my calf.

CHAPTER

19

ALDOUS

$\mathcal{F}$OR AT LEAST THE TENTH time, I shuffled past the picture window, then paused, peering through the glass. Across the street, Dakota sped down the sidewalk on his skates. His elated shouts pierced through my sealed house. The boy approached the edge of his yard, pivoted on the heel of one skate, then glided back toward his driveway. He turned in my direction and flashed a wide grin. I saw the gap of his missing tooth as he waved with broad strokes in the crisp afternoon air.

Stepping behind the draperies concealed within the shadows of my living room, I had come to believe that bratty kid disliked me as much as I harbored aversion toward him. What caused such an abrupt change in his behavior?

I pressed my thumb onto the joint of my aching hip—the price paid for that day's pacing. Nonetheless, anxious energy kept me from giving in to the pain and plopping into the recliner.

Oscar lay curled up on the couch with his head on a pillow. His tongue hung halfway out of his mouth. Somehow, I gained comfort from his rhythmic snores.

Careful to remain hidden, I craned my neck for another look. A spot of metallic green flashed before my eyes.

The hummingbird flitted before its empty feeder. He would have to find nourishment elsewhere today, for I didn't dare risk the exposure of journeying outside. By all appearances, Dakota prepared to pounce on me the instant I stepped out the door. I was not about to give him such pleasure. *Since when had I become a coward?*

The instant that question popped into my head, an image of Mariam's face sprang into my mind. The best way for me to protect both her and myself had always been to maintain complete control. The only way I could achieve that goal was to master dominance over her. In the beginning, Mariam resisted with the spunk of a young filly, but within a few short years, she had submitted. Along with her surrender came a douse to her internal fire.

At first, I missed her spunk, but soon I discovered that the sense of power over another placed a rush within my bloodstream as strong as a shot of adrenaline directly into my aorta.

As years passed and I perfected my tight authority over her, I discovered a devastating drawback—somewhere along the line, the love I once held toward her had transformed into contempt. Every time I took a firm stance, I expected her compliancy. I left no wiggle room for my sweet Mariam. The more she submitted to my will, the greater my repulsion for her grew. My capacity to control had become a powerful drug, vital to my soul. Before long, I had lost the ability to remember how compassion felt.

Why did those unwelcoming thoughts invade my mind? With a wave of rage, I willed them away. My courage raised a decimal. I crossed directly in front of the window, over to where the oval mirror hung beside the front door.

Oscar lifted his head from the velvet pillow. His molten brown eyes followed my motion until he snuggled back onto the cushion and re-shut drooping lids.

I froze before the looking glass—the same one my wife had inspected her appearance in whenever she ventured out. Never had I understood her impractical routine. Mariam always appeared perfectly fine to me. Yet, in time, her attention focused on the tender skin below her eyes as she swiped away mascara smudges.

A sense of shock struck me as if bludgeoned by the broad end of a baseball bat. *Had shed tears caused those frequent smudges?*

I gazed at my reflection, wrinkled by time, and remembered the day I first noticed the spark had vanished from Mariam's eyes. Regret's sharp teeth bit into the meat of my stomach. I blinked away the sting of tears. *What had I done?*

God had blessed me with a beautiful, loving wife who always remained loyal to me. Never once had I deserved such a blessing. She sacrificed to unthinkable measures on behalf of my selfish behavior, surrendering to the point that by the time she had passed, not a drop of joy remained within that fragile, shattered heart of hers.

I stared at my grayed reflection. Creases between my unruly brows deepened. *What was I thinking? How could I have lost such self-restraint that my mind would carry me away on the wings of outlandish lies?* Throughout all those years, I maintained the perfect image of a husband and father any wife or child would be honored to have.

If that were true then, why had it been almost four years since Lacey paid a visit or even called? Mariam's gravest heartbreak occurred the day Lacey announced that she no longer would bring her daughter, our only grandchild, over to the house. My wife had begged me to take her to what Lacey called a "safe meeting place" for a short half-hour visit with little Chloe.

I never did concede to her foolish wishes. If Lacey were to set down such outlandish ground rules, then I, sure as anything, would hold an even firmer stance and make it clear who remained boss around this place.

The head-butting stubbornness between my daughter and me had carried on since the day she left home at age seventeen. Not a direct word had been uttered between us for nearly two decades.

Mariam released a long sigh each time she passed a message between that stubborn ox of a child and me. With each roundabout exchange, a greater sense of sorrow had seeped into my sweet wife's rich brown eyes—once a perfect match to her thick, chestnut-colored hair. Not long after that, those luminous eyes, which once sparkled like priceless jewels, lost their luster.

Not once did Mariam ask me why. She would clamp tight her pretty red lips and, in silence, comply with whatever I bade of her. Sure as anything, I would never have explained, even if she had asked. Only a weak person would stoop to such an exploit. Weak-livered is something I had *never* been, nor would become.

I tipped my head toward my feet and examined the old, familiar fleece-lined slippers I treasured dearly. When I attempted to lift my gaze, for some strange reason, my neck stiffened and would not straighten, as if an invisible cable had fastened to my chin and pulled tight, wrenching my head into this downward position. This *cord of shame* bound me, rendering me too dishonorable to raise my sight. "God, how could you do this to me?" My balled-up fist shook in empty air.

With my neck frozen in that humbled stance, I ambled in front of the living room window and scanned the view. "Where did that Dakota skate off to?"

The boy stood affixed in the middle of his drive. An exaggerated pout plastered to his face as his father shoveled heaps of dirt and gravel, collected from our last bout of heavy rain, off their sidewalk and into an awaiting wheelbarrow.

I felt my wrinkled skin stretch as a sneer spread across my face. With it came an unexpected gush of strength and courage, enough to break through that unseen cord. My neck creaked. My chin jutted upward at a proud, sharp angle.

Dakota spun his head around and faced his mother as she stepped out their side door. A glow from the evening's setting sun highlighted tawny streaks in her hair. For an instant, my eyes tricked me into believing it was Lacey who stood across the street—a sadistic hoax to play on an old man.

The child hollered something inaudible to my ears, then raced toward his mother. Randy paused his labor and glanced toward the two of them. "I'm almost finished." Being far closer to my house than his son had stood, this man's voice sent minute rattles through my well-worn windowpanes.

Six gongs sounded from the clock on my wall. Fully alert, Oscar lifted his furry head and hopped off the couch. His short, stubby legs carried him across the rug until he stood at the base of my feet. This obnoxious mutt stared up at me with his tail, coiled like a snail's shell, in a perpetual waggle. How well this pesky animal resembled that tiresome boy across the street.

"What? Are you now able to tell time? Well, I might as well get it over with. Come on, boy, I'll get your supper before I leave."

CHAPTER

20

DAKOTA

*A*LL CLEANED UP AND READY for our guest, I sat tall on my knees and leaned over the back of our couch while I stared out the window at Mr. Aldous's front door. I wanted to catch the exact moment he stepped outside. In case Mommy or Daddy happened to come into the room, I keep my bounces on the cushions small. That way, if caught, I could explain it away as an accident.

Mr. Aldous's door swung open. He stepped outside onto his porch. I leaped off the couch and zoomed toward our entryway. "He's coming! I saw him leave just now. He's on his way!"

At the top of the steps, with both my hands, I held out Daddy's black bathrobe so that it draped around me like a cape. I leaped down all four stairs, not touching a single one. My Super-Bat cape gave me the power to do great things no one else would dare attempt.

Bursting through the side door, I held it open and, frozen like a statue on the concrete stoop, waited for our visitor. Isn't stoop the oddest name for a cement step? My mommy taught me the strangest words. I'll never know where she comes up with them.

I'm not sure why the change. I never used to like that cranky man very much. Then all of a sudden, I grew excited to have him over. When Mommy first came up with the idea, I thought she had cracked the big one. Yet the more I remembered his wonderful piano music, the more determined I got to ask him to teach me to play. That's my best guess why he no longer seemed so creepy.

Mr. Aldous stared in my direction as he inched across the road. I swore the closer he got, the slower he moved. Not once did Mr. Aldous take his eyes off me, not even to look both ways for traffic. I counted his footsteps as he crept closer. How could a man take so long to walk up one driveway?

Finally, he was just a few feet away. The thump of my hand as it slapped over my heart sounded much louder than I expected. "Welcome to the Bat Cavern. Before you enter, you must swear to keep our identity a secret." I stretched my neck and threw back my shoulders to stand as tall as possible so he would know I meant business.

Two gray hairs poked from the nostrils of his long, hooked nose, making him look more like a villain than a partner in fighting crime.

My dad stood in the doorway. "Welcome, Aldous. Dakota, are you going to let him in?"

"But Daddy, he hasn't repeated the sacred oath."

Daddy's ice-cold glare drilled into my eyes with power so fierce it could have frozen the flame of a burning stick. *Yep, I got the message loud and clear.* That expression was why I had given Daddy the superhero name, Iceman.

Mr. Aldous grunted as he plodded past us. I held my hand up to my mouth, next to Daddy's ear. "I'll have to keep an eye on this one."

Daddy's mustache twitched.

The intense focus Mommy kept as she prepared the meal made me think she must have wanted to make everything perfect for Mr. Aldous. She didn't even tell me to take off my Super-Bat cape before I sat at the table. I figured since she didn't mention it, neither would I. However, I flipped it behind my shoulders to make it a bit less noticeable, just in case.

Mr. Aldous seemed to work real hard to keep that frown pasted to his face. He must scowl an awful lot because the downward wrinkles around his mouth were carved in as deep as canyon gullies. When he wasn't looking, I placed my hands on each of my cheeks and pressed in on the skin to make my face resemble his. Too bad I wasn't near a mirror. I thought I almost had his expression when Daddy motioned at me to stop. A great dinnertime activity would be making faces. I ought to suggest that to Mommy. It's a lot more fun than all that boring talk those adults usually do, and Mr. Aldous doesn't seem to have near enough fun in his life. I'm positive he must be in such great need of it that he could use a whole dump-truck load of fun by now.

Daddy carried in steaks that still sizzled, straight off the charcoal grill. My nose twitched at the aroma as he set them in the center of the table, then slipped into his chair. Mommy crowded the rest of the open space before us with other yummy dishes. I sat across from Mr. Aldous and grabbed the serving spoon for the strawberry gelatin. It had mixed-up big juicy berries and whipped cream, just how I liked it. Mom shook her head at me and sat down, then folded her hands and closed her eyes. I bowed my head as Daddy said grace.

I stole a peek at Mr. Aldous. His eyes remained wide open as he stared at the serving platter heaped with juicy steaks. I understood how he must have felt, for I'd much rather be digging into the food too. I think God would understand. From the moment I get that first bit on my tongue, my taste buds say thank you to God with every bite that follows.

I'm grateful Daddy didn't say one of his long prayers. As soon as he said, "Amen," I reached again for the gelatin spoon, but Mommy again had that crinkly brow thing going on as she glared at me. "Let our guest have first dibs, Dakota."

Rats, he better not take too much. That dish was one of my favorites.

Mr. Aldous piled his plate full. His eyes grew big, ready to bulge clear out of his head as he gaped down at the food. He hovered his fork and knife over his meat as if he had never seen a steak and wasn't quite sure what to do with it.

I thought he could use a bit of help. "Here, Mr. Aldous. It's real easy. All you need to do is make a fist with your right hand and stick your fork in it, then stab the meat like this—till it's secure. Next, take your knife with your left hand and saw back and forth."

"Koty, no." Mommy had a horrified look on her face, much like the one she wore the day I had overheard her say how nice it would be for us to get a small house pet, so I went out and caught the biggest bullfrog I could find. For some reason, Mommy didn't like that very much. She sure can be hard to please sometimes.

I'm not all that convinced about Mr. Aldous, though. He may be easier to work with than I thought. As soon as I placed my knife and fork back down on the table, Mr. Aldous roared with laughter. For reasons I may never know, this crabby man had these laughing fits ever so often.

Mr. Aldous's shoulders stopped heaving. He picked up his napkin and used it to wipe his face, then began to take small, deliberate bites.

My parents tried real hard to get Mr. Aldous to talk with them, but I guess he knew such few games that he didn't even understand how to play the most boring one of all, *"Talk time at the dinner table."* Hardly a word left his mouth as he slowly swallowed every bit of his food. He scraped his plate so clean it looked like it had been washed. Then he refilled it again, heaped even higher than the first time. Good thing Mommy had made lots of food because Mr. Aldous downed it like he hadn't eaten a meal all year.

My stomach grew queasy as I watched him gobble down so much.

After his third serving, Mr. Aldous must have finally gotten full, for he shuffled what remained of his roll and potatoes around his plate as if chasing a hockey puck. Whenever I played that game, I got told to stop messing with my food. For some reason, Mommy and Daddy didn't have a problem with how Mr. Aldous acted. So, I figured I'd join him.

I stabbed my fork into a big carrot slice and ran it in circles along the edge of the plate. *Carl the Carrot took first place in the hundred-yard-dash.* I grabbed the handle of my spoon and shoved a celery piece around after the carrot slice. *Here comes Caesar Celery, catching up from close behind. Carrot and Celery, running neck and neck as they approach the finish line. It's an exciting race. Who will be the winner?* Maybe I ought to be a sports announcer when I grow up.

"Mariam always cooked the best steaks with mushrooms and onions, similar to yours. No one could sauté as well as she did," Mr. Aldous said.

Screech. Foul on the racetrack, abrupt halt to all actions! I jerked my head in his direction. Did he just insult Mommy's cooking? I stared at Mr. Aldous—somehow, his expression seemed a bit softer than usual—then I turned toward Mommy.

"You must miss her cooking very much."

Wow, she sure handled that well. Mom just got slammed, yet she turned it around. I pinched my lips together real tight to make sure I wouldn't say something I might regret.

"Oh, I do fine without her." The usual frown returned to Mr. Aldous's face.

I no longer could keep quiet. "Yeah, but I bet this Mariam couldn't cook anywhere close to as well as Mommy does."

"I don't need a woman to cook for me. Never did and never will." Mr. Aldous's eyes clouded over.

I leaned in to get a better look. Maybe Mr. Aldous is not a partner in fighting crime. Maaayybe he *is* one of the villains.

Daddy placed his hand on my arm and gave it a light squeeze. "Dakota, that's enough. Now go help your mom with the dishes."

Daddy must have known I was ready to give Mr. Aldous one of my special tests, the type that revealed where a person's loyalties stand. A bit disappointed, I stood up. Regardless of Daddy's request, I pasted my stare onto Mr. Aldous. "Aww, but Daddy, I've just about got it all figured out."

"Dakota."

"All right, Iceman, but you better take over now." I grabbed my plate and marched toward the kitchen. Mommy followed, her arms loaded down with dirty dishes. Behind me, Daddy and Mr. Aldous talked. Just in case our neighbor was one of those bad guys, I figured I better keep my ears tuned in sharp to what he might say. I never know when Daddy may need my help.

"That boy of yours can be quite obnoxious."

Daddy laughed. I always took his chuckle as assurance that everything would turn out perfect, regardless of how hopeless things may seem. So, I guess I should trust him when it comes to Mr. Aldous too.

"He has his moments, but he's a neat kid," Daddy said.

Wow, two compliments in one evening. My shoulders rolled back in pride.

CHAPTER 21

DAKOTA

"**I'M** OBNOXIOUS. I'M OBNOXIOUS . . ." I held Snippets, my favorite stuffed puppy, partway under the covers. "I know I'm obnoxious because Mr. Aldous told me so. And tonight was not the first time, either."

I flopped up one of Snippets' long gray ears to make it easier for him to hear. Snippets always listened well, even though soft fuzzy cloth and a bunch of stuffing filled his insides. His ears and the rest of his fur weren't gray because he had come that way. A long time ago, when I first got Snippets, he was all white and fluffy. But after many outdoor adventures, his pure white had turned dingy. Mommy tried many times to clean Snippets in the wash, yet nothing worked. But that's okay. I loved Snippets as a gray puppy just as much as when he first arrived, pure and white.

"I know Mr. Aldous must have enjoyed the evening. It took him forever to start talking, but once he did, the man wouldn't shut up."

Snippets listened to every word I said. Unlike people, Snippets never once took his eyes off of me.

"Mr. Aldous rambled on and on, so much that Mommy sent me to my room to get ready for bed by myself."

Snippets' ears turned toward the hallway.

"What was that . . .? Did you hear something . . .? I hear it too. It sounds like footsteps."

Daddy popped his head through the doorway, startling Snippets, but not me. I never get scared easily. It must be because of all my Super-Bat training.

"It appears you did a good job getting ready for bed, Dakota. Did you brush your teeth?"

"Sure did. See?" I spread my lips wide and clenched my teeth to give Daddy a good look. He hunched down and peered inside, then nodded. I could tell he was pleased.

"So, was the evening as bad as you expected it to be?"

"Nah, Mr. Aldous may be creepy, but he's also funny. Did you notice how he laughs at the strangest things?" I bounced up onto my knees. "I think he's beginning to like me. Did you hear? He called me obnoxious."

Instead of acting excited or proud as I expected, Daddy kept the strangest expression on his face, almost as if he didn't understand what I had said. "Dakota, do you know what obnoxious means?"

I grabbed my pillow and balled it up in my lap to help me think real hard. "Not exactly, but it must be something pretty neat. Mr. Aldous has called me that many times. Whenever he does, it seems to make him happy. It must be his favorite name for me."

Daddy's thick brows arched together, shading his green eyes. He sat down beside me on my bed. "Buddy, obnoxious is not necessarily a nice term to use on someone."

"Huh, what do you mean?" I held Snippets' ears out to assure we both had heard Daddy correctly because what I thought I heard didn't make much sense.

"Obnoxious usually refers to a person who tends to be difficult to be around, someone who gets on other's nerves, is irritating . . . things such as that."

Neither Snippets nor I were very happy about what we had just heard. Here, I thought Mr. Aldous was beginning to warm up to me. After all, I'm a kid. What's not to like about a cute, freckled-faced boy like me? Other people think I'm fun to hang around, so what Daddy said didn't make any sense. "Why would Mr. Aldous call me something nasty like obnoxious?"

Daddy put on his thinking face, which makes creases arched above his nose. Maybe he didn't quite know the answer. "Well, people, especially those a bit older, tend to grow comfortable with their lives . . . they get stuck in their ways. Then someone young and full of energy, like you, comes along." Daddy poked at my tummy.

I squirmed and laughed and then poked him back.

His nose crinkle disappeared. "You kids have a talent for jarring older people out of their comfort zones."

I stopped giggling and stared at Daddy's sand-colored hair, a bit mussed-up. If Mommy hadn't gotten on his case by now to get a haircut, she soon would. She sent Daddy to the barbershop anytime his hair got long enough to flop over his forehead. I didn't get why she wouldn't let his hair grow long like hers, but then, lately, a lot of things didn't make much sense. "So I'm obnoxious to Mr. Aldous because I make him do things and think things that he'd rather not do or think? Sooo why is that bad?"

Snippets wanted to dance, so I held him by the ears and swayed him back and forth. That must have been obnoxious, too, for Daddy took Snippets from me and set him down near the foot of my bed. "It's not necessarily bad. Sometimes that can be very good for a person. With Mr. Aldous, I believe that to be the case. He's set in his ways and has been so for a long time. I also get the impression he has many unresolved issues, and even though he may choose to ignore them, they would still eat away at his subconscious. Then you come along and shake up the mix."

With both hands, Daddy pressed down on the mattress many times, causing me to bounce. I giggled.

Daddy laughed. "You may be exactly what Mr. Aldous needs."

"So, obnoxious is good?"

"It can be if done right."

"How can it be done right?" *What would Super-Bat do?*

"Just by being yourself, Dakota. You have what it takes. You handle things pretty well on your own. You don't need coaching from me or anyone."

I stuffed my pillow behind me and leaned into it, feeling all glowy and proud inside. Super-Bat power must be shining through me. Mommy would call it a God spark, but my way of looking at it was far more fun. "Okay, then I'll go to Mr. Aldous's house every day and be as obnoxious as possible. You can call it a Super-Bat mission."

"Slow down, son. Remember, you're still never to visit him alone." Daddy tapped his finger on my chest.

I giggled some more, then caught my breath. "Why not? We even invited him to our house for dinner. He's no longer a stranger."

"There's still far too much we do not know about him for you to traipse over to his house by yourself. You will have plenty of opportunities to spend with Mr. Aldous, with your mom or me at your side." Daddy pulled the covers up to my chin.

I popped up onto my elbows. "While we're at it, do you think we could ask Mr. Aldous to teach me how to play the piano?"

"That's a good possibility, buddy. Are you ready to say your prayers?"

"Yeah, but I don't want your help. Tonight I want to do it all by myself."

"Okay, go right ahead."

I waited for Daddy to close his eyes and fold his hands, then I shut mine. "Dear God, thank you for Mr. Aldous. And thank you for making me obnoxious. Even though that may not always be the best way to behave, I can see how in Mr. Aldous's case, I'm doing him a lot of good. My obnoxiousness is just what he needs. Thank you, God, for choosing me as Your perfect obnoxious kid to help Mr. Aldous because he really needs Your help. He can act awfully crabby sometimes. He needs someone to remind him how to smile and have fun. I am grateful You chose me for that job. In Jesus' Name, Amen."

I opened my eyes.

Daddy must have liked my prayer because he grinned so wide, his mustache turned up at the edges.

Daddy grabbed Snippets from the foot of my bed and handed him to me, then leaned in and kissed me on the forehead. "Good night, Super-Bat. Happy crime-fighting dreams."

"I'll also have great dreams about being obnoxious. That way, I can help all the crabby old men in this world remember how to smile."

DAKOTA

$\mathcal{T}$HERE, SHE DID IT AGAIN. Even though I couldn't quite see, I felt her eyes on me while that new girl from the bus continued to stare. She burned holes into the side of my head. I craned my neck to peer over my shoulder. She shifted her gaze and glanced down at her worksheet. All morning I could sense her ogle me. Mrs. Miceli had introduced this girl the day she arrived, but I couldn't remember her name. She made it obvious she didn't want me to know that she kept gawking in my direction.

I twisted around to catch her. She avoided my glance, just like all the times before.

Determined to beat her at this game, I held my position. I wanted this girl to know I didn't care if she stared. I'm all about being friendly, and she could use a few friends, being new to this school.

Slowly, she lifted her face and tilted it toward me.

I gave her my best grin.

A stripe of pink streaked across her plump cheeks as if a paintbrush swiped over them. With a quick jerk, she turned away and un-tucked a wad of light-brown hair from behind her ear. It fell over her face, hiding it like a curtain.

I didn't know why this girl was so shy, but if she kept it up, she would find it hard to make friends.

"Dakota, is something bothering you? You appear distracted."

I peeked up. Mrs. Miceli towered over me.

Heat rushed to my cheeks. I figured they, too, must appear bright red. "No, ma'am. Nothing is wrong."

"Then you need to focus on your numbers. If you don't finish before the bell rings, you will spend recess inside to complete your work." She tapped her long purple-painted fingernail on my paper.

Cool color. I'll have to ask Mommy to paint her nails neat colors just like my teacher does.

Behind me, a bunch of kids snickered as Mrs. Miceli stepped away. Careful not to turn my head, I whispered under my arm to Roberta, who sat behind me. "Shut up."

"Why should I? You've got a girlfriend."

The fire in my cheeks flared across my entire face. I clenched my jaw to keep from yelling back. Maybe how Roberta acted was what Daddy had meant when he explained the meaning of obnoxious. Except I couldn't see how her behavior would do anyone any good, unlike how mine helped Mr. Aldous.

I clenched my jaw and tried to ignore Roberta and focus only on my worksheet. I would hate to miss recess just to finish this stupid math.

Only three problems left. A bit panicked, I glanced up at the clock. The long hand inched toward the number twelve. *Three plus five equals . . . seven. That must be the correct number.* I scratched a seven on my paper.

I peered behind my right shoulder and, again, caught that new girl staring at me.

"I saw that. See, you *do* like her." Roberta leaned up over her desk. Her *obnoxious* breath puffed on the back of my neck as she gave a great example of the bad side of that word.

Two plus three, now that problem, I knew the answer to—five.

A hand nudged the back of my head. "You better hurry up and finish that paper, or you'll miss out on recess."

"Then shut up and let me work!"

Mrs. Miceli glanced up from her desk. "Is there a problem, Dakota?"

"No, ma'am, everything's fine." "Thanks a lot, Roberta." I gritted my teeth. My eyes glanced to the side again, toward that new girl. Because of *her*, Roberta wouldn't leave me alone.

"Anytime, I'm always glad to help."

Yeah, right, Roberta's help I don't need.

Two plus four—The recess bell rang, jarring me half out of my seat. I didn't care what the correct answer was. I refused to miss recess, so I made a guess and scratched a five on my paper.

My chair scraped the floor as I fled from my desk. "Here you go, Mrs. Miceli, all finished." I dropped my worksheet on the pile of papers and took my place at the back of the boy's line.

My teacher flashed me a grin as she strolled past, then moved in front of the kids and opened the door. "Walk, or you'll come back for a second try."

Staring at my shoes, I willed them to slow down until I got to the big double doors that led outside. As soon as my feet crossed the threshold, I dashed toward the giant swings. It made no sense why, today, I tried to claim one. Of course, since I was the last kid from my classroom to leave the building, they'd all be taken.

I rounded the corner and, smack, plowed right into that same new girl who had stared at me all morning. Without thinking, I grabbed her by the arm. She toppled onto the hard concrete. With a thud, I landed on top of her. The rough ground scrapped the palms of my hands. My skin stung from the bite of loose gravel. But I was not about to cry, not now, not in front of the new girl. Her straight hair flew before her face, covering up tears as they flooded her eyes.

I leaped to my feet and jutted my hand out toward her. "Oh, I'm so sorry. Are you alright?"

She grasped it and rose to her feet, brushing dirt from her bright pink skirt. "I'll be fine."

A trickle of blood oozed from a mean scrape just below her knee. "That's an awesome gash. You need the nurse to clean that up. I'm Dakota, by the way, and I'm sorry I ran into you."

Her dirt-smudged hand swiped away a tear. "My name's Caitlyn." Her throat rippled as she swallowed back a sob, then clasped my hands in hers. Caitlyn turned them over and exposed the scraps on my palms. "Looks like you also need to see the nurse."

I jerked my hands from hers and scanned the playground, hoping no one, especially that pesky Roberta, saw. "Come on. I'll take you inside."

Caitlyn stayed beside me as she limped toward the school building. A question seared my mind, not a polite one to ask, but my ability to hold back failed as I gave in to the urge. "So, why did you stare at me all morning?"

Her footsteps paused. "It's hard to make friends. And you were nice to me the other day on the bus, so I thought maybe you could be my friend."

A mass of guilt dumped into my gut as I remembered how angry I had felt when Roberta sneered at me because of Caitlyn's stares.

A shadow flashed across Caitlyn's face. "I'm sorry I made you uncomfortable."

"Nah, don't worry about it."

"But I saw what that girl behind you did."

"Oh, you mean Roberta? Never mind her. She's just obnoxious. So am I, only I'm the good kind of obnoxious. Mr. Aldous tells me so almost every time I see him."

CHAPTER

23

ALDOUS

"WHY DID I EVER AGREE? I can't make a bit of sense out of this." I clamped my hands over Oscar's fur-covered shoulder blades and hoisted up the front end of his body. "Oscar, I must be losing my mind."

The animal gazed back at me. A helpless expression sprawled over its squashed-up face.

"Like it or not, I must follow through, at least with this first session. Maybe Dakota will hate piano and won't want to continue. If he does resume lessons, that child better practice hard. I won't waste time on anyone, especially a pesky, irritating kid." Tension inched into my fingers. With more intensity than intended, I jostled the helpless animal.

His befuddled expression bit a slice of regret clear through my flesh. So, cautious to gentle my mannerism, I set him back beside me on the piano bench.

The animal shook out his ears. They folded forward in typical fashion as he sat his small furry rump down on the polished wood.

I stared at my pug-nosed friend. With a tipped head, he gazed back. Dark brown eyes drilled into mine.

"I could always say I'm ill and can't possibly teach the boy."

Oscar lowered his torso. His chin rested on his paws, held together as if in prayer. A single whine escaped this otherwise silent pose.

"I know . . . you're right . . . Someday, I would have to get well again, and then that child would be back at my door, begging even more intensely for me to teach him to play. And *then* what excuse would I make up?" I threw my arms in the air and directed my question at this four-legged beast as if expecting an answer. The longer I existed alone without Mariam, the nuttier I got. It began to concern me.

Oscar raised his head and let out a small yelp.

I stared at the lump of fur beside me. Since when had this mutt become my confidant? Not long ago, I detested this very beast with great intensity. Somehow, something significant had changed within me. I wasn't sure what it was, and I did *not* like it.

I inhaled a long-drawn-out sigh deep into my awaiting lungs. "With my luck, Alexandra would still arrive at my doorstep, armed with some strange soup concoction and wild claims that her recipe cured all ailments. Why can't this lady and her pesky child leave me alone?" A groan throttled in my throat. "That's exactly the type of thing Mariam would have done." I snorted out a puff of air from my nostrils. A heaping load of tension left along with it.

"Well, I better get busy and find something we can use. Mariam stashed some beginning music around here somewhere. Go on, Oscar, move it."

I nudged the mutt off the piano bench, lifted the lid, and searched within. Finally, my fingers clamped onto the frayed cover of the *Thompson's First Grade Learner*, the same beginner curriculum Mariam had used with me years ago.

Footsteps, followed by a rap on the front door, sent Oscar into a full-fledged barking spasm while he darted off in that direction. He halted beside the welcome mat and spun in circles as if engaged in a frantic race with his coiled tail. Whether he or the stub would win, I never could tell.

"Move aside, boy." I shoved the spastic animal out of my way and held open the screen.

"Howdy, Mr. Aldous, sir." Creating an exaggerated wave, the eager child arched his hand above his head. A sweaty-boy aroma wafted past my nostrils.

"Just come on in and make yourself at home?" I cringed at the sharp tone of my voice. *Why should I care? I never used to.*

"I'm so sorry, Mr. Aldous." Alexandra bowed her head as she stepped over the threshold. "He's extremely excited for his piano lesson to begin. That's practically all he has talked about since that day you joined us for dinner."

"We might as well get this over with." To slow down the inevitable, I dragged my feet, weighted down with regret from having opened my big mouth on the topic of the piano.

Alexandra planted herself beside the piano bench, like a sentry guarding its castle.

Dakota scooched onto the bench, his erect spinal cord as straight as a signpost. A broad smile stretched across his freckled face as all his attention aimed toward the keyboard before him.

I lowered myself beside the boy and turned the first few pages of the *Thompson Learner* that sat on the music rack. My sight froze onto the treble clef, then darted to Dakota. *What was I thinking? I haven't a clue how to teach piano, especially not to a child.*

The boy remained motionless beside me. Expectancy glimmered in his wide eyes.

"I guess we'll start here." I placed my right finger on an ivory note, dead center of the keyboard. "This is middle C. When written in a music score, it looks like that." My left finger pointed to a blackened note on the page before us.

Even though I strained to focus on the enthused child, my glance wandered toward the young lady who remained stationary at our side. Something about her silhouette spooked me. From the corner of my eye, I swore that personage could have been my wayward daughter, Lacey.

I angled my head for a better view, with hopes of resolving the conflict conjured up within my aged mind. Sure enough, Dakota's mom stood just beyond this bench. Yet, the uninvited illusion persisted.

I squeezed my eyes and shook my head with hopes of willing my mind to end this cruel joke. I've always prided myself on my militant actions. Now would be the ideal time to apply that well-disciplined ability. My eyes reopened and all attention drilled onto Dakota. "With only these three notes, you can play 'Mary Had a Little Lamb' like this." My arthritic fingers feigned limber as they plunked out the familiar tune.

The boy's inflated grin extended even further across the small span of his rounded face. "Let me try!" His chubby fingers plunked out a tune comparable to the one I had just played—only his version consisted of multiple pauses and sour notes. His one remaining front tooth bit the pulp of his lower lip as he ran through a similar series of notes numerous times. Not quitting until he perfected this beginner's melody, Dakota displayed a level of determination I had not anticipated.

Impressed and annoyed at this child's persistence, I held my breath. Maybe he did have what it took to master this complicated instrument.

Not convinced what I wanted more—to further test his ability or scare the child off—I pressed my middle finger on the same note that began the first melody. "Now watch, with only two more notes added, you get another song."

Dakota's blue eyes widened. I stared at those saucer-shaped orbs, which gave the impression that God had carved two circles out of the sky and placed them on this child's face.

"What's the song, Mr. Aldous? Are you going to play it?" The boy squirmed as if bugs crawled beneath his clothing.

Pulling my rebellious mind back to attention, the ancient fingers on my right hand appeared surprisingly agile as I alternated each digit.

"I know that song. That's 'Joyful, Joyful We Adore You.' Mommy sings it when she washes dishes."

"Well, I guess you could call it that. But I prefer the title, 'Ode to Joy.'"

"Let me try. I want to play that song." The over-enthused child reached out his stubby, anxious fingers, knocking my hand off the keyboard.

Alexandra took a step closer—her mouth gaped as if to speak.

"No, don't . . . I want to see if your boy has it in him."

Her throat rippled. I assumed she swallowed unspoken words as, in silence, she stepped back.

With ease, the child replaced his fingers over the accurate notes so focused I doubted he retained awareness of having shoved me aside. Dakota pressed down on white keys, replicating almost the same musical sequence I had. After numerous attempts, Dakota's chubby fingers plunked out every note in its precise and correct order. The child pulled back his hands and beamed a grin that could have charmed Ebenezer Scrooge.

"Wonderfully done, Dakota." The vigor of Alexandra's applause rivaled her verbal acclaim.

In my delusional mind, Alexandra's ovation resonated from Mariam instead, as she would complement my awkward performances.

Mariam had never tired from extending large doses of patience. She would sit beside me for as many hours as necessary, an image of forbearance, while I plunked out sour notes. No matter how atrociously I had played, a loving smile always radiated from her tender lips.

How to master this complicated instrument still baffled me to this day. Yet never, in all those years, did she grimace at my muddled efforts.

Unlike my forbearing wife, I quickly grew impatient. The idea of Mariam teaching me anything had grated on every one of my already frazzled nerves. Regardless of the constant string of grumbles and complaints that fled my intolerant mouth, not once had Mariam diminished her love exhibited in countless ways. Every expression of devotion I eventually pushed away.

By the time the end of her life had drawn near, I not only achieved to shove her love aside but, without realizing it, killed her spirit. I condemned my beloved Mariam to live out her final years in an emotionless state as if her true essence had diminished into an empty shell.

Mariam had spent the better part of her life showering me with unconditional love, and I drove her to her grave as a depleted soul. God gave me an angel, and when her time to return home had arrived, I sent her back as a worthless corpse.

"That's enough for today." Surprised by the sharp pitch of my voice, I sprang to my feet. The bench scraped back an inch.

While still perched on its hardwood surface, Dakota flinched. He pierced his sky-blue irises directly toward mine. Fearful he could view the memory that dominated my thoughts, I spun my head and directed it toward the door.

"Thank you for your time, Mr. Aldous. I'm certain Dakota enjoyed the lesson very much." Confusion edged Alexandra's voice. She stretched out her hand toward her child. "Come on, Dakota. Let's go home. We've taken up enough of Mr. Aldous's time."

The child clasped his mother's hand. Together they marched to the door.

The seat of my pants magnetized to the solid, unforgiving wood of the bench. Alexandra and Dakota's voices faded to the back of my mind as if they resonated from an old radio left to play in a far-off room.

In the distance, Alexandra uttered a "goodbye." Somehow her voice morphed into Lacey's—an echo of the last time my estranged daughter had exited through that same door.

Air wafted through the entryway as the door closed behind them. An unexpected sensation lacerated my heart. For the first time in many years, I cared how my only child and grandchild faired. With Mariam gone, I no longer received indirect messages. I had not heard a thing from Lacey since the death of my wife three years ago. My insides overflowed with unexpected grief.

Over many decades I had constructed a solid wall around my heart with the sole purpose of concealing myself far away from the hassle of feelings. The sensation of a knife stabbed into me, slicing open my outer shell. I grabbed at my chest.

I staggered from that cold, firm bench, alone in my house, and sobbed. Just moments before, I had viewed this place as my hidden sanctuary, and now, for some unexplainable reason, it had morphed into my prison.

CHAPTER

24

DAKOTA

*T*HREE, THREE, FOUR, FIVE, FIVE, *four, three, two, one, one—* "That's it!"

"What's it?" Traven looked as surprised as if an alien had walked past us.

I didn't mean to speak out loud. I remembered the exact fingering to the song Mr. Aldous had taught me the other day during my first piano lesson. That one most excellent lesson had caused me to lose control of my excitement, and the words "that's it" had bubbled out.

Traven shrugged, then turned back toward Mrs. Miceli, who sat across the circle from us in her teacher's chair.

My hand stretched past folded knees as I sat crossed-legged on my assigned carpet square. The tips of my fingers, one at a time, drummed against floor tile. In my mind, those faint raps transformed into the notes to "Joyful, Joyful," played on an imaginary piano. As silent as possible, I hummed the tune so only my ears could hear.

"Dakota . . ." The sound of my teacher's voice droned as if far off in the distance.

Traven nudged my shoulder.

"Ow!" I grabbed the upper part of my arm and shot him my best glare. "What was that for? You didn't have to shove so hard."

"It's your turn. Pay attention." Somehow Traven kept a perfect opened-lip grin between his sunburned cheeks as his words spat through gritted teeth.

I glanced across from me in the circle at Mrs. Miceli. Beside her sat Caitlyn. Her feet rested on her thighs instead of beneath her the way the rest of the kids did.

Irritation coiled up my spine as almost everyone in that room stared at me. I shifted my sight from the odd placement of Caitlyn's feet to her blue eyes and caught her direct gaze. My cheeks burned as if they rested against a space heater. "I'm sorry—what was that again?"

"Larry Lizard . . . What letter makes the la-la-la sound that we hear at the beginning of Larry and lizard?" The tap of Mrs. Miceli's foot increased.

I hated those babyish word games. Doesn't everyone know the right answer? Either Mommy or Daddy had read to me almost every day of my entire life. By my first day of school, I had already learned how to read most of the books stashed on my bedroom shelf. "*L*, Larry and lizard both start with the letter *L*." *We were supposed to be in kindergarten, not preschool.*

"Dakota, you need to pay more attention. This makes the third time since recess that I had to repeat a question for you."

"Yes, Mrs. Miceli."

Someone to my left snickered. I turned. Roberta slapped her hand across her mouth.

Some people can be so rude. I tipped my head downward. My piano hand still stretched out over the hard floor. From the top of my eyes, so that no one could see, I focused on Caitlyn. Her cheeks blazed a fresh shade of pink, not there a minute ago.

"Well, let's go on. Jacob, what sound do you hear at the beginning of Billy Bear?"

Finally, the attention shifted off me. I never heard Jacob's answer. My ears tuned back into the pretend notes from the song Mr. Aldous had called "Ode to Joy." My fingers struck each note while I concentrated on memorizing its correct placement.

I stayed in my private world, filled with make-believe piano music, as the day sped by. So determined to master this song, I barely noticed the other kids nudge me as they fought for space beside the wall hooks where our coats and backpacks hung.

Roberta faced me square on, "Boy, Dakota, what's gotten into you? You sure didn't pay much attention today." Her hands perched on her hips while she chewed me out the way a teacher would.

Jacob elbowed in beside Roberta. His jaw clenched as he shoved her. "Why don't you leave him alone? Or are you unable to do such a thing?" He shot her a stare powerful enough to bend steel.

My jaw dropped to my shoes. Never had I guessed Jacob would come to my defense.

Roberta made a "humph" noise and stomped off toward the door.

Jacob's pudgy cheeks puffed out as he flashed a grin in my direction.

My stomach churned as if snakes made up my intestines. *Now, what does Jacob want from me?* I had never known him to be kind without expecting something in return. Full of suspicion, my jaw muscles tightened as I returned the loaded grin.

With coats on and backpacks in hand, my classmates and I jostled out the door and onto our assigned busses lined up alongside the school building.

Traven claimed the space beside me, then stashed his backpack under the seat in front of us. "What got into you today? You hardly paid any attention. You're lucky Mrs. Miceli didn't make you stay inside for recess."

I barely heard my friend's voice. My mind concentrated on the notes to "Joyful, Joyful." "Do you have a piano?"

"No." Traven's nose crinkled as he gaped in my direction.

Across the aisle and two seats up sat Caitlyn. Her hand pressed against the back panel of the seat in front of her. Her fingers danced in what appeared to be a well-thought-out pattern as they tapped dingy vinyl. Did she also play a silent melody on an invisible keyboard?

"Well, have you heard anyone play before?" I gawked at Caitlyn's hand.

Traven tipped his head in the direction I gazed, then back at me. "Yeah, my great-aunt Coral plays. Sometimes when our family gets together to celebrate birthdays or some other holiday, she'll play songs on the piano, and all we kids will sing along. It can get mighty wild."

I grabbed both his arms. "Have you ever wished to play? I mean, *really* play."

A pale tint inched over Traven's sunburnt face. "Never even thought of it. Why?"

I released my grip. "The neighbor who lives across the street from us plays piano. Mom and I overheard him the other day when we went over. You should have been there. Mr. Aldous sounded amazing. Anyway, he gave me a lesson, and I learned two songs. More than anything in this world, I want to play just like Mr. Aldous does." I held back the urge to again grab Traven's arms.

"Uh-uh, there's no way that's true. I know something you want much more."

"Yeah, right, you think you're *so* smart. Go on then, let me have it." I folded my arms across my chest and squeezed.

"You want that Super-Bat bike kit. The one you earned from the fundraiser."

My arms relaxed. "Well . . . maybe . . . but I already have that, so it doesn't count."

"Does too! You've earned it, but it's not yet yours."

Maybe Traven was right, but as sure as chocolate chip was my favorite type of cookie, I wasn't about to let Traven know. Even still, I wanted that Super-Bat bike kit so much I would have almost been willing to give up the puppy I had begged Mommy and Daddy for all year. "So, when do you think our prizes will come in?"

"Not sure, but it should happen real soon. It has been at least a couple of weeks since we turned in the order forms, hasn't it?"

Brakes squeaked. My head jerked and bumped onto the back of the padded seat that faced us as the bus jolted to a stop.

Traven and I snatched up our backpacks, then pushed in among the kids lined up in the center of the bus. The screech of a chaotic uproar pierced my ears as we elbowed our way down the aisle.

Caitlyn waited in her seat for another stop. Her fingers still danced to an unheard melody. To keep from being prodded forward by the mob behind me, I gripped the back of her seat. "Caitlyn, do you play?"

"What?"

"Do you play the piano?"

"I sure do. As soon as I get home today, Mommy will take me to Mrs. Zmich for my lesson. She plays the organ at the Saint Stan's Church."

"Move it, bud. I want off." A hand jammed into me, almost knocking me off my feet as I lurched forward. He kept bulldozing me toward the front of the bus and out the door. The rubber soles of my shoes landed with a thud on a familiar concrete sidewalk.

Traven slung his backpack over his shoulder. "How about I come over later today? We could go another round of backyard baseball."

"Nah, I want to practice my songs."

"But that's all you did the entire time at school. Don't you want to do something else, something far more fun?"

"Not much is far more fun than playing the piano. You ought to give it a try. There's only one way to get as good as Mr. Aldous, and that way is to practice every chance I get."

Traven pursed his lips and shook his head. "Keep this up, and you'll be better than your Mr. Aldous before you know it. But by then, you may not have many friends."

The thought of playing the piano better than my music teacher made me smile. But what did he mean by that *friend* comment? "See you tomorrow." I shot Traven a wave and ran toward my mommy, who stood in her usual spot at the end of our driveway.

A suspicious expression covered Mom's face as if her attempt to hold back a smile failed as the strain grew too much. "Dakota, I need you to do me a huge favor. Stay out of your room until after your father gets home. Then the three of us will go in together."

"But, why Mommy?"

"You'll find out soon enough. So, is it a deal?"

"I guess so." Wow, Mommy often sent me to my room when I did something naughty, but not once had she wanted me to keep out.

Mommy wrapped an arm around my shoulder and herded me like her little lamb toward the house.

I guzzled a glass of milk and my afterschool snack—cookies, oatmeal this time. I usually loved Mommy's oatmeal cookies just as much as her special chocolate chip ones, but this time, for some reason, Mommy put raisins in the batch. She said she did it to make them extra good for me. Mommy always finds some way to make me and Daddy's favorite foods extra nutritious. Sometimes it turns out okay, but now and then, it spoils a perfectly good recipe, and this was one of those times. I didn't know much about raisins and nutrition, but I sure knew how they goop up in my back teeth. I never could stand how that felt.

"You only ate one cookie. Here, have another." Mommy pushed the open jar across the table, within easy reach.

"No, thank you." As I watched the sparkle in Mommy's eyes, a twinge of guilt sprang up in my gut alongside a mushed-up cookie. Most of the time, I would have eaten two or three, but too many raisins had gummed up and filled all the grooves in my molars.

Mommy placed the lid on the cookie jar and carried it back to its usual spot, on top of the refrigerator where it belonged. "Well then, don't you want to go outside and play?"

"No thanks, I'd rather practice my piano songs." The yummy cookie taste faded from my tongue as "Joyful, Joyful" rang in my mind, tempting my fingers to join in on the dance.

"You sure have gotten a lot of enjoyment out of that one lesson. We definitely need to ask Mr. Aldous for more. I wonder how much he would charge to continue with weekly lessons." I swore that Mommy winked as she turned and grabbed the sponge.

The tune in my head, along with the motion of my fingers, came to a screeching halt. Mommy only winked when she was up to something suspicious. Now that got me to wonder what she might be up to.

Mommy leaned over the table and peered out the window. "I thought I heard the mail truck. Want to go get the mail with me?"

"Why not." I marched toward the entry and slipped back into my coat, then plopped down on the bottom step. Shoving my feet into my nifty new shoes, I concentrated real hard, trying to tie the laces. Lace tying was very difficult, yet our teacher—clear back at the beginning of the school year—had insisted that all we kids tie our shoes with no help whatsoever. One day she even sent home a letter to our parents, asking them *not* to tie our shoes. Mrs. Miceli had called it our first homework assignment—to learn to tie laces all by ourselves. Most of the time, I did pretty well. But once in a while, I cheated and folded my laces over, turning them into bunny ears and then twisted them into a knot. It came out looking the same, and no one caught on.

Mommy and I stepped out the side door and marched down the driveway. Mr. Aldous and his cute puppy dog, Oscar, trotted ahead of us toward the giant mailbox. I grabbed Mommy's hand. After a glance in both directions, I tugged her across the street. "Come on, Mommy, the road's clear."

"What's the rush?"

"I don't want to miss Mr. Aldous. I've got something important to tell him."

"Okay, okay. I'm certain we will get there before he leaves. Look, he hasn't even inserted his key."

I pulled on Mommy's arm like a dog tugging at its leash as we hurried across the street.

"Hey, Mr. Aldous!" I waved my free arm high in the air.

Our neighbor buried his head in the palm of his hand as if he had one huge headache.

"Mr. Aldous, I need to talk with you!" I dragged Mommy along with me down the sidewalk. She stumbled over her feet and giggled. I must have again entertained her.

"Mr. Aldous . . . Am I glad we caught up with you . . ." My words staggered among pants of breath as I sucked in much-needed air.

Mr. Aldous stared down, his head still held in one of his hands. Maybe he was concentrating on his feet? He was wearing that same old, worn-out pair of slippers from that first day we had met when he scratched me with his key. *That's it! He must be embarrassed to be seen outside again in such rags.* Mommy often made a big deal of not letting me in public while wearing worn, outgrown clothing.

Mr. Aldous lifted his head and tipped it in my direction. "Yes, Dakota, what do you want?"

I opened my mouth and gulped a breath of crisp air. The chill met the back of my throat, triggering a slew of coughs.

Mr. Aldous's eyes widened, revealing dull gray peepers before those lids returned to their usual half-slit, too heavy to hold up position.

I swallowed back a bucket of tears and caught my breath. "Thank you again for teaching me how to play the piano." I spread my lips wide to give Mr. Aldous my best smile.

He turned toward the postboxes and grunted something. I couldn't tell what. To keep the grin frozen on my face, I remained perfectly still as I waited. Mr. Aldous stuck his key in the lock, then pulled out a heap of mail. My cheeks ached, but I continued to hold the smile in place. Of course, Mr. Aldous would want to know how happy I felt because of what he did for me.

"Two lousy songs plunked out on five ivories do not mean someone knows how to play." He sifted through his pile of mail, uncovered a bright yellow envelope, and paused.

It felt as if a baseball whacked into my gut. The smile I strained to hold broke.

Mr. Aldous turned from the postal box. With his eyes angled well over my head, he started toward his house.

I moved in a bit closer and accidentally brushed against the hand that held his mail. A few letters tumbled from his grasp.

"I'm sorry."

Three items scuttled down the sidewalk, pushed along by a breeze. I snatched up two pieces that looked like newspaper advertisements, then ran after the third, the bright yellow envelope, grabbing it before it blew into the road. The envelope ripped. Bright sparkly print peeked out from the fresh tattered opening.

"It's your birthday. This card spelled out 'Happy Birthday.'" I held the three run-away letters out toward him. "Here you go, Mr. Aldous. You dropped these. I'm sorry. I didn't mean to rip this one open, but it says, 'Happy Birthday.' Is today your birthday?" I tried to bring back the same extra big smile I had used before, but my cheeks ached too much.

"Come on, Oscar." Mr. Aldous snatched the items from my hand. He turned sharply on his heels and stomped off toward his house. Oscar scampered after him.

Mommy rested her hand on top of my head. "It's all right, Dakota."

I felt like a deserted puppy waiting for his master as Mommy stroked my hair. "But he never answered. Why didn't he answer? We never even had the chance to ask him to teach me more lessons."

"I know, honey. We'll ask another day."

CHAPTER 25

ALDOUS

"*H*URRY UP, OSCAR, AND GET in the house." The pesky mutt paused in front of the door. With the level of interest that would warrant a scientific discovery, he inspected a simple black ant.

I propped the door ajar using the side of my foot and nudged the animal to hurry his pace over the threshold. He whimpered a complaint and scurried his short legs inside.

I knew better than to gather my mail during afternoon hours. I should have waited until dusk. Of course, the chances of bumping into that menacing kid were far too great this time of day. And whoever heard of a boy his size being able to read?

I dropped the bundle of mainly bills and advertisements onto the open secretary desk beside the staircase, then, as Oscar meandered around my feet, sidled over to the picture window.

Alexandra's arm enwrapped around Dakota's shoulder as she escorted her son across the street. The dual gave off a similar allure to a mother goose as she gathered her precious goslings.

Drawing in a breath to ease the mountain of disappointment within my gut, I plopped my tired body into the rocking chair. Wood scraped against the worn rug, grinding my frayed nerves as I shifted the chair to fashion the perfect observation perch. Oscar twirled beside me, then curled into a fuzzy ball on the carpet.

Today's encounter marked the first time I had seen Dakota outside all week. This meddlesome child's absence provided me with an unexpected yet highly appreciated vacation, one I regretted to see come to an end.

My insides twisted in confusion. If, with such intensity, I hated bumping into that pesky child, why did I battle this uncontrollable obsession to peer out the window in search of his small form?

Oscar's snore captured my attention. The canine's upper lip fluttered with each exhale. My stomach muscles jolted from a sudden chuckle. These foreign occurrences, which I'm not so sure I enjoyed, had lately become a frequent event. "Crazy mutt . . . How could an insignificant beast like you influence me?"

The pug's right ear twitched.

To quickly erase the curl from my upper lip, I resumed staring out the window. Dakota's side door swayed as he and his mother entered their home. Fear raged within. This boy held a power that tugged at the many scabs that covered my shameful wounds. A lifetime of vulnerability created these battle scars. A concrete wall had surrounded my hardened heart now for many decades. No tool could ever penetrate this well-constructed barrier, yet now an unwitting child threatened to knock it down.

Oscar leaped to his feet. His tiny body spun in a double circle on the teal carpet, then darted to the dining room and hopped on top of the piano bench.

"No! I've had enough of that instrument!" The sound of my voice roared with such volume I glanced out the window to assure no one else had heard. Certain aspects of one's life must remain private.

I had come to detest that monstrous instrument. Every time I ran my fingers across the keyboard, another carefully constructed layer had peeled away. Over the years, I invested far too much into forming my prized barricade, my masterpiece, to let it crumble. To remove my smokescreen this late into my life would strip away all sense of purpose. That precious barricade represented everything I possessed, my only mark of achievement acquired from a long and dismal existence.

Oscar let out a string of spastic yelps. The speed at which his tale wagged rivaled the rapid beat of a hummingbird's wings.

"I said NO!" Dry air stung my eyeballs as I stared down at the unassuming animal.

Finally, having gotten the point, Oscar laid his body down on the bench and rested his pudgy face on his crossed front paws. He relayed the perfect pout as a single tooth protruded over his top lip.

"It's about time you get the point. Remember, mutt, I'm in charge, not you." I straightened my aching bones and shuffled over to the deposited mail. The act of scuffing my slippers against the carpet acted as a soothing ointment to my frazzled nerves.

I plucked the torn, bright yellow envelope from the pile. It had held my attention since Dakota handed it to me. The last thing I needed was for this pesky child to make a fuss over my birthday. Such events were better left ignored. Throughout the years, I had burnt every bridge. No one should remember my personal information. Who would know that next week marked my seventy-second birthday?

Despite efforts to remain uninterested, my heart pounded a brisk rhythm within the core of my chest. I slid my finger into the torn envelope and opened the unexpected card. My heartbeat slowed. Commercial ink spelled out a generic greeting, mushy to intelligent ears. Purple crayon scribbled across the inside—"Love, Chloe."

The room spun before my eyes. I staggered to the staircase and dropped onto the bottom step—physical evidence of little Chloe, my only grandchild.

Countless times during her final year of life, Mariam wept because I had forbidden her to see her only grandchild. If Lacey demanded to stand firm and declare such outlandish lies, I would refuse her entrance into our home. Daughter or no daughter, it made no difference. No one would fabricate false accusations about me and get away with it. As a result of the constraint, little Chloe became a causality of friendly fire.

I kept a loose grip on the card. Something soft and wet made contact with my free hand draped over my knee. I forced my eyes to focus as Oscar licked my bony flesh.

Usually, I would have jerked my hand away, but for some reason, I allowed him to continue to lick. I barely detected the warm slobber while a part of my mind riveted onto an image forever burnt into my brain of the boy across the street. Another section of my mind strained to formulate pictures of how my grandchild today might look. She would be around his age.

Lacey had resembled her mother more and more as she matured, which proved detrimental, for she, too, needed to be put in her place. Her very appearance reinforced that need.

I slammed the card onto the floor. Oscar yelped and bolted away. "I don't want to remember!" The heel of my foot ground Chloe's scribbled signature into polished hard-wood boards. A crinkle obscured the smile drawn onto a brightly colored sun.

"I had to control them! It was the only way. Dear, God, you know I tried everything, yet nothing worked. I beg of You, don't unlock those memories!" I fell to my knees and buried my face in balled-up fists. Not even at Mariam's death had I cried so hard.

CHAPTER 26

DAKOTA

"MOMMY, DADDY'S HERE! HE'S FINALLY home!" Daddy pulled our car toward the garage behind our house. I leaped off the couch and raced to the back door.

"Slow down, Dakota, before you get hurt." Mommy turned into a streak of color as I sped past her.

"But now we get to see what this big surprise is all about." The screen door slammed behind me. I darted outside and soared down the steps in a way Super-Bat himself would have been proud of. My feet hit the concrete with a thud. I sprinted up the driveway and bounded to the side of Daddy's car as his door swung open.

Daddy's mustache twitched. Laughter rolled out from somewhere deep within his chest. "You sure are excited. What's up, Dakota?"

"Yeah, like you don't know." I grabbed his hand and tugged hard. "Hurry inside. I want to see what you and Mommy are hiding in my room."

"Hold on, little man. We'll be up there in a few minutes. But first, you have to let me out."

I hopped back and gave Daddy room, my insides twisting in fast gear. Too bad I didn't have on my Super-Bat cape. Mommy and Daddy held it hostage along with whatever else they had placed in my bedroom. With the strength that poured out of me at that instant, I could have soared off someplace adventurous and captured any villain. But to do that right then would have been crazy. It would slow us down even more from solving the mysterious case of why Mommy refused to let me enter my bedroom all day.

Daddy seemed to move extra slow as he unfolded his long legs and eased out of the car. My parents had told me that someday I would grow as tall as Daddy. Now that's tall! It would take a lot of work on God's part to stretch my small body way up to that level. But it sure would be pretty neat if it did happen. I've often wondered how things looked from way up there.

The car door shut. Daddy slid his hand in mine, and we hustled toward the house. Mommy grinned extra wide as she stood on the porch. Her arms wrapped tight around her as if to keep warm.

Daddy tugged at my grip. "You don't have to move so fast, Dakota. Whatever is in your room will remain, regardless of how long it takes us to get there."

"Oh, so you admit it . . . the surprise is a thing." I eyeballed Daddy, giving him an extra-big smile as we approached the porch steps. As I placed my foot against the first step, it scrapped the wooden lip and tripped me up. I began to tumble forward.

Mommy gasped. Her arms jutted out in my direction.

Daddy jerked me upright before I crashed face-first onto the hard surface. "Good thing you kept a tight grip on my hand. You could have gotten hurt there, young man. Now slow down and be more careful."

Mommy held the door open. We followed each other inside and headed straight toward my room.

We approached the closed door at the end of the hallway. Daddy twisted his body and blocked our entrance. "Now, Dakota, are you sure you want to go in? Who knows, you might not like this surprise. Once we step inside, there's no going back." His green eyes sparkled as his mustache twisted into the distinct outline of a grin.

If *I* had blocked the doorway, they would have demanded that I stop being so mischievous, maybe even called me obnoxious. I glanced at Mommy for help. All she did was laugh.

Finally, with a chuckle, Daddy turned the knob and moved out of the way.

I couldn't believe what my eyeballs saw. I squinted and rubbed them. I'm not this good at imagining things. I popped my eyes back open, and, sure enough, that same mind-blowing item I felt positive my mind had invented stood in my room.

Beside my bed, secured to a sturdy black stand, sat the most awesome keyboard I had ever seen. I stared so hard at this dream-come-true I had to blink to keep my eyeballs from drying out.

"Wow, would you look at that!" I darted toward this unbelievable instrument and ran my fingers over the keys.

Not a sound came out. "It's broken! Something's wrong with this thing."

"No, honey, you need to turn it on first. Here, let me show you." Mommy pressed a long gray button above the keys. Knobs lit up, and a faint hum rang from the speakers.

"By pressing these controls, you can make all sorts of sounds." Daddy pushed a bunch of switches, then ran his fingers across the black and white keys.

I expected a piano tone similar to what I had heard at Mr. Aldous's home. But instead, the clash of a drumset spat out. "Cool, how'd you do that?"

"Press these buttons, see? You can make this thing sound like just about anything." Daddy beamed wide, looking like a kid as thrilled as I was, maybe even more.

His fingers danced over the notes, turning all kinds of unexpected sounds into familiar tunes. My excitement soared with each key played, yet a load of disappointment tugged at my joy—the same way a bucket of rocks yanks at the string of a circus balloon tied to it. "But, can it sound like a piano?"

"It absolutely can. This knob here will do it."

I watched which buttons Daddy pushed, burning the information into my brain. As fun as all those other settings were, especially the way Daddy played them, I still wanted to make the same music as Mr. Aldous.

"Go on, Dakota, give it a try." Mommy nudged me closer.

Daddy pointed to the button that turned this cool transformer into my favorite instrument. "There, it's set on piano, ready and waiting for you."

I placed my fingers on the correct keys my mind had pictured every day since Mr. Aldous's lesson. That very song, which not once had left my head, now rang forth as a melody even more beautiful than I remembered. My thumb pressed the final key. "I love it! Is it mine?" I gaped at Mommy, then Daddy, and back again, pleading in my heart to keep this fantastic instrument.

"Yes, Dakota, the keyboard is all yours." The arch of Daddy's brows, combined with a sparkle in his eyes, confirmed his answer.

My insides buzzed with such force it made me bounce on my tiptoes. I spun toward Mommy. "It really is?"

She nodded. "As your Dad said, it's all yours."

"But how?"

Daddy picked up an instruction book and started to flip pages.

Mommy slid a strand of hair behind her ear. The ring of green in her mostly blue eyes glinted brighter than usual. "We noticed how much time you've spent practicing an imaginary piano. Because you're so dedicated to learning how to play, your father and I figured you need the proper equipment."

Daddy slid his index finger into the instruction manual's binding and held it closed. "I went online and found this baby." He rubbed the top of the keys, like how he brushes my forehead before kissing me at bedtime.

Mommy lowered herself onto my bed and pressed the palms of her hands to the mattress. "Tomorrow, while you're at school, I thought I'd call Mr. Aldous and see if he'd be willing to continue with weekly lessons."

"Really, Mom? And now that we have this"—I patted the keyboard—"that means I can practice every single day on the real thing."

"That's the whole idea, son." Daddy winked as the left edge of his dark blond mustache jerked.

I tugged the sleeve of Mommy's oatmeal-colored sweater. It made me think of the cookies I ate after school. "But why wait till tomorrow? Can't we go ask now?"

"We could, but I don't want to put Mr. Aldous in an awkward position. If he doesn't want to teach, it may be difficult to say no to our faces, especially yours, Koty." The soft skin of Mommy's hand pressed against my cheek.

I stretched out my arms and ran my fingers over the keys, switching from larger white ones to skinny black ones, and created a never-before-heard melody.

"Why should Mr. Aldous teach me? Caitlyn, a girl in my class, takes lessons from a real teacher who plays the organ at her church. Wouldn't that be much better?"

Daddy lowered his body onto my bed and turned all his attention to the print inside the instruction booklet.

"Your father and I discussed that very thing. I even called a few piano teachers to get an idea of what they charge. We decided it might be best to ask Mr. Aldous first. He appears so lonely, and since we've already reached out to him, it would be nice to give him our offer. We hope not only would you learn how to play but also that Mr. Aldous might find joy in teaching. Everybody needs a purpose, and I get the impression Mr. Aldous has lost his. Maybe we can help him get it back."

"Well, okay, if you think he's the best choice. But what if he says no?"

"Then we'll find someone else."

Filled with excitement, I sprang back onto my toes and bounced, then stopped and stared straight at Daddy. He lowered the booklet and gazed back at me.

"Mommy and I made a great discovery today. When we got the mail, we bumped into Mr. Aldous. He dropped some of his letters, and the wind blew them away. I ran after them but accidentally ripped open an envelope as I grabbed it just before all the letters blew into the street. That's when we discovered the yellow envelope was a birthday card. Do you know what that means?"

Daddy placed the booklet in his lap and let out a deep chuckle. "No, Dakota. What does that mean?"

"It means Mr. Aldous is going to have a birthday." I rested my hands on Daddy's knees, using them to bounce from as a springboard. "We need to buy him something special, especially since I'm going to be his piano student."

I paused in mid-bounce to think real hard. "Every time we see Mr. Aldous, he always has on that same worn-out pair of slippers. I doubt he even owns any shoes. He could use a new pair. Could we buy him slippers, please?" I moved one hand onto Mommy's knee and continued bouncing with my other hand still on Daddy's.

Mommy patted my hand. "We could do that. Maybe even bake him a cake."

ALDOUS

STARTLED AWAKE FROM A DEEP sleep, I shot straight up in bed. Unconsciously, my feet kicked from beneath neatly tucked-in blankets.

Oscar stirred. "No, no . . . stay asleep." My words came out in a whisper, barely audible to my ears. It was the middle of the night. I did not want to disturb the mutt.

How rare we get what we wish for. The now aroused animal pulled out of its tranquil, curled-up position and hopped off the bed. Wide awake mocha eyes stared up at me, bulging like glass orbs.

With clenched fingertips, I clutched both sides of my throbbing head and kneaded at thinned-out, gray hairs matted down by sweat onto each pulsating temple. I used all the willpower I could muster and forced my foggy sight to focus on the confused mutt who now—I was sorry to say—stood with ridged legs in a full-alert stance beside the bed.

"It was only a dream. It was only a dream." The punctuated words tagged onto short, quick puffs of breath as a chill itched up my spine.

I threw back the covers and tossed my bare feet onto the frayed Persian rug. Oscar yelped and scuttled out of the way.

My calloused soles scuffed a trail across the hallway, then into the bathroom. I paused in front of the sink, turned on the faucet, and splashed cold water over my clammy face.

Droplets rolled off hollowed cheeks as I gazed into the mirror. "Pull yourself together, bud. You're acting like a helpless fool. It was just a dream, nothing to get upset over."

The sallow complexion of a stranger gawked back as if an imposter was mocking me. I scrutinized ashen-tinted irises that once glimmered clear blue. The reality that those royal-blue eyes had long ago lost their luster struck like a mallet to the solar plexus as I labored for breath.

The reflection of Oscar's flattened muzzle as he peeked around the doorframe caught my attention. One glance at that familiar form was all it took to coax out a low-rumbling grunt from deep within my chest. "Who am I trying to fool? I know as sure as that squashed-up, prune-like furry face that belongs to you that what awoke me was not a dream." My words hung thick in the air. Oscar whimpered. It boomed out of place in the hushed atmosphere that twisted my alert nerves.

"No!" I slammed my fist onto the porcelain sink. Oscar darted down the hall, out of sight.

"I have labored most of my life to conceal that shameful reality! For over fifty years, I held in place the perfect grandiose cover story. Not even Mariam suspected!" My words spat out through gritted teeth. I glared at my reflection as if staring down a malicious villain. "I did it so well that *I* even began to convince *myself*."

I pulled away from the sink and turned around. My eyes riveted an empty gaze onto the blank wall. "It can't all come crashing down. Not now!"

I spun my body ninety degrees and placed a tight grip on either side of the mirrored medicine cabinet. Blood within my veins flowed from each bony knuckle, leaving behind pasty white flesh.

"Not ever!" My jaw clenched as I hissed the venom-spiked words into the mirror, showering an already marred reflection with even more unsightly blemishes. Leaning within inches of the looking glass, I pinched my eyelids and formed two narrow slits, resembling a vicious hawk as it stared down unfortunate prey. "I will not go there!" The chilled punch of my voice provoked goose bumps on my exposed forearms.

My fist collided with the edge of the sink. The basin shimmied on narrow steel support rods. I spun on my heels and stormed from the room, slamming the door behind me in an attempt to shut out all threats as wood jarred against the framework.

All this time, Oscar lowered his head, cowering in the hallway. The loud slam sent his short legs beneath his pudgy body, scampering as he darted out of my way. The frightened animal remained almost unnoticed as it fled for cover in a far corner beside the closed door that had once been Lacey's bedroom.

A brash twang announced protest from worn-out springs as I threw my distressed body on the disarrayed blankets arranged in a massive tangle over my mattress. Every muscle within me vibrated with rage.

A beam of light cast by the moon seeped through the hallway window, spilling across the entrance to my room. Every fiber within my being screamed, begging me to ignore the illusion. But no matter how hard I tried, my inner will rebelled. My moistened eyes fixated on the deific ray that had not existed moments before.

Oscar hesitated in the doorway, then sheepishly tramped through the celestial beam painted over scuffed-up floorboards. His folded back ears cast a shadow that transfigured into the form of angel wings.

As I stared at the apparition, all control of thoughts ripped from my tormented mind. A torrent of tears spilled forth. My body heaved with the sorrow of a dying soul. When that life-altering event occurred, I was only a young, innocent child, not unlike the small boy who this day lived across the street and had become a daily pest.

Why had no one come to my defense? I tried with all my will, yet could not imagine Dakota's parents ever violating their son the way my boyhood self had been.

"I entrusted that man with my life." *Doesn't every child trust in their father?* Like every other son, I had placed my dad on a pedestal so high not even the tallest rung could stretch to such a lofty elevation. *How does a person heal once trust has shattered into countless pieces, each a razor-sharp shard gored within his weeping heart?*

Visions of me, Dakota's age, flooded my memory. Far too long, sandy-brown hair fell in my eyes. Every morning, like clockwork, Mother would dampen a comb and draw a sharp part on the right side of my head, then sweep my bangs aside—a feeble attempt to keep them out of my face. *"God blessed you with such beautiful bright blue eyes. It's an insult to your Lord to hide them."* Mother had died many decades ago, yet I still heard the rote tone that clung to her voice, as if she quoted well-rehearsed scripts.

Mother's efforts never lasted long, for in only a short time of boyish play, my sculpted hair, true to its unruly self, fell back into my face. As I returned home for dinner each evening, Mother chastised my disheveled appearance. *"How could you do that to us? What would the neighbors think? You look like a street urchin."* She always took great care in outward appearances, claiming it *"honors our Lord,"* yet even the messiest inward wound never drew a breath of attention from her.

As an innocent child, I many times had tried to tell, yet nobody heard my cries. No one would have believed me anyway. No one protected me.

"Lock your lips and remain mute."—the callused chant of my only advice received—*"Reputations must be preserved at all expenses."*

Even if that expense meant my innocence?

Tragically, *yes.*

Young, innocent, and alone in my silence, that first monumental violation had marked the key predominant element that began my life's journey, ultimately resulting in the final sale of my soul.

At first, this "don't see, don't tell" silence had disguised itself as a rueful friend. For many years, I dwelt in its comfort. I had used this repentant companion to create fantasies of a more joyous time. A time when I believed my parents loved and cherished me. Yet somewhere along the way, this mute comrade had morphed into a vicious enemy that foamed from its jowls.

No matter how hard I had tried to contain this poisonous froth, in the end, it ultimately bubbled forth like putrid acid. It burnt everyone who came in contact with it. The heaviest coating of this toxic spume had spattered sweet Mariam and precious Lacey. It devoured their flesh like a mottled spew of chemical burns, dictating their every action, even consuming their very spirit, just like, long ago, had happened to me.

"How could I have done such a thing? I had forced onto the two people I claimed to love more than any other the same atrocity that my parents had afflicted upon me."

Like words burnt into wood with a branding iron, an even more horrific deliberation seared within my brain. *This time* I *had become the monster*—I alone *oppressed my loved ones and crushed their spirits.* I despised Mariam and Lacey's free-living nature with the same disgust a person demonstrates when he squashes a repulsive bug.

But worst of all remained the violations committed to my precious Lacey. For over thirty years, I rationalized those horrendous actions with lies. My illusion that Mariam never knew trumped my stack of falsehoods.

Emotions attached to these scorned memories smashed into my gut like a battering ram. I bent over in dry heaves. My timeworn body hung off the edge of the bed as I retched from this sudden attack.

In no way could Mariam have *not* known. Anyone with the slightest twinge of intelligence would have figured out the truth, yet she played along as if nothing had occurred. Did I repress my beloved wife to the point where Mariam sacrificed her innermost instinctive morals? Was she no better than I? Did this explain why she never protected Lacey but feigned ignorant all those long years? *"No! Not my sweet Mariam! . . ."*

The gags subsided—a hollowed sensation in my heart replaced nausea.

Did Mariam pretend not to know out of loyalty to me? Could she have loved me to such a pathetic degree that she sacrificed her own child, the same as my mother had sacrificed me? All these shattered lives to protect the reputation of a pitiful husband?

I slid off the edge of the mattress and sank to the floor on my knees. How could I conceive of placing the word "love" anywhere near such atrocity? Such cold-hearted behavior could only originate from one thing—pure, unadulterated evil.

Everything grew still. An all-encompassing silence encircled me. Even the sound of my heartbeat remained mute as secrets melted away, revealing an ugly, naked truth that stared into my shameful face.

A chill of fear trickled down my spine. In that sacred moment, only God and I existed. He stripped away all illusions, granting me a clear view of my past.

Oh, Mariam had known alright. I guaranteed that fact for *my* protection. This time *I* was the one who conspired and made Mariam swear never to tell, the same as a generation ago when my mother had plotted against me. A cruel shift of fate had spun events around, demanding I protect *my* reputation, regardless of the cost, just as my father had done. Only this time, the price was our child, our precious Lacey.

No wonder Lacey proclaimed she would never have anything to do with her mother or me again. Who could blame her when Mariam and

I *together* had committed the worst crime a parent ever could toward their child?

The curse had trickled down from one generation to the next like a boulder rolling down a mountain slope. With each successive rotation, this massive, granite scourge gained speed until, somewhere along the way, it crashed into the tender trunk of an innocent sapling, splitting its slender shaft down the center. Such a collision would ultimately cause irreparable damage to any guiltless seedling, rendering it impossible to grow magnificent and tall as God intended.

What would it take to stop this family curse? How many saplings must we chop down before someone stands firm and eliminates this out-of-control ritual?

The vague memory of a long-forgotten Bible verse elbowed its way into the forefront of my tormented mind. "The Lord is longsuffering, and of great mercy, forgiving iniquity and transgression, and by no means clearing the guilty, visiting the iniquity of the fathers upon the children unto the third and fourth generation." My life existed in the center of this prophetic curse. Through how many generations had the plague spread? When will it stop?

I buried my face in the palms of my hands. All warmth drained from my fingertips, rendering them ice-cold. My connection to God's love appeared to have vanished with the escape of this heat. Tears streamed out in torrents between curled fingers as if water from a pitcher poured from my cupped hands. I fervently attempted to contain the foretelling moisture. An all-encompassing sorrow threaded through my aching cells, wrapping me in the drapery of uninvited truth.

My heart bled with fear as I plummeted into a chasm of dismay. Could I gain enough strength to climb out of this abyss before its jagged claws penetrated my flesh?

The worn rug I curled up on did little to cushion me from the cold, hard floorboards. *How can I face this revelation? How do I live with such gripping grief?*

My heart continued to split open and expose more deep dark secrets. How could I go on? After a lifetime spent carefully manipulating my environment to cloak those truths, every confession now spilled from my soul in this river of tears.

The eastern sunlight peaked through paisley curtains. How long had I remained curled like an infant in the middle of my bedroom floor? I lifted my head and glanced at the windup clock on the nightstand. It showed almost seven-o-clock. I must have spent the entire night on the floor, encased in sorrow. Time had evolved into the next day without my noticing its arrival.

A quick review of the night's events flashed through my mind. I recalled what brought me to such an unusual position. I squeezed my eyes shut, expecting to be re-engulfed in the shame of my past. Instead, a radiant beam from the new day's light shot through the windowpane and immersed me in warmth.

While soaking up this healing light, unconsciously, my body began to sway. The vivid illusion of me as a young, innocent child enwrapped in our Lord's gentle arms took over my imagination. Could senility have seized my mind? How could this be? My being had spent the entire night split wide-open, and my most hideous memories had poured out. Yet, instead of being consumed with regret, I bathed in the light of God's love, pure and clear, for the first time I could remember.

A string of unspoken prayers, which sat dormant for years within my heart, spilled from my cracked lips.

ALDOUS

SOMETHING WARM AND WET SLAPPED against my left cheek, jarring me from a sound sleep. Hot putrid breath assaulted my nostrils. My eyes popped open to discover Oscar inches from my face. I shoved him back a foot and then searched my disoriented brain to remember. Oh yeah, I must have fallen asleep while deep in prayer. No wonder. After last night's escapades, pure exhaustion had taken over.

Another tongue-swipe slapped over my face, drenching the right cheek with slobber. My arm flew up in defense. "All right, already. That's enough!"

My achy knees creaked as they unfolded, pulling me to an upright position.

Oscar whirled around, hurling out a succession of yelps.

"I know, you've got to go outside." Grabbing my robe off the bedpost, I slung it over my shoulders and knotted the sash. "Come on, boy, let's go."

His stubby legs slid beneath him as sharp toenails scrapped the already scratched-up hardwood floor.

"I really should trim those claws someday."

The crazy mutt steadied his footing and darted from my bedroom. By the time I wandered into the hallway, this mutt's persistent barks—shrill to the ears—bellowed from the bottom of the staircase.

"That's enough. You sure could use a bit of patience." I had no clue how this animal could conjure up such abundant amounts of energy. "I'm coming!" Dragging my exhausted body, I descended the stairs.

With each step I took, the anxious animal bounced higher over the crumpled welcome mat before the front door. I shoved him aside and held the door open. "Go on now."

The spastic mutt shot outside, fled down the porch steps, then into the bushes beside the hummingbird feeder, all in one fluid motion.

Pulling my robe tighter, I closed the door and followed him onto the front porch. I anticipated a greeting from the familiar nip that accompanied the autumn's dawn, yet instead, unexpected sunlight caressed my face. Brilliant beams glinted off a large orb-shaped yard decoration in the middle of what once had been Mariam's flower garden.

I never could comprehend a purpose for that ugly globe with its bold red, blue, and green swirled together like a bucket of paint before being blended by an industrial mixer.

Mariam had insisted that this odd contraption would attract hummingbirds. She loved it. I guess that's all that mattered. I, sure as anything, couldn't argue with that fact. Less than two weeks ago, a lone hummingbird had flown above that hideous eye-sore while feasting on nectar.

Whatever made her happy had eased my job as head of the household, especially once Lacey decided to end all contact, and smiles became a rare commodity.

Whether caused by the unexpected warmth of the sun, or my delirium from the rough, sleepless night, I couldn't discern, but an unignorable desire to take a walk ate at my heart. "Oscar, back inside."

Used to being allowed far more time to sniff around the yard, the confused animal flashed a startled gaze in my direction before he obeyed my command.

I shut the door, the pesky mutt safely inside, then fled upstairs to throw on appropriate clothes.

Oscar followed my every move, remaining no more than two steps behind. He tipped his pugged head to one side or the other with an expression of curiosity one would expect from a human.

Back downstairs by the front entry, I slipped the leash out from a rarely opened drawer of the secretary desk and clipped it onto Oscar's collar. "All right, boy, this time we are going for an honest-to-goodness walk."

The bewildered mutt shook his head and defiantly tugged back against the restraint item as if demanding release from the alien object.

With a tight grip on the other end, I reminded Oscar that, like it or not, when I make a command, he better submit.

The now compliant animal trotted beside me in perfect heel formation as we strolled past the lineup of steel mail slots and continued further up the sidewalk. We approached the end of the block. A car sped past, splashing muddy water, remnants from last night's thunderstorm, in our direction.

Disgusted by the grubby mottled spray that streaked my pant leg, I lowered my scuffed loafer onto the splattered pavement. The leash, which only seconds ago had hung slack between my dog and me, now tugged at my clasped fist. I turned around. My glance locked onto Oscar's marble-shaped eyes.

They glared back at me in rebellion.

My fisted hand yanked at the leash. "Come on, mutt . . . let's go."

Oscar plopped his fur-covered rump down in the middle of the sidewalk. A look of resistance masked his pug face.

"We are not heading back home. You might as well get up and move it." I snapped the leash. The tags on Oscar's collar jingled. For some unknown reason, I remained determined to venture beyond our usual walking pattern, whether Oscar agreed or not.

The stubborn mutt gave in and remained only inches from my heels as we plodded across the street and roamed through new territories.

Uproars of high-pitched voices from what sounded like a herd of children interrupted our tranquil stroll. Oscar perked up and quickened his pace toward the racket.

We rounded the corner. Chain link fencing lined the local schoolyard that came into view. My chest puffed out while I drew a deep breath, then released it in a long-winded sigh. If I had remembered the elementary school was in this direction, I would have turned the opposite way, at the top of our street.

A crowd of enthusiastic children outside at recess enticed Oscar. He pulled the leash taut, tugging me toward their throng of activity.

Any other day at the first sign of these unruly kids, I would have turned around and proceeded back home. There I would resume my long-established mission to remain a hermit as I withdrew into the comforts of my castle.

I stood there and glared at these hooligans. If only I could mute their racket with the simple touch of a hand-held remote. That wish spread through me like flames blazing from the toss of a match on a pile of gasoline-doused brush. Any positive outcome that may have resulted from last night's escapades sizzled under that bonfire's intense heat.

All fight within me melted away. I gave in to Oscar's anxious attempts and allowed the eager animal to lead us toward the playground.

The continuous roar of rowdy kids escalated as we approached. I leaned into a steel post. The cold trapped within penetrated my hands, a quick reminder of their arthritic condition.

My eyes latched onto a familiar lad with mussed-up sandy-blond hair. He sat crossed-legged on woodchips near the base of a slide.

I watched Dakota stare down at his lap. A girl in a dirt-smudged dress lumbered beside him. Words I could not decipher shot from her mouth, directed toward the same child who lived across the street from me and possessed such a keen knack for pestering.

Dakota shot up from the ground, scattering stray woodchips as he jutted a pointer finger toward this youth. He hollered an inaudible phrase, then ran toward the basketball hoops on a paved courtyard.

Ignoring an earnest desire to turn my back and march away, my eyes fixated on this exasperating youngster. How could someone as irritating as this boy weasel into my sealed heart? A surge of compassion—a foreign emotion due to the fact that it had been so long since I had allowed my soul to feel—swelled within.

My sight blurred as my mind focused on a mirage of myself at the same age as this pesky boy, who would not go away, no matter how diligently I tried. As I stood on that concrete sidewalk, where the whole world could see, my heart bled for the years of atrocities I had endured while just a lad.

Enough of that nonsense. I blinked twice, pulling out of the daze.

A clear present-day awareness returned to my feeble mind. Even still, I could not entirely shake that delusional fog as I ached for the opportunity to relive my past through this child who, for some reason, continued to carve his way into my heart. If given a chance, I would do things very differently.

A long-rejected fraction of my soul jarred me to recall Lacey and my methods of parenting her. God *had* granted my wish through her childhood, and I threw it away. I could have done much more for my precious child, yet I had failed.

I shifted my eyes upward. Bright sunlight peeked around the edge of a large, cumulous cloud and burned into my retinas. I forced my lids to remain open. "Oh, dear God, please, forgive me. Grant me another chance to make things right in Your sight."

My eyes swelled.

An unexpected wave of anger surged through my veins. The last thing I wanted was for a bunch of brats to catch me with tears streaming down both cheeks.

With a hooked knuckle, I swiped my face dry. I refused to become vulnerable to the gossip of egotistical young'uns who strut about, flapping their tongues, as with great conviction they declare false accusations that supposedly exist as truths.

To make things worse, those who have found their way into positions of power wave that same egotistical, unwitting sword. Based on that addictive ill-informed high, they slash monumental changes into our society. They never see the damage resulting from their arrogant yet ignorant efforts. I only recognized the damage I created long after it became too late.

Anger's energy pounded within my bloodstream as vodka to the alcoholic. I jerked Oscar's leash. "Come on, let's get out of here. It's past time we go home."

Oscar let out a faint whimper, then scuttled behind me. His head tipped downward in submission.

CHAPTER

29

DAKOTA

"**H**EY, I HEARD YOU GOT a keyboard."

My fingers froze as the piano piece that played in my mind screeched to a halt. Not sure whose face matched that voice, I glanced up from my spot on the courtyard pavement.

Caitlyn hovered over me. Her shadow blocked the warm sunlight. "My cousin has a keyboard. The last time I saw her, I got to try it out. I loved messing with all the cool settings."

"It's pretty fun." My foot slipped out from beneath me as I stood up. Warmth flashed to my cheeks, even though, just seconds before, the chilled air bit at my face.

"I saw you . . . just now . . . moving your fingers as if on a keyboard." Caitlyn motioned toward my hands, which suddenly forgot all ability and hung stiff at my side like alien steel robotic probes. "You do that a lot. I figure you also play."

"Yeah, I do." With lightning speed, my high-tech brain programmed orders into both arms. Now with ease, I folded them across my chest.

"I practice that way myself, that is when I'm not near a piano." Caitlyn drummed her fingers in a distinct pattern on the hard metal basketball post. A high-pitched ding arose from each tap.

Set on recognizing what song matched the tap tapings of her fingertips, my mind scrunched up in deep thought.

Before I figured it out, Caitlyn's movements stopped. "I saw Roberta give you trouble again, just over there." Her pointer finger jutted toward the playground, infested like a swarm of insects by all the other kids.

"Yeah, she does that." Roberta bossed everyone as if she owned them. My highly imaginative mind saw her as a giant queen ant that held the "Evil Witch" title in a fairytale.

"But why? I've never seen you act mean toward her." A piece of Caitlyn's hair blew into her opened mouth. She spat it out again.

Ah-ha, that explained everything. Caitlyn must have drunk the evil potion, mixed up by this wicked Queen Ant Witch. Her brew caused all who drank it to see ant people as human beings. That way, they would never believe in Roberta's evil plot. "That doesn't matter much. She's just angry with me from when I was nice to Jacob a while back."

"Why wouldn't you be nice to Jacob? He is your friend, isn't he?"

Poor disillusioned maiden, I couldn't help but feel sorry for Caitlyn. After all, it wasn't her fault. I mean, she did only arrive at this school two weeks ago. I once heard how Queen Roberta, the Evil Ant Witch, slipped her wicked potion on unsuspecting victims. She hid her toxic brew inside the milk cartons. The same ones our lunch ladies pass out. It's impossible to tell which cartons she laced with poison and which remained safe. Neither taste nor smell could give it away. I had to hand it to Queen Roberta—she's one clever witch. No one would ever suspect.

"He is now, but it hadn't always been that way." There was a time when he, too, fell victim to Queen Roberta's evil plot. But Jacob had become one of the lucky few, rescued the moment he climbed aboard that giant swing and launched into space. Good thing I had offered it to him. The pure atmosphere swept him clean, inside and out, from every trace of her vial concoction. My space ride must have made me immune to Queen Roberta's potion, for not once have I been affected even with all the cartons of milk I've drunk.

Caitlyn scrunched up her nose and gazed at me. An obvious question slapped across her face.

I bit the inside of my lower lip to keep from laughing. "Yeah, that's why Roberta messes with me. She's angry because I was nice to Jacob. He used to be a bully, one of the meanest, but one day—for no particular reason—I gave him my swing. Ever since that time, he changed. I guess Roberta doesn't want to admit that people can change."

"You were nice to me too, remember, that day on the bus? That was my first day here. I was so scared, but your kindness made everything much easier."

"Really? All I did was help you pick up your things. No big deal."

"It was a big deal to me."

I stared hard at Caitlyn. Her last statement stunned me. Maybe it was brave to have helped her. I never thought of it that way. My mind flashed pictures of me dressed head to toe in armor, ready to fight off the evil Queen Ant Witch.

The bell rang. I turned toward the school building to head inside, but among the racket of other kids, as they ran like an angry mob, I swore I heard the bark of a familiar dog. My feet stuck to the asphalt as if caught in melted tar.

"Dakota, aren't you coming?" Caitlyn reached out her hand, about to tug at my coat.

"Did you hear that?"

"Hear what? We're surrounded by noises."

"Oscar." I pointed beyond the schoolyard fence. A small dog pulled on his leash while Mr. Aldous tugged back in the opposite direction.

CHAPTER

30

DAKOTA

*T*RAVEN SWEPT PALE BANGS OUT of his eyes. "You can try all you like—you'll never make this bus move any faster. Might as well slide up against that seat before Charlie sees and writes you up." A smirk spread across Traven's suntanned face.

It didn't matter how much he or anyone else teased me, the sooner I got home, the sooner I could turn my ordinary bike into Super-Bat's fantastic, new, secret, crime-fighting machine. The top edge of the opened package peeked out from the paper bag handed to me by my teacher as we had left our classroom. "If Charlie knew how pressing this was, I bet he'd drive much faster." Clutching the bag tighter, I scooched back an inch, just in case Traven was right.

"Yeah, like that would ever happen." Traven flashed that crazy gaze he liked so well—the one where his eyes rolled up and jiggled.

Only *I* understand how important this Super-Bat bike kit would be.

Finally, the long-drawn-out squeal of hydraulic brakes sounded. Daddy had told me all about them the day he replaced the brakes on our car. I slid off my seat and into the aisle. Worry poured into me, flooding my cheeks like scorching lava. We were to remain seated until the bus came to a complete stop, which had not yet happened. *Get over it, Dakota. Super-Bat would never be afraid of rules.* Wow, I had a lot to overcome if I were to pull off this superhero thing.

Bodies sprang up, surrounding me in the center of the bus. I let out a big breath as my shoulders relaxed.

"One at a time. No need to rush." Charlie pulled back on the lever. The door folded open. Like one humongous glob of toothpaste pressed from a giant tube, everyone getting off at this stop oozed down the center aisle and onto the pavement.

"See you Monday." Still squashed among the mob of kids, I waved back at Traven, then hopped off the bus.

Since my first day of kindergarten, whenever I arrived home from school, my mommy stood at the base of our driveway waving with a smile. But today, I stared at an empty spot. Glancing around, I almost fell over my toes. Mommy was not there. A lump formed in my throat. I gulped and fled to the side door of my house.

"Mommy, I'm home!" The door slammed shut behind me. "Mom?"

"I'm right here, Dakota. Did you have a nice day?"

I set the sack Mrs. Miceli had given me on the bottom step. My backpack slid off my shoulder and onto the floor. "You weren't outside to meet me?"

"Sorry, Koty." Mommy stepped out from behind the bathroom door. "I was ready to go out when I suddenly felt ill." Her face looked a bit pale.

"You can close that gaping mouth of yours, Mr. Worries-A-Lot. I'm okay. Now put your stuff away and move on up those stairs. Your afterschool snack is waiting on the kitchen table."

My stomach rumbled.

"Our orders from the fundraiser came in." I kicked off my shoes and tucked them under the coat rack. "Mrs. Miceli handed me this great-big bag, filled to the brim. Look, even my backpack is jam-packed." I stomped my foot in frustration. It took two tries to hang my coat up on the hook. "And I got my Super-Bat bike set. Even though Mrs. Miceli told us to wait till we got home before going through our stuff, I peeked while on the bus. But I didn't pull it out of the bag. Still, I could tell it's far more awesome than I thought!"

"Bring everything to the table. We'll go through it there." Mommy giggled. A splotch of color returned to her cheeks.

As I rushed to drag everything up the entry staircase, my right sock, which hung halfway off my foot from when I had kicked off my shoes, tripped me up.

"Slow down, Koty. I don't want you to get hurt."

I yanked the sock the rest of the way off and flung it to the floor, then plopped both bags onto the table beside a plate of crackers smothered with peanut butter and raisins. My stomach grumbled again, reminding me of how starved I felt. I shoved an entire cracker in my mouth and began pulling objects from the bags.

"Dakota, slow down before you choke."

With a stuffed mouth, I glanced up at Mommy. She didn't understand the responsibility of owning Super-Bat's exclusive bike kit. No other kid in my classroom earned one.

My fingers grasped the secured cardboard box that held this most-important reward. "Here it is, see?" I held it up high and smiled with a grin so big my cheeks instantly ached. "Isn't this great?"

I yanked at the plastic packaging. My tongue clamped between my teeth as I grunted, yet I could not get those craved items free.

"Just hold on." Mommy dug a pair of scissors out of the junk drawer. "Hand it over."

A bit discouraged, I passed her my prize.

With a few carefully placed snips, she freed the rewards. A water bottle, knapsack, whistle, mirror, and many more excellent items tumbled onto the table. First, I grabbed the water bottle. Then I had to try out the bell. I made it ding when I spied the horn. "Look, Mom, there's both. Can we attach everything to my bike right now?"

A piece of hair swayed in front of Mommy's shoulder as she shook her head. "Wait for your father to come home. He'll want to help you. However, as soon as you finish your snack, we can go deliver to those who are home this time of day."

"Like Mr. Aldous?"

"Like Mr. Aldous."

I plopped down in a chair and crammed another peanut butter-smeared cracker into my mouth. As I reached for a third, Mommy shot me a narrow-eyed glare, so I set it back onto the plate and chewed. "Which item did he buy?"

"Swallow first. Then you can talk."

I choked down my mouthful and, careful not to break anything, shuffled through the heaped pile of what looked like useless junk, unlike the Super-Bat treasures set aside to attach to my bike when Daddy gets home. From all the oohs and aahs our neighbors gave when they had placed their orders, they must enjoy that untouchable, knick-knack type of thing, why I may never understand.

"This is it." Mommy picked up a rectangular box. She folded back the flaps and removed a chocolate-brown vase with pictures of hummingbirds etched onto it. Holding it delicately, she turned the fragile item in her hands. "This sure is lovely."

Brilliant colors painted on each tiny bird gave the appearance that they could fly right off the vase. I drew my finger across emerald-green details, half expecting to touch soft feathers. Instead, hardened ceramic met my hand. I swallowed a lump of disappointment.

"When you finish your snack, let's go deliver this." Mommy placed the item back in its box. Her eyes scanned the order sheet. She glanced at me and flashed a wink.

"Uh-huh," I stuffed three remaining crackers in my mouth and gulped, but instead of going down, peanut butter stuck my tongue to the roof of my mouth.

Mommy's glare burnt into me.

After many tries, I choked back the last bit of that stuck-up glob and guzzled some milk. "I'm ready. Let's go."

"Slow down. You seem extremely excited." Mommy pulled a cloth shopping bag out of the cabinet and slid four of the ordered items inside. "You haven't even asked about Mr. Aldous's response to giving you weekly piano lessons."

"Oh my gosh, I forgot all about that." I felt my eyes dry up as they grew big and round like golf balls.

Mommy laughed and handed me a napkin. Assuming that was my hint that a mess covered my face, I swiped the napkin across my mouth. "So, *did* you ask? What did he say?"

"One question at a time, Koty, before you trip yourself up again. Yes, I asked, and he seemed willing but did not commit yet."

I took one last gulp of milk. "Oh, I almost forgot. During recess, I saw Mr. Aldous. He and Oscar were out for a walk."

Still prattling on about our across-the-street neighbor and his cute dog, I wandered toward the entryway, grabbed my ditched sock, and motioned for Mommy to follow me as I put on my shoes and coat. I handed Mommy her lightweight, purple jacket.

She slipped her arms into the sleeves and shot me that same humored expression, which usually meant I again did a grand job entertaining her.

Mommy bent down, slid her feet into a pair of white canvas shoes, and tied the laces.

"You know, Mr. Aldous's birthday must be any day now. So, what do you think? Can we throw him a party? I bet he'd love a new pair of slippers. The ones he wears are so ratty. Let's go shopping tonight and buy him a pair."

Mommy grasped the packed bag, then held the door open as I stepped outside.

"I bet if Mr. Aldous agrees on piano lessons, he'd want me to call him something far less formal. What do you think? I know. I'll call him Al—Good Ol' Buddy Al—Hey, since Good Ol' Al will be my teacher, how about I deliver his order all by myself? After all, he's not a stranger anymore." I drew in a well-needed breath and gaped at Mommy.

The space between her eyebrows crinkled. Instead of heading down our drive as I had expected, Mommy sat on the concrete step outside our door. "Sweetheart, Mr. Aldous may no longer be a stranger—however, there still is an awful lot that we do not know about him. Far too much for me to feel comfortable letting you go over there on your own."

"But why not?"

Mommy ran her hands over the zipper of my coat as if to smooth out a wrinkle. "Our instincts sometimes tell us things we don't understand. Some people refer to it as a gut reaction. I like to think of it as a God whisper. I've learned to pay attention to and obey that still, small voice. Too often in the past, after an event has occurred, I discovered a valid reason to have followed 'God's whispers.'"

I stopped chewing my bottom lip. "Well then, can I at least carry the vase as we walk to Mr. Aldous's house?"

"Yes, darling, be careful. It's very fragile." Mommy pulled out the box that housed his vase from her cloth bag, then handed it to me.

CHAPTER

31

ALDOUS

I PULLED THE CURTAINS OVER THE picture window and stepped back. "Why are you staring at me? I haven't a clue why they would come over." Oscar gazed up at me and whined. His ear twitched, the same way as when Mariam would scratch him on the head.

The drapes' translucent material made it easy to spot Alexandra and Dakota as they marched across the street. A determined bounce accompanied each step. "Fine, maybe I do have an idea. But I'm not ready to give them an answer. I should have told Alexandra *'No.'*" I refused to make a regular commitment to that bratty kid of hers, or any kid for that matter. A second glance through the thin curtains confirmed my suspicions as their shadowy figures proceeded up my drive.

Even as the declaration left my mouth, somewhere within, a part of me threatened to betray every word, as for some absurd reason, the desire to accept Alexandra's ridiculous offer ripened. Why would I ever consider becoming Dakota's piano teacher? To teach anyone would be a foolish endeavor.

Another glance through the sheers confirmed that the source of heavy footsteps came from Alexandra and her son as they trotted up my porch steps.

Mariam would have gleefully accepted the offer. She began to teach me as early as our first year of marriage. My sight wandered onto the well-polished piano located within the dining room. Some of my fondest memories consisted of my beautiful bride and me, side by side on that bench as we plunked out duets together. It never mattered how many mistakes I made. My sweet Mariam had more patience than a seventeen-year cicada.

Air rattled my chest, making it hard to catch my breath, for those cherished moments had dwindled soon after Lacey's birth. Dear Mariam had ached for a baby. Her heart broke with each miscarriage. I wondered if God did not want us to have a child, but all that doubt dissipated four years into our marriage when Lacey was born.

My sight locked onto the door, awaiting the inevitable knock. About a year after Lacey announced that she wanted nothing to do with us, Mariam had begged me to allow her to teach lessons. She insisted it would ease her lonely heart. I felt my nostrils flare with each intake of air. That first time she had confessed her loneliness, it hit like a sledgehammer to the gut, as if she had been unfaithful.

Mariam had no right to feel lonely—after all, I remained at her side. So, doing my manly duty, I put my foot down and forbade her to bring up such topics as piano lessons and loneliness.

A tap of knuckles rapped on the door. Oscar bounded to his favorite spot on the doormat and yelped with each spin.

I shook my head and grasped the knob. The last thing I wanted was a misbehaved hoodlum to take over my home. To ask me to teach? I hardly knew the instrument well enough to play. Mariam was the expert, not me. What a ridiculous notion for Alexandra to even have considered.

"Back up, boy. I might as well get this over with." My foot pressed against fur-covered ribs as I shoved the spastic beast aside.

I opened the door. The same pesky lad, spied earlier that day on the other side of the schoolyard fence, beamed up at me. I had become far too familiar with this child and his mother for my comfort zone.

"Hi, Mr. Aldous, sir." Dakota held his hands behind his back, his toothless grin as big as the one on the Joker's face. "Boy-o-boy, are you ever going to be happy."

"Now what?"

His mother stood a foot behind him. His exaggerated smirk persisted while he revealed his hands and, in them, a box. "Here's your order. It came today."

My breath lodged in my chest. Maybe the kid didn't know of his mother's phone call? I had forgotten about that vase I ordered.

"I hope you don't mind. Mommy and I opened the box and peeked inside. It's very nice. I think you will like it." Dakota's eager blue eyes, wide as golf balls, sparkled.

I cleared my throat. "No problem." My uttered words came out as no more than a grunt.

I grasped the box from the stubby fingers of this scrawny child who stood before me. It wouldn't matter how much this lad stretched his physique. He would always remain too small to amount to anything.

Turning from Dakota and his mother, I pulled the forgotten item from its box. My sight glued onto brightly colored hummingbirds painted on the side of the ceramic vase. The visitors who occupied my front entryway faded from comprehension. "That's perfect. Mariam will love this."

"Who's Mariam?" Dakota pushed past me and stepped into the house.

"That's not polite to ask. Dakota, come back here. It's none of our business." The young mother scrambled toward her son. Instead of grasping the red fabric of his jacket, her outstretched hand snatched empty air.

"I guess you were right, Mommy. There is a lot we still don't know about Mr. Aldous."

Alexandra's cheeks blazed rosy red.

My teeth clenched as my sight followed Dakota. Anger mounted at the familiarity reflected in his actions. Then, for some unexplainable reason, the hostile emotion dissipated, and a spark of warmth penetrated my ever-so-proudly etched, cynical heart. As if an uncontrollable reflex activated my hand, it patted the light-brown hair that covered this child's head. "Mariam is my wife." A foreign, tender tone camouflaged my words, making them difficult to recognize as my own.

Dakota craned his head and peered toward the kitchen. "I didn't know you had a wife. I thought you lived all by yourself."

"Dakota." Alexandra stepped over the threshold. A look of horror spread across the young mother's still flushed face.

Instead of anger—my usual reaction to a situation like this— laughter roared from my chest. Every ounce of control I had spent a lifetime perfecting melted away. It didn't matter how tight I grasped at this meticulously fostered treasure—my feeble attempt mirrored one who strived to contain water in a sieve. Every last drop slipped through.

"That's quite all right." I turned from Alexandra to Dakota when my crafty mind began to play tricks on me. In place of the intrusive child who shattered my peaceful sanctuary, my shrewd brain perceived this freckled-faced boy as a composite of my younger self. Compassion took over regardless of my strained effort to prevent the impulse.

Dakota planted both hands on his hips, appearing satisfied with what he found. "So, Mr. Aldous, Mom tells me she talked to you about piano lessons."

So, he *had* heard.

A gasp sounded from the woman behind me. I turned and took in the shocked expression on Alexandra's face. Another unexpected snicker squeezed from my diaphragm.

"Dakota, now is not the time to talk about this." A ridged tone cloaked her words, spoken through clenched teeth.

"Oh, but I think this is the perfect time to discuss the matter." Determined to be firm, I gathered every ounce of strength that remained. But for some peculiar reason, it no longer served me. "Dakota, I hear you have been practicing a lot on a new keyboard your father bought you."

The child's teeth glimmered as he beamed.

"I also heard that you practice every opportunity you get. I only provide lessons to those who show great dedication. It appears you match that bill." I pined to glance around the room, half expecting to see my deceased wife, for those words sounded as if they had come out of her mouth. *I* would never have spoken that way. My heart pounded a thunderous tone as I awaited a response from that scrawny, yet—and I regret to admit—intriguing lad.

"Oh, Mr. Aldous, that's great! Does this mean you'll continue to give me lessons? That I have my own real live teacher?"

"Well, I'm certainly not a real dead teacher." *However, due to the comments that have escaped my mouth lately, I have to wonder.* "Yeah, I think I can do that. Do you remember the song we went over in our first lesson?"

"Uh-huh, that's what I have been practicing, at least most of the time."

"Good. How about we get together each Monday after school? That will allow you a few more days to perfect it and anything else you may want to bring along."

Even as the words filtered through my lips, they rang out foreign, as if from a stranger's mouth. I had lost control of my responses. I must have gone crazy! Why would I commit to this pesky lad and his mother? When Alexandra proposed her idea earlier that day, it horrified me. Yet, here I am, committing to teach the boy.

Dakota bounced on his feet as if springs affixed to the soles of his shoes. "That's amazing. Mr. Aldous, now that you are my piano teacher, I decided to call you something far less formal, like Good ol' Buddy Al. What do you think of that?" The kid gazed at me, his missing tooth prominent in the ridiculous smirk that gapped from his mouth.

What had I gotten myself into? My mind jarred as if shaken out of a nightmare. My head pounded. This foreign Aldous, who had invaded my being only moments before, disappeared, allowing a return of my familiar callous self.

The boy spewed excitement from his every cell. Was this how it looked to be five? No matter how hard I searched my memory, it contained nothing that resembled this carefree, excited child before me.

The yellow birthday card my only grandchild had sent flashed within my memory as bright as a sunbeam. *Does Chloe behave in similar manners?* I would never know, at least my Mariam never would.

Many more invented images of my only grandchild elbowed into my already crowded mind. All those alien abilities to act pleasant and polite drained from my bloodstream.

Dakota darted back toward the door and tugged on his mother's sleeve. "Mommy, we have to set a date for Good Ol' Al."

My ears burnt like acid at the sound of this new name.

Alexandra clenched her son's shoulders. "Okay, take it easy, Koty. You're overwhelming Mr. Aldous."

Her gaze shifted to me. "Yesterday, we noticed that you have a birthday coming up. We wish to honor you with a party. Would you be okay with that?"

"Yeah, Good Ol' Al, what day *is* your birthday? We know you're having one because I saw the card. How old will you be?"

Anger's flame scorched another cell within my chest with every word this young lad spoke.

"Dakota, that is enough. You shouldn't ask that type of question." Alexandra's forehead creased as her eyes narrowed.

"Why not? People ask *me* how old I am all the time."

"I'll explain later when we get home. Mr. Aldous, I am so sorry. I don't know what has gotten into him." A splash of fresh blush splattered her cheeks. "We would love to have you over. Would you, please, at least think about it?"

"Sure." The uncomfortable silence that followed pricked my every cell. I wished they would hurry up and leave.

"Well, all right then. Come on, Dakota. We've taken too much of Mr. Aldous's time." She seized her child's hand. "Thank you, Mr. Aldous, for your willingness to teach piano to my son."

"Don't worry, Good Ol' Al. I'll make it worth your time." Dakota flashed a salute with his free hand as he and his mother marched out the door.

The click of the latch as I secured the deadbolt echoed in my head. Or could it be blood pulsating through my veins? I turned and caught sight of the vase placed on the secretary desk. The metallic teal paint glistened. I picked up the decorative item and held it in my hand. "This is for you, Mariam, one more hummingbird for your collection."

Oscar stared up at me. His short tail, coiled like a spring, wiggled. "Come on, boy. We might as well make room for this among all her others."

ALDOUS

*A*LEXANDRA'S INVITE ATE AT MY intestines. Every time the phone rang or I heard a sound that resembled footsteps, a wave of nausea hit. Soon she would expect an answer.

I had no good reason to decline her offer, especially since I had made that ever-so-stupid move of agreeing to give Dakota lessons. I had hoped the first lesson, given to the lad over a week ago, would have been an isolated occurrence. I never dreamed they would request more.

For the hundredth time that day, I peered out the peephole of my front door. No one trekked up my driveway. Each time I obtained that desired validation, I expected a breath of relief, but instead, a peppering of disappointment filled my heart.

This insane behavior continued throughout the entire weekend. Each time it arose, excessive discontent within me blew the air out of my lungs. I brushed it away as if nothing had happened. Yet, despite my resistance, life persisted in drilling into my head the harsh fact that

I would fail, no matter how much effort I expelled in my futile attempt to deny reality.

With each successive glance came an even larger serving of bitter letdown than the previous time had dished out. As distress increased with every blow, my enragement toward this stranger within—who did such stupid things as agree to teach piano lessons—inflated. I took every chance I could to ward off this villain-self, who had invaded my being, yet I flunked every occasion. I no longer knew who I was.

Oscar's bark alerted me to man my watch post. My luck ran out—Dakota and his mother trotted up the drive as disappointment's anvil landed with a thud in the pit of my stomach. Muscles in my forehead tensed, delivering an instant headache. How ludicrous the hopeful part of me had been, which now stung with surprise at their arrival. After all, the clock on my wall indicated three-o-clock on a Monday afternoon, the agreed-upon time of Dakota's lesson. Nevertheless, I awaited their knock before opening the door, hoping they might change their minds and turn around.

A sharp pound of knuckles assaulted my hearing—darn the luck. "Move over, Oscar. Let me get to the door."

I held it open a crack.

Dakota grabbed the door from my fingers, swung it wide, and marched inside. "Howdy, Good Ol' Al. Yeah, that works. 'Good Ol'' is far more fun to say than 'Mister.'"

Ears stinging from the name Dakota had designated for me, I snapped around and tracked the lad's abrupt movements.

Alexandra trailed in after her son. "Young man, you better remember your manners, or we will go back to our home. Do you understand me?"

"Yes, Mommy. Good Ol' Al, I'm sorry. I'm just excited for my lesson." Dakota tucked his chin onto his chest.

"I'll forgive you this once. Now hop on over to that bench." What

I *really* wanted to tell the child and his mom was to return home and leave me alone. And, by all means, stop calling me 'Al'!

"Thank you, Good Ol' Al. I knew you wouldn't mind." A grin the size of the Cheshire Cat's bridged the span between Dakota's ears. With both feet held together like a rabbit, he hopped to the piano bench and sat down. I need to remember to avoid animated phrases.

I scooched onto the bench beside the boy.

Alexandra straightened a cushion on my couch, then sat in full view. Great, that's all I needed, a spectator.

Highly uncomfortable and conspicuous, I shifted while my phrase "I'll forgive you" restated in my ears. Lacey had voiced those exact words shortly before she announced that she would never again enter our home. Why had all my foolproof methods of self-control failed me? I pinched my eyes shut, hoping to squeeze that memory out of my mind. "So, Dakota, what do you remember from our last lesson?"

"Oh, I remember it well. Here, I'll show you." The child bit his bottom lip as his pointer finger darted like an arrow to the center key. "This is middle C, and by adding just two more notes, D and E, I can play 'Mary Had a Little Lamb,' like this." The overzealous lad plunked each note in perfect rhythm.

"You have been practicing. I'm impressed." The man I had always held pride in being would never speak like that. Why were my rambled words sounding as if spoken by Mariam?

I glanced at Alexandra, seated with an alert posture on the edge of the couch. Pride sparkled in her smile.

I hated being under the microscope.

"See, I told you. I'll do the work. These lessons won't be a waste of your time. I promise." Dakota's determined eyes gaped at me.

"It appears you won't." Darn, I'm stuck with this crazy commitment. I pressed against my left ear to silence the argument in my head. One internal voice cheered at this fixed opportunity with Dakota and his mother, while another roared in agony at my loss of solitude.

"Let me show you what else I know." Dakota ran stubby fingers up and down the keys as he played a mishmash of notes.

That same compelling voice, propelling me to provide Dakota lessons, now demanded that I open the *Children's Hymnal*. A sufficient beginner's piano lesson book sat opened and ready on the music rack, but that blatant fact did not matter. I placed my hand on Dakota's wildly moving fingers to silence them. "Are you ready to learn a new song?"

"You bet."

I pulled down the *Children's Hymnal* and stared at protruding blue tabs. I flipped pages and stopped at page eighty-seven. The assortment of notes I gawked at appeared far too complicated for a boy with Dakota's skill level, yet somewhere in my head, that voice, which led me to believe a stranger resided within, now insisted I teach Dakota this song. "How Lord?"

"How what?" A glimmer in the child's sky-blue eyes resembled the morning star.

"Oh nothing, I was just thinking out loud." *Had I just uttered a prayer?* I had given up praying while still a young child. Right after— No loving God would allow such a thing to occur. He had ignored me, and as a result, I ignored Him right back. It had been that way now for over sixty years. Why, after all that time, were my well-cemented ways changing? Certainly not by my own accord.

The solution of how to teach a five-year-old this overtly complicated hymn popped into my head. *Did God answer my prayer?* "Dakota, I need you to stand up for a moment."

The lad scrunched his nose and slid off the bench.

Neglected hinges groaned as I lifted the piano bench lid and sorted through forgotten contents.

"What are you looking for?"

"A special type of paper."

Sifting through a jumble of sheet music, I uncovered the tattered notepad of lined staff paper. I pulled it out and flipped past sheets inked over by Mariam's hand-drawn notes. Near the back of the tablet, I uncovered a blank page.

I had never been good at writing down music, but due to ceaseless taunts within my ears, I gave it a try, anything to shut up that uninvited voice only I could hear. One by one, I blackened in single notes to the melody of "Jesus Loves the Little Children." Why I must put so much effort into this task seemed ridiculous. Plenty of easy-to-play songs existed within the beginner's lesson book. I should stick with that suitable curriculum, yet, as if I had lost my mind, that still small voice relentlessly chanted out the familiar tune printed on this page.

While holding open the *Children's Hymnal*, I shut the lid and propped the now marked-up staff paper over the beginner's lessons book I should use if any brain cells functioned within my head.

Dakota slid beside me and stared at my work-in-progress. His sleeve clamped between his teeth as he sucked the fabric.

"Dakota, have you heard 'Jesus Loves the Little Children'?"

"You bet I have! We sang it just yesterday, during Sunday School."

"Well, I will teach it to you, but first, you need to learn some new notes. This song is by no means what one should teach in only the second lesson. Are you up for the challenge?"

Dakota dropped the sleeve from his mouth, hitched back his shoulders, and stretched his spine. His height rose an extra inch. "I can do it, Good Ol' Al."

There he goes with that Good Ol' crap again. I drew in an exasperated breath. "Well, okay then. Your three new notes are F, G, and A. This song has a far more advanced beat. When played, it should sound like this." I placed my hands on the keys and ran through the notes.

Dakota kicked off his shoes and pulled his legs up beneath him. "That was great. Do it again."

Without hesitation, I started the song over from the beginning.

Dakota's child-like soprano rang out the familiar words. He waved his mother over. In seconds she stood beside us, and her angelic voice joined her son's.

When, for the second time, I approached the end of the song, for some odd reason, I continued again from the starting point.

Dakota and Alexandra resumed singing in unison, this time with slightly different words. I had never before heard more than one verse to this time-honored song.

The songbirds beside me held out the final note extra-long, then fell into joyous laughter. Even I chuckled. I dropped my hands onto my lap and breathed in a pleasant silence. A rhythmic pound thumped against my breastbone with each beat of my heart. I couldn't remember the last time I had participated in such merriment.

"That was great. There's a piano in the youth room at church. Once I learn to play as well as you can, Good Ol' Al, I could play this song for the kids in my Sunday school class. Oh, thanks so much for teaching it to me." The child wrapped his tiny arms around me, pressing his head against my shoulder as he squeezed.

It had been years since I'd received a tender touch, and even then, such sentiment had rarely, if ever, originated from a child. Since that horrible day, I had spent much of my life avoiding touches, especially from children.

I handed Dakota the drawn-up sheet music. "Take this home and practice. I know you will do well."

"Thank you, Good Ol' Al. I won't let you down."

For some odd reason, this time, Dakota's annoying "Good Ol' Al" neglected to singe my nerves.

Alexandra took my hand. "We still haven't received an answer about when you want to celebrate your birthday."

"Thursday would be best for me." Before I could lock my lips, the words fell out, spat from that same stranger who had lately invaded my body.

"Well then, Thursday it is."

CHAPTER

33

ALDOUS

*W*ITH AN INTENSIVE GAPE, OSCAR'S head tipped to the side. He whined while Dakota and Alexandra stepped out the door, then closed it behind them.

A wave of loneliness pierced my heart like a thorn. I had wanted nothing to do with them only an hour before, yet now, a treasonous desire for their company plagued me.

I gazed down at my pug, who continued his pathetic whimpers. "Oh God, what is happening?" My own spoken words startled me. I had not intended to utter another prayer, yet that was exactly what I did.

My stomach rumbled, reminding me I had not eaten. "You hungry, boy?"

Oscar responded with a yelp and scrambled to the kitchen. I plodded behind the determined animal who, once reaching his destination, pressed his flattened nose against the cabinet doors that concealed his food.

"I'll take that as a 'yes.'" I bent over, stroked his silky fur, then scratched behind his ears. The mutt groaned—the dog's version of a purr.

"Okay, boy, move over." Oscar slid his stubby feet to the side, allowing me access to open the cabinet. Any other day I would have just shoved him out of the way, but for some strange reason, a foreign tender nature dominated my actions.

I dumped Oscar's food into his bowl, then opened the refrigerator. Stashed on the top shelf inside a plastic grocery bag, I found a steak, fully encased in its original packaging.

Ever since that evening when Alexandra had invited me over for a steak dinner, I had grown obsessed with trying to duplicate her delectable results. Each of my various efforts had failed. This lone raw slab of beef remained, begging for one last attempt.

I glanced at Oscar, who scarfed his food down in huge gobbles. How could he taste a single morsel? That crazy mutt had profited from the frequent bones that resulted from my many botched cooking experiments. While inhaling every mouthful, how could Oscar decipher ordinary kibble from an extra special treat?

"I better cook up this last steak before it gets old. You want another juicy bone for your collection, boy?"

Oscar knew the word "bone." He abandoned his half-empty dish and scampered to my side. His spring-like tale bounced on the end of his rump.

"Okay, okay. I get the point. You have to let me cook it first."

I set a pan on the stove and turned up the burner. No reason to have another go at sautéed onions and mushrooms. All my other attempts concluded with a charcoaled mess.

As I ripped open the slab and plopped it in the pan, my mind wandered from the task at hand and instead reviewed the piano lesson with Dakota. Oh, how I hated the way that child persisted in calling me "Good Ol' Al." I refuse to be that boy's Good Ol' buddy. No one had the right to address me by any name of affection—no one except Lacey and Chloe.

How had my heart softened to such a degree? My exhausted mind struggled to conjure up a mental picture of my grandchild. Having never seen her, the best I could do was to imagine a cross between Lacey and that idiot she called her husband.

Disgusted with the direction my mind had gone, I pressed away all thoughts of my grandchild. Yet instead of leaving, they mingled with recent memories of Dakota and his mother.

For a person who prided himself on certainty and absolute control, many questions invaded my mind. Questions like, why did I find myself wrapped in a blanket of comfort after Dakota and his mother sang every verse to "Jesus Loves the Little Children"? And, from where did that feeling come? That foreign creature that had raided my soul enjoyed their serenade. At that time, I wasn't even bothered when Dakota called me "Good Ol' Al." *What was happening to me?*

Not paying enough attention to my cooking, I dumped a glob of seasonings on the sizzling meat. Absentmindedly I had removed the cap instead of snapping open the shaker holes. "You idiot." The words grumbled deep in my throat like the growl of a beast. Am I to go through this confusing torment every week? Oh, why did I agree to teach that brat?

As if answering my question, Alexandra's sweet voice sang in my ears. *"Hurt people hurt people."* I had hated that phrase the first time I heard it, and this replay fared no better. "Hurt people hurt people. What the heck did that mean anyway?"

Oscar darted from the room. I couldn't tell if he had left due to the angry tone in my voice or because I had not yet relinquished his bone from the frying pan.

"So, if you're out there, God, answer me." Since two prayers so far that day had unwillingly slipped from my lips, I might as well take back control and shoot off a third. But of course, I never expected an answer.

"Hurt people end up hurting other people. They are those who hold onto deep wounds while they live out their lives." That definition described me. A gasp for air caught in my chest as I realized how my myriad of unhealed wounds have caused me to hurt many people. This idea slipped in with no warning. Yep, I had lost all control.

"What do you mean? In no way could that phrase refer to me!"

Every sorted detail of every incident that resulted over multiple decades flashed through my tormented mind as if I were watching an old-time movie reel. A lifetime of excuses I had so carefully constructed crumbled before me.

I had enjoyed nectar's sweet taste of control as it played out in so many ways over the years. The last tactic was the new vase I had purchased to add among the abundant hummingbirds Mariam had loved. Whether figurines of hummingbirds or those very much alive, it didn't matter—they all vied for a spot at one of her feeders. Little had Mariam realized how her innocent feeders, the same ones that nourished her unsuspecting feathered friends, robbed her of personal power while injecting me with even greater authority.

How could something as sweet as nectar cause such commotion? And how often had I exploited that control over Mariam and Lacey? I would have done anything to sustain that extreme dominance like a drunken fool, pining after his next taste of alcohol.

The truth was I *did* whatever it took. Mariam was naive to the point of being deaf and blind. She saw every person and thing as good and blotted out any trait clashing with her fantasy. Mariam's fantastic characteristic fueled her ability to enable my self-serving actions. It was no wonder that since Chloe was born, Lacey had wanted nothing to do with neither her mother nor me. How could Mariam have been an accomplice to something as horrible as . . .?

My anger toward this beautiful, tender woman—my direct gift from God—soared. Blinded by rage, I stabbed the seared steak with a fork and flung it across the room. It smacked against a cabinet door, slid down its smooth painted surface, then landed on the countertop below, leaving a greasy trail behind.

I stared at the mess. So much for dinner.

The fury vibrating within my cells melted like a pool of liquefied plastic. Mariam's behavior resulted as a method to survive living with me. Yes, my sweet Mariam had played the part of the innocent accomplice, but I starred in this production as the villain she protected. The real monster was *me*. With my back pressed against the butcher's block, I slid onto the floor. The trail left behind, this time, consisted of a far messier content than mere grease.

CHAPTER 34

DAKOTA

"*J*ESUS LOVES THE LITTLE CHILDREN, all the children . . ." Without thinking, I whispered the words to the song Good Ol' Al had assigned to me while my right hand tapped out imaginary notes. At the same time, I balanced upright on my knees and stacked a blue rectangle block on top of the tower that Traven and I were building.

"Yeah." My fist punched the air. With this piece, only five more to succeed. "All the children of the world."

"What'd you say? You're mumbling again. You've been doing that all day," Traven said with a curled upper lip as he held out another block to me.

I stared at the yellow, triangular shape. Rats. Another hard one to set in place. I felt my nostrils flare as I sucked in a big breath.

So far, every structure we had put together during this indoor recess had toppled before we could complete it. Most had collapsed while trying to position one of these stupid triangles. Even so, Traven and I grew more determined with each attempt to include every block stashed within this storage bin.

While still on my knees, I snatched that stupid piece of wood from Traven's grip and stretched to put it on the tower but could not reach the top. So, I stood up, pinched my lips together, and held my breath, then I propped the triangle in place and slowly removed my hand.

The tower swayed a tiny bit and then stabilized.

"Oh, Dakota's just rehearsing his fingering. He does that all the time." Caitlyn, who acted as foreman, flipped up her empty hands. A hint that a bit of confidence had soaked into her former shy self.

Grateful for understanding, I took Caitlyn's comment as an okay to continue with my song. "Red and yellow, black and white . . ." I flashed her a grin, then balanced a green square near the tip of that annoying triangular block. As I withdrew my hand, my finger brushed the tower. "Rats!"

It shimmied and tipped to the left. I held out my hands to steady it. It toppled, scattering wooden blocks in every direction.

Traven sprang to his feet. "Fingering, what do you mean by fingering? Maybe if you paid more attention to what you were doing, our tower wouldn't have fallen."

To keep from snapping back, I bit the inside of my cheek. He had a point, though I refused to admit it. That same melody had run through my head all day, nonstop. It drowned out nearly everything, including the ting of raindrops pattering against the window throughout most of the morning hours. This entire afternoon recess, my thoughts focused on perfecting this new piece Good Ol' Al had given me.

"You know . . . to practice his piano lesson." Caitlyn acted oblivious to Traven's frustration. She dropped to her knees and scooped up a pile of blocks scattered among reflected pieces of a rainbow.

"All you do anymore is practice that stupid piano of yours, even when it's not around. You're no fun at all." Traven's mud-brown brows pinched together, forming an outline of his far more pale-colored bangs.

I held my breath.

Traven glared at me, then stormed off toward the book corner.

"It's okay. Traven will get over it. He always does." Caitlyn shrugged her shoulders.

I felt my jaw drop as I stared at her. I couldn't tell if I was more shocked by Traven's reaction or Caitlyn's sudden show of self-assurance.

She grinned back with her chin held high. Her blue eyes sparkled as they met mine.

When had she stopped playing the part of the shy newcomer?

I twisted to view the clock. In a few minutes, the bell would sound to end recess. Shortly after that, we would load the buses and head home.

With a swagger to his step, Jacob Downing moseyed past. "Hey, you missed one." He flung the wayward block our way.

Caitlyn snatched at the airborne missile but missed. It landed near her feet. "Thanks." She picked it up and tossed it into the tub.

Roberta slunk low in her seat at the table as she scribbled on a coloring sheet. Her dark pupils darted from her project and followed Jacob's carefree movements before returning to the page in front of her. She then glanced up at me and scowled.

Mrs. Miceli stepped away from her desk, where she had kept busy grading papers. The bell rang. "Okay, kids, recess is over. Time to pick up. Then gather your things and line up at the door."

I peeked at Traven, hoping he would return to help Caitlyn and me clean up our mess. Without a peer in my direction, Traven snapped the book closed and stashed it in the caddie. Then he stomped his feet with every step as he returned to his desk.

Caitlyn and I gathered all the blocks and placed them in their tub. I secured the lid. Together we shoved the heavy container into its labeled space beneath the toy shelf. I wiped my sweaty hands on my pants, and we hurried to our seats. The rest of our class hustled about as they continued to pick up.

I turned toward Traven and revealed my biggest and best grin. I hoped he'd remember me as his buddy and would respond in the same way.

So much for hopes. Traven braced his elbows on the desk while his chin rested in the cup of his hands as he tipped his head away from me as if I didn't exist, squashing my wishes.

All I could see was the almost white hair that covered the back of Traven's head. How could he treat me like that? Since the beginning of this school year, that guy has been my best friend. Why now would he give me the cold shoulder?

Jacob sat at Traven's other side. He stretched his large body over the top of his desk. "I saw that tower you built . . . before it fell over, that is. You did a great job."

"Thanks." I didn't know how to respond. Why would Jacob act so kindly? Could he and Traven have somehow switched bodies? Nah, that would be nuts.

My "used-to-be friend" carried on in exaggerated form as he craned his neck in the opposite direction from where I sat. I've never known Traven to act so rudely. Maybe Jacob *would* make a better best friend.

Now might be the time to blame Traven's behavior on the evil schemes of that horrible Ant Queen that had taken over Roberta. But I had no desire to let Traven off easily with an excuse. Friends should remain friends, regardless of wicked ants and their evil schemes or anything else.

"Okay, kids, come line up." Mrs. Miceli moved to the front of the classroom and pushed open the door. The room filled with thunderous feet as everyone jumped from their desks and piled in line, each vying to be first.

I slid my chair back and flashed one last glance at Traven.

He jutted his nose in the opposite direction, away from me and the door.

Roberta shoved back her chair. Instead of placing it on the desk, she left it and butted her way to the front of the line.

Traven continued to gawk in the opposite direction from which he was heading. He took two steps, then banged into Roberta's chair.

I swallowed back a laugh. "All are precious in His sight." I guess that even means ex-best friends. Maybe I *should* continue paying more attention to my fingering. The piano treats me far kinder than Traven ever had.

I grabbed my backpack, then pushed along with everyone else for a place in line.

The kids finally settled down.

Our teacher raised her eyebrows and moved aside.

I had seen that expression on Mrs. Miceli's face many times before. It meant she was not pleased with the way our class behaved. She tomorrow would probably make us sit at our desks an extra five minutes into recess.

The herd of kids shot through the doorway, down the hall, and out to where the busses awaited.

I felt like a football in mid-play as I got shoved along. Relieved to break away from the crowd, I climbed the steps of my bus and found an empty seat, hoping Traven would claim a different spot instead of beside me as usual. I slid to the window and stared outside. Two can play at that game.

"You know, Traven, just because Dakota and I like the piano doesn't mean he's no longer your friend. He can be my friend and yours, both at the same time."

Could Traven be jealous? With a jolt, I turned toward Caitlyn's voice. She slid beside me onto the dingy-green vinyl. Her eyes pointed toward the rear of the bus.

A spring twanged as Traven plopped on the seat behind us. He slammed his lunchbox down beside him. "I don't know about that. I never heard of a piano-playing baseball player." His upper lip pouted like a kookaburra's beak—I saw one once at the zoo. It looked cool—unlike Traven's behavior.

If this were any other day, I would have argued Caitlyn's point with hopes of putting Traven at ease, but not today. At that moment, I didn't care much how Traven felt. So I clamped my mouth shut, turned to the left, and stared out the window.

As Charlie pulled the bus onto the street, the wheels' hum blended with the whispered melody within my mind. Good Ol' Al's party was only two days away. For a present, I wanted to play in perfect form on my keyboard the song he had assigned me.

Traven and Caitlyn's bickering voices faded into the background. The ride seemed to take extra long, but finally, brakes screeched as we pulled to a stop just past the entrance of my drive. "Excuse me, Caitlyn."

She pressed her knees against the edge of the seat.

I squeezed past. "See you both tomorrow." I nodded first at Caitlyn and then Traven before darting off the bus. Halfway down the sidewalk, I glanced back.

Traven hopped off the bottom step and gawked after me.

Forgetting all about our spat, I flung him a quick wave, then sprinted toward Mommy at the base of our driveway, where she waited in the driver's seat of our car. "I'm home, Mommy. Let's go."

"Well, you seem excited. Your snack's in the back seat." She motioned behind her.

I opened the door, tossed my backpack onto the floor, then hopped inside.

The bus pulled away from the curb and rumbled down the street.

"Are you sure you're ready? Is there anything you need at the house before we leave?

"I'm sure." I opened the snack sack Mommy had prepared. "Oh yummy, muffins! You must have baked today."

CHAPTER

35

DAKOTA

$\mathcal{I}$ KNEW WHAT I WANTED TO get Good Ol' Al and exactly where to find it. I pushed through the heavy glass doors, my feet ready to race to the far end of the store when a tug on my snapped-up coat collar stopped me.

"Slow down, Dakota. There's no need to rush." Mommy loosened her grasp and spun me around. She then undid the zipper to my coat. Her eyes bore into mine as her lips pressed together in a straight line. I knew that glare well. It shouted that she meant business, and I had better listen or later would regret it.

My feet wanted to dart ahead, yet I forced them to stay glued to the floor. Mommy undid her own coat and flung it over her arm. "Okay, Koty, lead the way."

I bit my bottom lip, a reminder to slow my pace and place one foot in front of the other. We cut down aisles and wove through what appeared to be hundreds of clothing racks toward the shoe department.

Like an over-excited puppy held back by a taut leash, I plowed ahead of Mommy. Her hand no longer grasped hold of me.

She paused before the perfume counter and picked up a sample bottle. Mommy pressed the pump, releasing mist-like water droplets that spritzed the air. Her nostrils flared as she sniffed twice. "That's nice. How about some cologne? I bet Mr. Aldous would like this."

"No, he won't. He needs a new pair of slippers." My coat, hanging loosely over my shoulders, gave off far too much heat. "You saw how he always wears that old ratty pair. I'm certain Good Ol' Al would love some brand-spanking-new ones. A good reminder of how nice his old slippers used to be."

"Okay, if you're sure." Mommy set the cologne back on the display counter, readjusted her purse strap, and followed as I continued to lead the way.

Finally, we located the shoe section. With Mommy still behind, we snaked through heaps of display racks, each filled with ladies' high heels. All that footwear, yet nothing resembled a man's slipper.

I stretched my neck as far as it would go to see over the top of those shoe mounds, but it was no use. "Where are they, Mommy? I can't find a single slipper around here anywhere." A thing I hated most about being short was that while shopping in big stores like this one, it became impossible to peer over racks and shelves to spy on anything.

"Don't worry, we'll find them. It has to be around here someplace."

"There it is, Mommy. Over in that direction." I grabbed her hand and tugged. "There it is! That's just what I want for Good Ol' Al." I jutted my pointer finger toward a pair of brown suede slippers lined with what seemed like genuine lamb's wool.

"They look like the ones he has now, only brand-new." Mommy wore her hair pulled to the side in a loose clip. Dark blond strands bounced off her shoulder as she turned and drifted down the aisle.

"How about this pair?" Mommy lifted a green and blue plaid slipper off the shelf. It had no back to it, making it easy to slide in a foot.

"But, Mommy, that's the point. As much as Good Ol' Al loves his ragged, old slippers, he's certain to be glad of a brand-new pair that's almost the same."

"I don't know . . . It seems to me Mr. Aldous might enjoy something different." This time Mommy turned a black corduroy slipper over in her hand.

"Uh-uh." I darted to the shelf. Stretching onto the tips of my toes, I snatched the opened box that contained what I had searched after. "Oh yeah, these are it." I set the box on the floor, well, dropped it. I needed to slow down my movements again, or Mommy would shoot me another one of her glares. Before she could respond to my over speedy action, I handed her a spanking-new slipper. "Here . . . feel it. It's sooo soft."

Mommy ran her hand over the golden suede, then touched the lining. "Well, all right, if you're that sure about it."

"Yep, I'm sure." I threw back my shoulders and straightened my spine.

Mommy picked up the box, which still contained the left slipper, and held it out to me. Carefully so as not to mar the smooth, spotless suede, I returned the other to its partner. I placed the lid onto the box and then carried it to the nearest checkout counter with such care one might think I held a priceless treasure.

A grandma-type lady stood behind the cash register. As I handed her the box, an ache settled in the plump of my cheeks—the type I get whenever I smile too big for too long.

"Hello there, young man. What do we have here?" A chain speckled with miniature ladybugs hung around her neck. The narrow pair of pointed glasses, attached with rubber pieces to the ends of the links, swayed back and forth like a metronome keeping beat to some unheard song.

I began humming the same tune that had haunted me since my last piano lesson.

"All the Children of the World." The checkout lady's voice rang in a crisp, deep tone. She piped out the words as I hummed the melody. Each note left her wrinkled lips with a vibration that matched the plucked string of a guitar.

This lady lifted the lid off the box and ran a scanner over the zebra label. Mommy once said that those black and white strips were some code only computers understood. Its purpose was to tell people how much an item costs.

I hummed the final note. On the next beat, by pointing my finger in the air, I counted six brightly colored ladybugs—a perfect match to the cherry red lipstick she wore.

"Goodness, I haven't heard that song in a long time."

"I'm learning it for my next piano lesson." I motioned toward the box. "We're buying these slippers for my piano teacher. I call him Good Ol' Al because he's my buddy. He's having a birthday, and we're throwing him a party." The same ache settled back into my cheeks.

"What a lucky person he is for someone as nice as you to enter his life. Not everyone has the blessing of people to regard them the way you honor your friend, Al."

"It is easy now, but it hadn't always been that way. When we first met Good Ol' Al, he was mean and cranky. I didn't like him much at all. Mommy made me act nice to him. It was hard at first."

"Dakota, that's enough." Mommy rested her warm hand on my shoulder.

"What's enough?" Confused, I turned around. Mommy's face shined such a deep shade of red it made me wonder if, somehow, she had gotten a hold of this checkout lady's lipstick.

"No reason to bother . . ." Mommy's eyes popped upward, angled past my head, and aimed at the nametag pinned to the checkout lady's dress. "Judy. No reason to bother Judy any longer. I'm positive she has better things to do with her time."

"Oh, no worry. Your son's a delight." Judy placed our purchase into a large shopping bag, then handed it over the counter to me. "I imagine *you* will want to carry this."

"Absolutely!" I grasped it with both hands, feeling like I sprouted another four inches in height.

CHAPTER

36

RANDY

*J*TIGHTENED MY GRIP ON THE screwdriver and forced one final twist. After dropping the tool on the concrete drive, my callused fingers clutched the blunt edge of the Super-Bat license plate, attempting to wiggle it like a loose tooth. Good, just the way I wanted. The bolts held tight, leaving no room for play. "There you go, Dakota. That's the final item." I flashed my son a wink, confident I had secured all his bike accessories.

My assistant remained at my side. Eager anticipation poured from his every cell. Dirt smudged his speckled nose, which twitched as patience drained from his little body. Dakota's pale blue eyes—shaped like his mother's—bulged as he strained to hold back a bucket load of pent-up excitement.

I chuckled, no longer able to contain my amusement. "Well, hop on and give it a try." I released my grip on Dakota's mountain bike.

"All right!" With a grin as wide as a canyon, he grabbed the handlebars and hopped onto the seat.

Dakota's feet barely touched the ground as they straddled the framework, keeping perfect balance while he inspected every newly attached item. Both freckled cheeks puffed out like twin balloons blown to maximum capacity. "Wow, Dad, my bike looks even better than I had imagined!" His small hand caressed the chrome bell—first blemish to its polished shine. With a flick of his thumb, Dakota rang the bell and then, in one swift motion, squeezed the bulb to the horn, releasing a sound similar to that of a sick cow.

"Go on, little buddy . . . take it for a spin before your mother calls you inside to help make a cake for Aldous."

"All right, make sure to keep an eye on me. You're about to witness a ride that will go down in history. The first trip on Super-Bat's one and only Bat-bike—far better at fighting crime than the Bat-car ever could be."

Dakota flung each foot on a pedal and took off in one swift motion as if he and his bike merged into a single entity. He spun around and glided to the end of the drive, where pavement met asphalt. With multiple successive rings to his bell, my son swerved around and soared back up toward me. At only five years of age, that child rode with expertise many modern-day, computer-savvy teenagers never achieve.

The bike's new horn blared, followed by the squeaking hinges to the back door. Alexandra glided across the porch and paused at the top step. "Dakota, it's time to come in and bake the cake."

"I'll be right there." Dakota stood on the pedals and pumped, driving his petite forty-two pounds into a force used to create superhero speed as he flew up the length of our driveway, then swerved into the opened garage. He hopped off his bike and, in one swift boot, tapped the kickstand in place, leaving his prized crime-fighting machine sandwiched between the concrete wall and my parked Dodge Avenger.

"Thanks, Dad, everything works great." My son threw a wave in my direction. Unmindful of the evening's crisp air, Dakota unzipped his coat and flung it over his shoulders, mimicking a cape, then darted up the steps toward his awaiting mother. Alexandra wrapped her arm over our child's shoulder, and together, they strolled through the back door and into our house.

My heart swelled. Nothing illustrated God's magnificent love better than the moments I pause to watch my beautiful wife and our precious child. I've often wondered what I did to deserve such rich blessings. And every time, God reminded me that this was merely a demonstration of our Lord's magnificence—His love poured out to us, His undeserving children.

The porch screen swung shut with a clatter, followed by the muffled sound of wood against wood as the inside door closed behind it.

I picked up the screwdriver and placed it inside my toolbox, then carried the vessel to the far end of the garage, setting it on my workbench. For the next hour or more, Alexandra and Dakota would be busy with Aldous's cake for tomorrow's party.

Earlier that day, Alexandra had called me at work. Her excitement sprang through the phone as she confided an unshakable feeling that somehow, her deceased grandfather smiled at her from Heaven because of our efforts to pay tribute to Aldous with this party.

As I brushed debris from my hands, I moved to the front of our garage and tugged the suspension rope. The retractable door clambered down in front of me, barely missing my toes.

I turned and marched toward the house when I remembered Alexandra had asked me to retrieve the mail. Grateful to have not forgotten, my feet, tired after a long day of repairing computerized networks, carried me down the drive and across the street.

Mr. Aldous stood in front of the cluster of mailboxes with his dog at his side. His shoulders hunched, forming an exaggerated swayback I had not before noticed.

Dakota had, only last month, confided his suspicion with regards to our across-the-street neighbor. The boy's overactive imagination conjured up the crazy notion that this neighbor I approached was Super-Bat's greatest enemy and the pug as his evil sidekick, both in supreme disguise.

I drew closer and stared at Aldous's hooked nose, stifling a laugh. Somehow, in my son's eyes, this man had gone from a mortal enemy to a well-beloved grandparent substitute. How he achieved such an extraordinary leap? I would never know—one more reason to marvel at God's mysterious ways.

Tugging on the end of his leash, Oscar pranced to my feet and sniffed my pant leg. I stooped and patted the pint-sized pup on his head. Then straightening back up, I faced his owner. "How's it going, Aldous?"

The elderly gentleman glanced at me. His thin lips pinched shut. Saggy skin surrounding his eyes bagged far more than I had remembered. I witnessed no change during the short time I knew this man, nothing to explain my son's drastic transformation in attitude.

Aldous lifted his angular chin shrouded with gray scruff. A bundle of newfound creases joined the existing collection that crisscrossed his forehead. All evidence confirmed my skepticism—He remained just as cranky as always.

"My wife and son are in the kitchen this minute, preparing for tomorrow's party."

Furrows around his elderly mouth deepened as his line of eyesight roved down my pant leg and landed near my shoes. Why does my family insist on exerting such effort for this grouchy old man, who would probably never extend a drop of appreciation? I may never understand.

I pulled keys from my pocket and opened our designated mail slot, box number 1217. My effort to instigate friendly conversation had been a waste of breath. I removed a handful of invoices and unwanted ads, then re-secured the small metal door with a twist of its key. Hopefully, Aldous doesn't plan to stand us up. If he does, I'm not sure who'd be more brokenhearted, Alexandra or Dakota. I stuffed the keyring back into my pocket. "Well, I'll see you tomorrow evening. Dinner will be on the table by six. My family is working hard to make the event special for you." With any luck, Aldous got my hint and would follow through.

My shoe squeaked as I pivoted on its heel. I took one step in the direction of my home.

"Wait . . . can we talk?"

CHAPTER 37

RANDY

*T*HE SHORT DISTANCE FROM THE mailboxes where Aldous and I had stood to his front door extended with every step. Muffled thumps from the soles of my shoes as they hit the pavement sliced through stifling silence as we inched forward. Tension hung like a living entity, heavy in the air. Wondering what Aldous had in store, I clamped the knuckle of my forefinger between my teeth as I followed him up the porch steps to his home.

Aldous gripped the edge of his door. I crossed the threshold, and he slammed it shut behind me as I leaped out of the way.

During the short timeframe I had known this sullen neighbor, he had impressed me little. Despite my wife and child's persistent efforts, this "cranky old man," as Dakota had once called him, continued to show little interest in anyone.

With my nose so frequently buried deep in a computer screen at work, I often wondered what it would take to convert into the life of a hermit. At times, I desired that secluded existence until I remembered how much I adored my wife and son and the joy life would lack without their ever-persistent interruptions.

Why this self-satisfied hermit wished to confide in me, I did not get. And why my family insisted on reaching out to this same hard-nosed man remained an even greater mystery.

Aldous stooped and unlatched the tether from Oscar's collar. A roadmap of veins protruded from the sallow skin of his wrinkled hands as he looped the leash onto an empty peg beside the door.

The small dog darted off to the kitchen, then scampered the length of a butcher-block island and out of sight. Food remnants scattered the top of the well-worn wooden surface.

Aldous lowered his hand, then paused. His eyes bored into an oval mirror beside the row of pegs that acted as a coat rack. Something within that reflection froze him in place.

I choked down a knot lodged in my throat. Was I about to catch a glimmer of the inward soul who captured this man's attention? I glanced behind me and noticed the door's deadbolt turned to its locked position.

As Aldous broke away from the spell of his reflection, his stature sagged. He moved across the room, then wilted into a worn-out recliner. With shoulders hunched, he buried his drawn face into those same hands, marked by years of travel.

"Dear God, only You know why I am here. Please, guide me." The spontaneous prayer whispered on a breath of air drawn deep into my lungs.

Aldous remained still as if his body had hardened into the position he held. I settled into the seat across from him, a wooden rocker in front of the picture window.

The silence drove knives deep within my toes as I waited for something, anything, to happen. Concerned Alexandra would wonder what happened to me, I pulled out my cell phone and glanced at the time.

Aldous raised his head. His face streaked with tears, like parallel runways. "*You* are God's answer to my prayer."

Did I hear him correctly? He had muttered the words so quietly that I wondered if I imagined them. I tipped my head to better angle an ear in his direction.

"I couldn't bear the torment any longer. I begged God for relief. Something had to break and set me free." Aldous's voice filled with sorrow. He peered up. His eyes glazed over. "Something must change. It has to!" The desperate man's words pounded out as an angry growl. "I can't! I'm old and as solid in my ways as those stones that edge the flowerbed outside that window. Yet, I *need* release. I can't remain silent any longer!" His fisted hand thumped his chest as emotion boiled to the surface.

My gut shouted a warning to leave. But this wretched man's dull eyes, framed by unruly brows, stared into mine with such intensity they pinned me to the chair.

"I have done some horrendous things within my lifetime. And throughout those many years, I justified everything." The pause of his voice suspended in the air like a cannonball dangling over my head. "I protected my family. And I did it by taking complete control. You must understand that for you, too, have a wife and child. You must know the drive to do whatever it takes to protect them. We men are bred like that." Aldous punctuated each word. His last sentence hovered, thickening the tension that filled the air.

As if the man before me groped for approval, an awkward urge to answer his unspoken question twisted at me.

"Yet, everyone knows that to protect, one must first gain complete control. Long before I became a husband, I discovered I had little power over the outside world. That left me with no choice other than to dominate within the walls of this home." The hardened man leaned in toward me. "I could no better control what happened to my family outside those doors than can you."

Acid from the sting of what sounded like a threat singed my gut. My imagination ran off in multiple directions. What part of this outside world did this man need to control? He had used that word with such force as if he owned it. What was I missing? What horrible element existed that I must control for Alexandra and Dakota's safety?

Aldous relaxed back into his chair. His gray eyes glazed over as he stared off into the distance. "Mariam was so beautiful . . . a kid of only nineteen the year we got married. But not me—I was much older, wise, and sophisticated at thirty-one." The corner of his upper lip curled in arrogant pride and then relaxed. "I never understood what a pretty, young thing like Mariam saw in me, except . . . she had often mentioned how she felt safe with an older man." Aldous drifted back into the silence of his inner thoughts.

I leaned in, waiting for him to continue, but Aldous sat motionless in his recliner with his lips clamped shut. About to question whether or not he was okay, I gasped for a breath.

As if breaking free from a frozen capsule, Aldous's sedated form took on new life. "Her desire for safety fed my overabundant need to protect. I took both mindsets to the extreme and did whatever deemed necessary to keep her secure. My hunger to safeguard her grew as I felt the need to shield Mariam from everything, even herself. I monitored my wife's every word and movement. Then came the day Mariam lost our first child. That uncovered an area my efforts could not influence." Aldous's voice faded.

"Oh-oh no . . ." The tone of Aldous's voice intensified with each shake of his head. "That did not discourage me. In fact, my protective instincts grew even more when she fell into severe depression. She needed to get pregnant again, as soon as possible, to take her mind off the miscarriage." Lean muscle bulged from Aldous's jowl as it clamped tightly. "My idea backfired! She lost a second child and then a third."

Sandra and I had been trying for another baby over the past three years. An ache shadowed my wife's heart each time our efforts proved unsuccessful, and a tear ripped deeper into me with each failure. I dreaded to imagine the intense pain Aldous and his departed wife had experienced.

"We began to believe we would never have a baby. Mariam withdrew from me, demanding she was to blame, and I recoiled back at her in a chain reaction." Aldous's soot-colored irises darkened like two lumps of coal peeking through narrowed slits. "She *had* to have done something very wrong, or God would not have punished her with such ferocity! The louder I voiced this belief, the more she pulled away in shame, proof of my suspicion."

Shock stung my cells as if hit by a taser. How could the man profess love for his wife and at the same time place such spiteful blame upon her head?

The soles of Aldous's worn-out slippers pressed against the floor with each groan of his rocker. "Oddly enough, the more Mariam withdrew, the louder my past shouted back at me. The two timeframes blended so much that they became impossible to differentiate." He nodded toward the front entry. "I'd look in that mirror over there—my reflection blotted from sight with a stamp of disgrace. Oh, God punished alright—He punished *me*, not Mariam."

Maybe more integrity existed within this man than I had given him credit for.

Sagging skin around Aldous's mouth hardened. His lips parted, revealing clenched teeth. "I fought and fought to banish those memories that crowded my mind. God has a strange sense of humor . . . Funny thing, while I waged my war, Mariam became pregnant for the fourth time." A callous chuckle broke through that stone-cold mouth. "Four years to our wedding day, Mariam gave birth to our only child, Lacey.

"That moment should have been a time of rejoicing. However, instead of joy, my urge to protect and shelter my wife and now daughter had multiplied. Lacey grew like any other child. With that came rebellion. No child of mine would rebel!"

An anxious spasm jerked my breastbone.

"Flashbacks from my youth returned, further distorting our present reality. All my success gained at repressing the two of them proved short-lived. My father had kept me in compliance with the back of his hand and a switch. His method didn't work any better, for I also was no easy child to contain. Sometimes I wondered who I strived to control, Lacey and Mariam, or myself . . . maybe my father. He had no choice but to keep the stakes high . . . after the day he first entered my room at night with everyone sound asleep in their beds."

Demand for air forced me to breathe. My hardened heart toward this man began to melt.

"I was only twelve years old! I learned to remain completely silent during those sessions. Somehow that made everything easier to bear. . . . My father's secret demands continued until age fifteen. As a strong, fully-grown man, he no longer could handle me in such a vile manner. I thought my maturity had freed me, but it hadn't. The shame within multiplied and, in time, took on a personality all its own." Aldous's chest expanded as he sucked in a large breath. "My baby sister was only eight . . . I could no longer stand it. The angry monster within swelled with such fury that I lost all sense of myself. Before I could stop it, this evil beast sought out little Helena."

Aldous paused. Repulsed by what he had divulged, my heart skipped a beat.

"The entire time, I diverted my eyes from hers. . . . Once it was over and I could look at my baby sister again, the brokenness caused by my betrayal reflected off every tear that flooded her eyes."

I sat exhausted, invaded by a range of emotions as Aldous's story unfolded. My heart switched from melted sorrow over what he had endured to a fiery rage. How could any man do such a thing? Fifteen or not, the age did not matter. This very person seated before me had violated an innocent child! Aldous had prefaced this conversation with *"control"*? Well, it took complete control of every one of my muscles to constrain myself from flying off this chair and beating this creature before me into an unrecognizable pulp! My wife and our son have had multiple encounters with this fiend. If he ever placed a finger on either one of them . . .!

"I couldn't stand it." Aldous's eyes pierced mine like the fangs of a poisonous snake. "I couldn't stand *myself*." The words spat out like deadly venom from between his clutched teeth. "That day, I ran away from home. No longer could I allow my father's toxin to invade me. Knowing that his defilements had turned me into a vicious monster, no better than him, sickened me."

The putrid taste in my mouth testified that I knew how he felt. My stomach churned with the threat of vomiting.

"For the first time in my life, I see things clearly." Aldous planted his feet covered with those same ratty, old slippers he wore every time I'd seen him solid onto the floor. He stretched out his hunched back, straight and firm. "To contain my wounds and shame, I needed to maintain complete control over myself. The day I molested Helena, I failed. That calamity proved that I strove for an impossible task. So, since I could not restrain myself, I resolved to control everyone around me, mostly my wife and child."

I stared at this man. My eyes stung with disdain. Today's revelation proved my initial instincts correct. My mind's eye envisioned multiple strands of shame entangled among his DNA, transforming him into a fictional villain, yet flesh and bones constructed this person who sat less than ten feet away.

Repulsive words, which I detested to hear, continued to roll out of Aldous's weathered mouth, unaware of the scorn I held toward him, shackled within my soul. He dared to brag of *control!* Good thing that man remained oblivious to the *control* I exercised that very minute.

"Over the next fifteen years, it seems all I did was run. I ran from that villain residing beneath my flesh. I had fooled myself into believing I'd beaten that monster when I met and married Mariam. That was when I discovered that no matter how long or far I ran, I would never escape that evil beast. That creature didn't just live within me. *It was me!*"

I felt my nostrils flare with every drawn-in breath. In my hand, I held an imaginary stake ready to plummet into Aldous's evil heart.

"Little did I know, this villain had remained dormant within me the entire time. Like black mold, abandoned in a dark, dank corner, it multiplied in strength and cunningness. Undetected, this monster overtook every aspect of my being, my thoughts, my actions, my emotions. Cloaked in solitude, this creature matured in such a clever way it gave no warning as to what to expect. Slowly, bit by bit, this disgraceful beast made itself known as it leached out in minute actions toward Mariam, disguised by clever means such as, 'It's for your own good,' or 'It's for your protection,' and the best one yet, 'Because I love you.'"

A wicked act gave birth to this beast, and seclusion had fed it. The hermit existence I had savored now tasted like a decayed carcass. A rapid beat pounded in my chest. The fleeting ambition, which had met me at the door as we entered, to embrace Aldous's hermit lifestyle now blended in with the words that poured from his wretched, half-decayed lips. *How dare a person compare any part of my existence to this deplorable beast! In no way am I anything like this vial man.* My ears bled from the vibration of Aldous's voice as he further described his inward battles. A conflict of my own clashed within me. My animalistic instincts craved to eliminate this personage who, at that very moment, professed to be a threat to society. At the same time, something forceful within held me back, compelling me to listen with compassion while this man talked.

"The monster's abilities increased, and with it, its fury. As Lacey grew, she, too, developed into a rebellious child. And just as my father had felt the impulse to control me, I, too, fought unbridled instincts to control her." The tattered chair creaked as Aldous's stature slunk low within its frayed fibers. A tear escaped those sinister, hardened eyes that stared off into a world only he perceived.

Confusion skirmished within me.

"I lost the battle. The first time it happened was as if I had separated from my body and witnessed a sinful piece of myself violate my innocent baby. Each time the defilement occurred, I merged even more with the beast. Before I realized it, *I* held the reins. *I* now ordered the monster to continue its evil ways. *I had become the monster.* By that time, I held Mariam well under my power." The glassy gaze returned to his ink-black eyes. "Oh, she knew what was happening, all right. She played the part of ignorance so well that she could have earned an Oscar. Yes, she knew! She also knew that if ever she had tried to stop me, I would turn on her with a rage so strong that with all certainty, she never again would attempt."

The same stiffening silence engulfed Aldous and me as when we trudged up the sidewalk toward his house. It twisted a tight knot in my intestines.

Aldous clenched fisted hands and shook them before his chest. "Help me, God, even though I am entirely unworthy of You and Your help." He dropped them in his lap and stared down at the floor. "No wonder Lacey disowned us once she grew up and became a mother. She had no other way to protect her child." He raised his face toward the ceiling, streaked by the glow of a single light bulb encased within a yellowed fixture. "I deserve every bit of your punishment, dear God, but, please, not Mariam. She was an innocent victim caught up in the middle of my nightmare. Please, spare her. I left her no way out! . . . Oh, why?" Grief drained from his cells and rose in putrid puffs of smoke.

My sight locked onto Aldous's anguished face. Disgust coated my tongue, yet a taste of compassion seeped through the barricade. This tormented man never had a chance to heal. No matter how deeply the boyhood Aldous had long ago buried his wounds, they ultimately leached to the surface and spewed forth daggers that lunged into the bodies and souls of his loved ones. How true the phrase rings, which my wife many times had repeated, "Hurt people hurt people."

CHAPTER 38

ALDOUS

*A*NGUISH CASCADED FROM THE DEEPEST crevasses of my soul at what I had done. While gasping for breath, I lunged toward my final chance for mercy and begged God to hear my pleas. I had needed to divulge my story, no matter how horrific. For far too long, I had carried these secret burdens. They weighed me down like concrete blocks. But now, as I exposed my innermost secrets and chipped away this concrete, the weight lifted.

My insides screamed out, imploring Randy to say something. The silence hung in the air like heavy, damp curtains, smothering our faces and impeding airflow to our lungs. With the same effort it takes to turn a rusted lug nut, I twisted my head and stared into Randy's moss-green eyes. He stayed motionless in the rocker, I feared, frozen from shock. I had just spilled into his lap my most private, inner secrets. Could he read my plea for compassion? The silence tore at me like sharpened claws to bare flesh.

Randy twisted his head. Two flawless malachite eyes pointed in my direction. Whether they harbored disdain or compassion, I could not tell. I ached for the latter yet deserved the first. Randy's mouth hung open. Time stopped as I awaited a comment—anything—to fall from his lips. Instead, thunderous silence met my ears.

The deafening hush continued as Randy tipped his head toward his lap. He then, in painstakingly slow motion, lifted it. "Jesus died on the cross to absolve you. God hears your anguish, and I believe He mourns for you. He has mourned since that first day you were violated. Today, He hears your appeals for forgiveness and rejoices."

My eyes strained as I stared at this young man. The final beams of the low setting sun illuminated his silhouette, highlighting golden hair that arched across his forehead.

Randy blinked twice. A look of stunned disorientation distorted his features. "It took great courage to tell me this. Why did you?"

I no longer could hold it in. I didn't know what changed, but the person whom I had perfected to be somehow cracked open, shattering my carefully formed outer shell. Now all I had left was this fragile, vulnerable creature with whom I didn't know what to do. What just happened to me?

A sudden compulsion to share further took over my sensibilities. I leaned in toward Randy like an old hen and clucked out word after word. "I believe it was your son that first day he knocked on my door. When I opened it, a sense of dread rushed through me, but at the same time, something illuminated like a flash of bright light. From that very moment, my life began to change. Your child somehow broke through every barrier I constructed throughout my seventy-one years. He crumbled them into piles of dust, then swept the mounds away. I feel as if a stranger to myself. I have no clue what to do with this new person inside me." My fist thumped against my chest.

An expression of merriment splashed across Randy's face as he chuckled. "That does sound like my Dakota. He has a way about him that I will never understand. He always could walk through any barrier like it never existed."

"How do I move forward? My life is a mess, and I haven't much time to clean it up. Is it too late for me?"

"It's never too late for anyone. Jesus, the Great Carpenter, can fix anything. All God wants of us is to humble ourselves and ask for forgiveness, then allow Him to do the cleaning." Randy's pencil-thin mustache wiggled as he snickered and gave a wink. "God has a special crew set aside specifically for that kind of work."

"Will all those whom I have hurt ever forgive me?" Images of my precious Mariam and our dear, sweet Lacey flashed through my mind. Then I viewed little Helena, only eight years old the day I had molested her. I still could see her pigtails flying as she ran. My darling little sister had always appeared so happy, far cheerier than me at that same age. Oh, how I had envied her carefree nature. Even more, I resented how much Mother and Father loved her. My out-of-control jealousy had caused me to shatter Helena's carefree life. That same day, I fled home and never returned. This nightmare doused me with so much shame I could not bear to look into the eyes of Helena or our parents. Could they ever forgive me? "Would God forgive me?"

"God already has. He now asks you to do your part. Once you accept true forgiveness, no longer will you pine for a different past. Instead, you will fully live and move toward a better future with God." Randy shifted, angling his body in my direction as he leaned over his knees. "Just now, you confided in me, but have you asked God for forgiveness?"

Lumps swelled within my throat. "I don't know how."

"I'll help you."

The wooden rocker swayed forward, then lurched backward again as Randy slid off its seat. He folded onto his knees in the middle of the living room rug. His hands stretched out toward mine. "Want to join me?"

Even though I could have been this man's father, maybe even grandfather, I felt like a child as I gaped down at Randy's broad fingers spread open in invitation.

My body moved toward him with little effort, as if a Being, mightier than I, manipulated my muscles, commanding them to perform. Without remembering how I got there, my knees bent on the rug in front of Randy. He placed his hands on top of mine and closed his eyes.

I kept my eyes wide open and gawked at this personage sent by God. Warm air puffed over my face with each word Randy spoke. So taken in by astonishment from the moment, my mind barely registered Randy's petition. A foreign sensation of comfort draped across my shoulders. I relaxed into it, bowed my head, and let my eyelids drop.

In silent beats, my heart spilled out a petition to the harmonious hum of Randy's prayer. *Please, dear God, forgive me for all the evil I have done. And even more so, heal those whom I have harmed. And, dear Lord, in the short time that I have left on this earth, before I pass, please, guide me so that I leave this world having blessed it with Your goodness and honor.*

Thank you, dear God, for sending this man and his family to help me heal.

In Jesus' name, Amen.

DAKOTA

$\mathcal{M}$OMMY GRIPPED THE HANDLE OF a wooden spoon. It scraped the bottom of the pan while she stirred thick chunks of chocolate that melted into liquid pleasure.

I ogled the desired sweet as it dissolved, bubbling in a saucepan on the stove. My tongue swiped across my upper lip, ready to taste. Itching to dip in and snatch a sample, my bare toes hooked onto the rung of the kitchen stool. I began to stretch out my pointer finger but, knowing Mommy would never allow it, pulled back and sighed.

Happy birthday to you, happy birthday to you . . . In my mind, the words chanted to the perfect rhythm created by each scratch sound made by the spoon as molten chocolate swooshed around the sides of the pan. Could Mommy hear it too? "Do you know which part of a birthday party is the best?"

"No, Koty, tell me. What is the best part of a birthday party?" She lifted the pan off the burner and set it in the center section of the stove.

"The cake! We should celebrate somebody's birthday every week!

Just so we can eat more cake." I topped off the brilliant idea with my biggest smile, knowing she would agree. I don't know why, long ago, no one else came up with it.

"Part of what makes a birthday cake special is that we *don't* have one every week. If we did, they'd be as commonplace as vegetables." Mommy mussed up the hair on top of my head.

She couldn't fool me—she must be nuts to think that scrumptious cake could ever become as boring as broccoli and carrots. Corn-on-the-cob is a bit fun, though. Now that's one food it's okay to make a mess with while eating.

I hopped off the stool and stood beside Mommy at the counter.

Into a large, prepped mixing bowl, Mommy poured the pan of melted chocolate over a heap of sifted flour, then held the spoon out toward me, still coated with my favorite yummy treat. "Ready to stir, Batkid?"

"It's Super-Bat!" Sheesh, when was she going to get it right?

"Forgive me. Super-Bat, get stirring." She winked, then slapped the spoon into the palm of my opened hand.

The mound of white flour became more ooey and gooey with each swoosh as I stirred. "Do you think Good Ol' Al will like the party?"

"I don't see why not. Most everyone likes a party, especially one meant for them."

"But Ol' Buddy Al is awfully *old*. What if, by now, he has had enough and is tired of parties?"

Mommy held an egg, ready to crack, on the lip of a large glass measuring cup. "Just a moment ago, you said we should have a party every week. Now you're concerned that Mr. Aldous would be bored from too many parties? So, which is it, Dakota?"

"Hmm . . . I guess that doesn't make much sense, does it?"

Mommy crinkled her nose and shook her head. "No, it doesn't."

She whacked the egg on the glass edge. Raw yoke and innards oozed from the shell, then, with a plop, dropped into a ready mixture of milk and vinegar. Mommy had once explained how that combination of ingredients substituted for buttermilk when none was on hand.

The bright yellow yoke parted a sea of white. Relief that we never seemed to have any of that yucky stuff in the house washed over me.

"I get the impression, however, that it's been quite a while since Mr. Aldous has had a party." With the back of her hand, Mommy swiped a strand of hair from her face.

"Why do you say that?"

"Oh, just a feeling."

Long ago, I learned to pay attention to Mommy when she got one of her feelings. Usually, she ended up being right. "Well then, he had better enjoy this party."

"Stop stirring for a second." Mommy poured the sour milk and egg mixture into the big, stainless steel mixing bowl in front of me. "What is taking your daddy so long?"

I glanced out the window facing our back porch, not a soul in sight. It had been far too long since Daddy had left, considering he only went to pick up the mail.

The final drop of egg liquid mix trickled from the measuring cup and plopped into the bowl. I pressed the edge of my spoon into the center of a yoke. Like molten gold, bright yellow ooze bled into the chocolaty glop. With the aid of the spoon, I folded in the rich, ooey gold. "Maybe Daddy's been busy fighting off the Mailbox Thief. I heard he struck again, another job for Super-Bat." My hand, which had held the mixing bowl steady, fisted up and punched the air.

"Cute, Koty." Mommy patted my back and chuckled.

"Yeah, I thought it was a pretty good one too. Remember earlier today when we were shopping, and I told Judy, the lady at the check-out counter, about Good Ol' Buddy Al and how he hadn't always been so nice? You know, when we first met, and he was mean and cranky?"

"Uh-huh, I sure do." With trickling water and a sponge, Mommy wiped down the inside of the sink.

"Why do you think he changed?"

She crammed the stopper into the drain, then squirted in some green dish soap. "That's a hard question. I'm not sure I know why." Mommy turned up the faucet. Steam arose among bubbles, releasing a smell that reminded me of Granny Smith apples. "Maybe Mr. Aldous has a reason similar to why your friend Jacob made his big change."

"Wow, there it was again, another person called Jacob Downing my friend, just like Caitlyn had done almost a week ago. I guess maayybe he is." I rested the spoon's handle against the inside of the bowl and, in a daze, watched suds rise within the sink. "It seems Jacob's change came after that day when I gave him my swing. Is it possible that all it took for him to be nice was for me to do something nice for him first?"

Mommy plopped dirty measuring cups and different-sized spoons with markings on their handles into the hot, soapy water. "I'm certain your act of kindness had a lot to do with Jacob's change. However, transformations as drastic as his are usually far more complicated than that."

I forced my eyes to focus and examined the batter in front of me. "All done."

Mommy peered into the big bowl. "Looks good." She picked up the mixing bowl and, with the aid of a spatula, divvied the batter into two round cake pans.

"But I can't remember having done anything extra nice for Good Ol' Al, nothing that would make him want to change . . . except . . . we bought him those new slippers, but he doesn't even know about that yet. He's the one who's done nice things. He played the piano and began to teach me."

"We may never know what caused Mr. Aldous to change, just like we will never fully understand what made him bitter and angry in the first place. What's important is that you follow God's promptings and reach out to others. By doing so, God uses you as His instrument in other people's lives." She scraped the last bit of batter into the cake pans, then set the empty bowl on the counter.

"I'm an instrument?! Like a piano?"

"You can say that. I know I can tickle you, similar to how you tickle the keyboard." Mommy ran her fingers over my ribcage.

We chuckled as I squirmed. I grabbed Mommy's hand, and the tickling stopped. "I guess I, too, can make music. Oh, I remember—my Sunday school teacher once said that 'music heals the soul.' She told us that just before teaching us the same song I'm learning on the piano for Good Ol' Al. You know, 'Jesus Loves the Little Children.' If music can heal, and doing nice things for others also heals, then tomorrow evening, when Good Ol' Buddy Al comes over, we need to make certain and sing 'Happy Birthday' extra loud because it seems like Good Ol' Buddy Al needs a lot of healing. If God gave me this job, I want to do it right, all the way."

"Sounds great to me. Now let's stick this batter in the oven and bake it. Hopefully, your dad will walk through that door any minute. You know how much he loves the smell of baking." Mommy gave me a wink.

CHAPTER 40

RANDY

$\mathcal{T}$HE SMOOTH GLASS MY HAND pressed against supported my body as my attention riveted to the house across the street. A beam of light cast through Aldous's living room window, illuminating painted floorboards on his porch.

I peeled away from the window and gazed at Sandra as she lay peacefully in our bed. Her sandy-brown hair draped over covers pulled partway up her chest. For an instant, the horrors of that evening's visit vanished as I soaked in her beauty. God blessed me with a wife who is even more lovely on the inside than this exquisite lady my eyes feasted on every day.

The driving force to protect this family God had blessed me with pulled at my attention and called me back to the window. The light in our across-the-street neighbor's living room clicked off. A few seconds later, an upstairs window illuminated.

Air rasped past my ribs as I drew in a deep breath. I had to say something to Alexandra, but what? I blinked hard, confirming to my suspicious self that the scene that I gaped at reflected reality. To an unknowing eye, that structure remained just a house. To some, it would even seem warm and cozy. No one would suspect the nightmare that resided within those silenced walls.

"Honey, come to bed." Sandra's last word stretched out, caught up in a yawn. Her pillow yielded to her head, which pressed an indentation as she nuzzled into its soft fluff, preparing to enter dreamland. "Are you going to tell me what kept you so long?" The glow from the bedside lamp reflected off her milky complexion, enhancing soft, delicate features. How do I tell her? If I let her know what had kept me, that peaceful exhaustion about to claim my wife would, undoubtedly, vanish.

My fingers shook as I let the curtains drop. "I bumped into Aldous at the mailbox. He wanted to talk and invited me into his home."

"How nice, Mr. Aldous has warmed up to us." A glimmer of pride glinted from Sandra's closed-lip smile.

"He needed to come clean with some events from his life and, for some reason, chose me for his confessional."

"That's great. He must have felt safe with you. Positive results to our efforts." Sandra's eyelids fluttered close—a shield to protect her innocence.

I crammed my fisted hands deep inside my pockets. Nothing was nice about what that man had said. Yet I needed to know—to protect Alexandra and Dakota. "I'm not sure what to do with the information Aldous gave. He certainly has complicated things."

Sandra's eyes opened, and she stared at me. I held my breath, hoping she could read my silent pleas for help.

"Aren't you coming to bed?" Sandra flung back the covers on my side. "Lie down and tell me what happened."

I slipped off my outer clothes, then sat on the edge of the mattress.

"Sandra, I'm not sure we should go through with our plans and have Aldous over tomorrow.

Sandra propped up onto her elbows. "What do you mean? Everything is all set. Dakota will be heartbroken if we cancel the party. Mr. Aldous is such a special friend to Dakota that he now calls him 'Good Ol' Al.' Our son is so excited to honor him. We can't let Dakota down."

I turned and faced my wife. All signs of sleepiness had vanished from her alert eyes. "Aldous shared some very personal facts about his past. The kind of things one usually does not tell their neighbor."

With slow precision, each gruesome detail spewed from my mouth. "I don't want that man anywhere around our son. Aldous has a history of inappropriately touching children."

Alexandra's eyes bulged. "Mr. Aldous is a child molester?" Covers fell back as she shot straight up in bed, her back as ridged as a goal post. "The man lives right across the street. Dakota plays in full sight of his front window every day. Randy, *I'm* the one who encouraged all of us to build a relationship with that, that man." Tears pooled within her eyes.

Sandra buried her face into my chest. I wrapped my arms around her.

"Dakota has grown to love Mr. Aldous. We would never have known who lived in that house if it wasn't for me. That—molester teaches our son piano lessons." Sandra stumbled over the words as if a far-too-hot morsel occupied space within her mouth. "We can't have him in our home . . . but Dakota is so excited about the party. The cake is baked and ready to be frosted. We even purchased a gift. Our son can't wait to give Mr. Aldous the slippers we chose. It would crush Dakota if we canceled. What do we tell him?"

A peaceful sensation brushed across me as if touched by a fresh breeze. The skin on my forearms prickled. "Calm down, honey. Most importantly, we will protect our son. Under no circumstances would God want another child harmed.

Alexandra lifted her head. "What does God have to do with this? I felt convinced God had brought that man into our lives as a way to reconcile my grandfather."

"God has far more to do with this than either of us could realize." I pulled back and stood up. "Sandra, there's much more to this story than the knowledge we received tonight. When I spoke to Aldous, I suppressed a rage so intense that if I had let myself, I could have torn that man limb from limb." My biceps flexed, then relaxed again. "It was the strangest thing as if God's peace shrouded my anger. 'You must help this man *forgive. You* must help this man *forgive.*' The words repeated over and over again, almost auditable in my head. They drummed out in perfect rhythm with each pound of my heart. It drowned out all my anger, so as I spoke to him, only words of comfort and forgiveness spilled from my mouth." I glanced down at my wife.

She stared at me, a slight quiver to her bottom lip as her mouth hung open in confusion.

"Sandra, the words that came out of my mouth were not my own. The only logical answer I have is that God spoke through me. *He* commissioned me." I stooped down and captured my wife's slender shoulders in my broad hands. "God commissioned our family to help this man . . . yet, we must make certain Dakota never is harmed. There has to be a way."

Green flecks of color floated in Alexandra's blue eyes as they pleaded for a logical answer.

Baffled as to how we move forward from here, I sat back down on our bed and pulled her slender hands into mine. "We need time to think about this. Rash action will not help. There has to be a reason God chose me to be the one whom Aldous confided in."

Sandra jerked back, out of reach from my touch. "Yes, to protect Dakota from becoming his next victim."

Her panic hung thick in the air, yet once again, all I felt was peace. "Yes, there definitely is that, yet I still feel there's much more." I shifted my body and stared into her wide, cat-like eyes. "Sandra, when Aldous shared his past with me, I had never felt more inadequate. As I responded to him, I couldn't feel my lips move. The words I said did not come from me. Everything I spoke was about forgiveness, and not once did I mention the consequences of his horrendous past actions."

Alexandra's posture relaxed. Green flakes glinted within ocean blue irises.

"I don't know why . . . the outward feeling I battled had nothing to do with compassion, yet forgiveness was the running theme I spoke of. It was like the words had come from another person, but Aldous and I were the only two in sight." I rested my hand on my wife's forearm. "The words that spilled from my mouth filled that man with promises of mercy." I pulled away and searched Alexandra's face, hoping for signs of understanding. "I can't turn around now and declare he is never to enter our home. That would make me no better than a common hypocrite." My hands balled into tight fists. "Believe me, a part of me is enraged with hatred toward that man, so much so, I'd just as soon see him rot in prison than allow him into our home." I loosened my grip and took her hand in mine. "Yet I can't ignore this other part of me . . . the part that says we must forgive. Don't worry, honey. God would never want us to place our son in danger.

ALEXANDRA

*E*VERY OUNCE OF SLEEPINESS VANISHED as my husband and I talked late into the night. While he continued to describe his encounter with Mr. Aldous, silent prayers pleading for guidance occupied my overloaded mind.

Randy's voice faded to a low drone in the background. My head bogged down with conflicting emotions that swirled within my gut at a pace that caused me to want to vomit. My eyes stung, congested with tears aching for release. In confusion within my mind, images of Mr. Aldous intermingled with those of my grandfather. Disgust slammed me in the pit of my stomach as if walloped by a sucker punch. My grandfather may have been cold and distant, but by no means had he ever inappropriately touched me or any other person. In no way would he ever have performed such a heinous act. The fact that my mixed-up brain confused my grandfather with this foul man tied me up in a blanket of shame.

"One of the cruelest things any human being could do to another was to cause them to believe themselves as unlovable." Randy's strong jaw hung ridged.

His last sentence hung thick in the air as if printed in large, bold font. I could almost touch each letter. Every one of my defense mechanisms sprang to full attention. "No. Grandpa never made me feel unlovable!" Even as those words rolled off my tongue, I knew it was a lie.

Randy's mustache twitched. "What? When did we start talking about your grandfather?"

I jolted my attention back to the present. "Oh, I-I'm sorry. Please go on."

"That's exactly my point. Didn't you tell Dakota that because you could not bond with your grandfather was the entire reason you encouraged him to build a relationship with Aldous?"

"Yes. The apparition of my grandfather's pleasure toward me, as a result of our embracing Mr. Aldous, felt so real. I had no idea! I told our son I wanted him to bond with Mr. Aldous because Dakota has no grandparents. I didn't want him cheated out of that experience." Tension in my jaw alerted me to the heap of defense I fought to tame.

"Just as you were cheated out of a relationship with your grandfather."

How could he say such a thing? Every muscle in my body screamed to slap Randy. I sprang from the bed and stomped toward the window. My arms locked across my body.

Randy moved beside me and gently massaged my shoulders. "It's okay, Sandra."

Tears gushed from my eyes like a dam bursting. "I'll never know why my grandfather remained so cold. Could his reasons have been as horrific as Mr. Aldous's?" I spun around and glared at Randy. My eyes stung like acid, begging for an answer. "What if Grandfather had carried a secret as horrendous as Mr. Aldous's all his life? Is it possible that could be why he distanced himself from Grandmother and me and rejected our love and affection?"

"We can't do anything for your grandfather. However, we can help the man you dubbed Dakota's surrogate grandparent. Sandra, remember how it says in the Bible, 'many are called, but few are chosen'? Every one of us has severe wounds within ourselves, wounds so intensive, if left unhealed, they could destroy us and everyone around us."

Randy's olive-green eyes acted as a screen for the home movies from my past that played in my head. "My grandfather's bitterness had bit into every one of his loved ones."

"God calls us all to face our wounds and allow Him to guide us into healing. Our Lord beckons us to forgive unconditionally and love as Jesus loves. Only by extending that love and forgiveness can we help each other overcome such deeply seeded wounds." Randy stepped toward our bed and picked up an open Bible from his nightstand. His large fingers riffled through well-marked pages. "Here it is, Matthew 22:14, 'many are called, but few are chosen.' It's sad how few respond to God's call. Most never humble themselves and ask for God's help to muster the courage and strength to face their wounds. That step is necessary."

"Yet, Mr. Aldous did just that." Shame toward the intensity at which I had detested that man just moments before pierced my heart.

"He did. It takes monumental courage to confide in sin such as his. For that alone, I must honor him."

Panic roared to the surface. "But Dakota is still our number one priority!" I swallowed a hurricane of emotions to steady my voice. "How do we help Mr. Aldous while at the same time keeping our son safe?"

"We *always* use caution to protect Dakota, the same as before we knew the truth of Aldous's past." Randy placed the Bible on his nightstand and crawled back into bed. "I believe God wants us to offer him the olive leaf. Our friendship must have helped Aldous unbolt that door to his past, or he would never have confided in me. We can't abandon him now." The whiskers of Randy's mustache spread apart as he yawned. "Maybe by remaining friends, we can provide Aldous a safety point to heal from and move forward. We're called to love as Jesus would. As humans, we're all subject to fall." Randy patted the vacant space beside him on the mattress. "We will remain cautious and never, not even for a second, leave Dakota alone with Aldous."

My feet skimmed the floor as I moved to my side of the bed. "From the start, even as I encouraged Dakota to be friends with Mr. Aldous, I sensed our son should not be alone with that man. Dakota often questioned me about that." I snuggled in beside my husband. "God has protected us from the very beginning. . . . What do we tell Dakota? And what about the party?"

CHAPTER

42

RANDY

*E*XHAUSTION FOGGED MY BRAIN. MY clumsy fingers fumbled to secure the metal clasp on my belt. In only half an hour, I would leave for work. I still needed to wake up Dakota. The shortened night due to our lengthy conversation was bound to affect my workday.

Alexandra smoothed out wrinkles on our bedcovers while a new crease formed between her eyebrows. "So . . . what do we tell Dakota? Today is the party. We haven't much time."

I sat on our bed and stretched for the rolled-up socks seated a few feet away. Funny how the simplest tasks seem monumental when overtired. "We keep it appropriate for his age. At five, all Dakota needs to know is that, in some ways, Aldous is a friend, yet in others, he remains a stranger. Dakota should understand that we do not know much about the man, so we must use caution." Against my strong desire to forget that day and lay back down, I rose from the bed and wrapped my arms around Sandra, confident she would handle things well when Dakota brought up the topic.

The sweet smell of strawberries met my nose as Sandra rested her head against my shoulder. I inhaled deeply. The awareness of our son's vulnerability struck hard. "We need to remind Dakota that, for his protection, we will never leave him alone with *any* stranger."

Alexandra pulled out of our embrace. She picked up a pillow and fluffed it, then returned it to its original location, on top of the covers. "You know how our son is. He might say something that would embarrass Mr. Aldous, especially now that he has confided in you."

"We don't have to say anything right away. When the appropriate moment arises, we will know. And when it does, we'll keep things as simple and generic as possible."

Alexandra placed a quick peck on my lips. "See you downstairs for breakfast." She turned and paced out of the room.

Dakota, I need to wake him. My body ached as I started toward the door. Does Sandra feel as worn-out as I do? She got no more sleep than I did, yet she is starting the day as alert as if she woke from a solid eight hours.

"Hooray! Today is Good Ol' Buddy Al's party!" Dakota shuffled down the hall, scuffing his padded feet on the carpet. He stood in my doorway. A huge grin dominated his freckled face. "You don't have to wake me this morning. I got up all on my own."

Great, the day I'm extra tired, my son bounds with mega amounts of energy. "Come on, Kid-O. Let's go get you dressed."

I followed after Dakota as he sped from the room, peeled off his pajamas, and tossed them on the floor in front of his closet. "Do I have to go to school today? There are so many things left to do for Good Ol' Al's party, and Mommy may need my help. Like, we still need to frost the cake." His sky-blue eyes pleaded up at me.

I reached into my son's closet and slipped a green striped shirt off a hanger. "Yes, you have to go to school. After you get home, there is plenty of time to frost that cake." I held open the shirt in front of him.

Dakota slipped his head and arms through the holes. "Well, since he and I are such special friends, when I get home and, after the cake is frosted, can I go over to Good Ol' Al's house and escort him across the street? He might like that special treatment since it is his birthday."

"No, Dakota, you know you are not allowed at his house without your mom or me." I sprang to full attention. To sharpen my focus, I squinted. This reminder was supposed to come from his mother, not me.

"But why not? You and Mommy let me go to Traven's house. I play there by myself all the time. What's the difference?"

My heart pounded. Dakota wasted no time in seeking an explanation. *Please, God, direct my words.* "The fact that Traven is a little boy makes things safer for you."

Dakota's eyebrows rose.

Please, God, I need to do much better than this. "Yes, you and Aldous have built a good relationship. Yet Aldous has lived many years and experienced a lot, both good and bad. We have no idea how those events have impacted him."

With one foot in the air stuffed through a pant leg and the other balanced on the floor, Dakota crinkled his nose, similar to how his mother often did. "Sooo, what does any of that matter?"

"Well . . . that is a good question." *Okay, God, I need Your help here.* "Think of Caitlyn, that new girl in your class. When she first came to your school, she acted all shy and reserved-like, right?"

Dakota's forehead relaxed. "She sure did. And back then, some kids picked on her."

"However, you made it a point to be friendly toward her, and she responded well."

"In no time at all, Caitlyn opened up. Someone who didn't know could never tell she used to be that same shy girl."

"That's what I mean. Caitlyn's experiences influenced her actions."

Dakota gave me a blank stare.

"You acted friendly toward Caitlyn, and she rewarded you by being friendly back."

"Yeah, Caitlyn is one of my best friends now."

"It is possible a harmful event in Caitlyn's past caused her to be so shy. However, she seems to have overcome. Some people's pasts are too traumatic for them to heal fully. A person's experiences color how they react. We have no idea what is in Aldous's past, and we cannot predict his actions. So, for now, your mother and I feel we should be around whenever you visit." Sweat coated my palms. Would Dakota be satisfied with this awkward explanation?

My son gaped up at me, silent.

With my fingers, I combed through wild, sandy-blond hair that stuck straight up from his scalp—the perfect indicator that Dakota had just gotten out of bed. "It is a part of how we parents care for our children."

"Why not just ask him and get it over with?"

"Aldous may not want to talk about that, and it's not our place to pry. People need the freedom to bring up such issues in their own time, often only with those they choose."

"So, if you and Mommy are so worried about my buddy Al's past, why spend any time with him? Maybe you're right. Maybe he has done something horrible."

"I'm not saying he did, or he didn't. And we're not going to ask. Whether he has done something or not doesn't matter, we need to exercise proper caution. It is not our place to judge what exists in another person's past. God expects us to love everyone, regardless."

"Even when they've done terrible things?"

"Yes, even if they've done terrible things. Remember, Jesus is our model. He loves us no matter what. We cannot erase our pasts. However, because Jesus died on the cross for each one of us, for *all* our sins, we are forgiven." I gazed into my son's eyes. Was I getting through? *Help me, God. I must do this right.*

Snippets' filthy, gray fur caught my attention as it stuck out from under the disarray of blankets on Dakota's bed. I grabbed a floppy foot of that well-loved stuffed puppy and yanked him out from under a tangle of bedding. I smoothed down matted fur. A calm sensation entered my soul. *Thanks, God. This just might work.* "It's pretty much the same as your love for Snippets, no matter how ragged he has become. Jesus loves Mr. Aldous, even after everything in his past, no matter how horrendous. That is the reason Jesus died on the cross for our sins." I straightened out Snippets' folded-over ear. "It doesn't matter how dirty and grayed a person may be. We, too, are called by God to reflect onto everyone that same love Jesus pours out for Mr. Aldous and us all. But at the same time, God expects us to remain wise as we extend love."

Dakota bounced in front of me, pointing toward the filthy toy. "You know what's really cool? Even though Snippets is all dirty, I love him twice as much now than the day when I first got him, when he was all clean and pure white."

"Do you know why?"

Dakota snatched his stuffed friend from my hands and gazed into its black button eyes. "Well . . . because . . . we've shared so many adventures that, by now, he has become a part of me."

My dry lips cracked as they curled back into a grin. Maybe my boy understood more than I had given him credit for.

"Mommy has tried many times to wash Snippets, but he never

comes out looking clean. Nothing takes away the dirt, proof of *his* past. Therefore, I've had to accept him as he is and move on."

I shut my eyes and breathed in relief. *"Thank you, God. Dakota gets it."* The words of gratitude whispered from my lips.

"What did you say, Daddy?"

"Just a quick prayer to thank God."

"Huh?" Dakota shrugged his shoulders and glanced up. "I don't know what for, God, but thank you."

I chuckled at his blunt mannerisms and held out a hand. "Come on, your bus will be here before we know it, and you still need to eat breakfast."

Dakota planted a kiss on the tip of Snippets' black plastic nose, then returned his well-beloved friend to my opened hand.

I propped the stuffed animal up against Dakota's pillow.

My son tipped his head upwards and wiggled his freckled nose as he sniffed. "I smell bacon!"

CHAPTER 43

DAKOTA

I STUCK THE SPATULA INTO THE tub of yummy frosting and slathered on another thick glob. Not a bit of freshly baked cake peeked through, yet I wanted to be sure a generous amount of creamy chocolate frosting covered every inch. I set the spatula on the counter and stepped back. "Good Ol' Al's birthday cake is ready, Mommy. I sure hope he loves it."

"I'm sure he will." Mommy stepped away from the pots and pans steaming on top of the stove and inspected my delicious work of art, then turned toward me. A half-stifled chuckle burst from her mouth. "Koty, you're wearing as much frosting as you spread onto that cake. Go to the bathroom and clean yourself up. I'll apply the lettering."

"I better hurry. Our birthday boy will arrive real soon."

Mommy filled a funnel-shaped bag with white frosting. "No need to worry. There's enough time."

Mommy and Daddy made another attempt to involve our honored guest in conversation, but just like the time before, the most response Ol' Buddy Al gave was a simple grunt or nod of the head. Whenever I called him "Birthday Boy," his eyes narrowed, forcing me to dial down my excitement. My Good Ol' Buddy showed no sign of enjoying his party other than scarfing down food almost as fast as I've seen his dog, Oscar, do. I didn't get it—doesn't everyone love a birthday party?

The Adam's apple on the outside of Good Ol' Al's throat bobbled with each greedy swallow. He shoveled in spoonful after spoonful at a rate suggesting that he hadn't eaten anything decent in over a week.

I stared at my empty plate, smeared with evidence of green beans, Mommy's awesome meatloaf, and homemade mashed potatoes. My parents—also with cleared plates—started up random conversations. Each chat pointed toward Good Ol' Al fizzled into an uncomfortable silence.

The worn mark on the belt around the birthday boy's pants hinted he had drawn it in another notch. How could someone that skinny eat so much? I hoped he wouldn't make himself sick.

Good Ol' Al overloaded his fork with a hunk of meatloaf, spread a glob of mashed potatoes on top, and then shoved the disgusting mixture into his mouth.

Yuck. Would he ever finish?

I pulled up onto my knees and craned my neck, hoping to catch a glimpse of the luscious chocolate cake that sat out of sight on the kitchen counter. "Be sure and save room. We'll have cake as soon as you finish. Then you can open the present we bought you." That should entice the man to stop gulping his food and show a bit of excitement.

"Dakota, let him eat." Mommy's cheeks flushed pink.

Good Ol' Al jutted his chin toward Mommy—his plate smeared

with mashed potatoes, gravy, and traces of meatloaf. "Could you pass me another roll?"

"Certainly. Dakota, please, pass these to Mr. Aldous." Mommy handed me a serving dish that contained one last dinner roll.

Faint whiskers on Good Ol' Al's chin gleamed white as he snatched up the roll. He ripped a piece off and wiped it across his plate like a sponge, sopping up every last drop.

Before our birthday boy could request anything else, Mommy rose from her seat and started to remove dirty dishes from the table. She saved Good Ol' Al's plate for last. As she lifted it away, his lower lip stuck out a tad further than usual. Never before had I seen a grown man pout. I rubbed my eyes and took a second look to be sure.

Mommy brought out the cake with lit candles. I used my biggest voice as she, Daddy, and I sang, "Happy Birthday." Good Ol' Al stared at us through glazed-over eyes and a blank face as if we all had gone mad.

Wax dripped down the sides of the candles and onto the chocolate frosting. "Go on, make a wish." I grabbed his hand and tried to pull it toward the cake. Maybe he didn't know what to do. Did nobody ever give him a cake like this before?

Good Ol' Al jerked his hand from mine. His bushy eyebrows stuck straight out as he gawked at the flames and the muscles in his jaw contracted.

Daddy leaned forward and, one by one, pinched out the candles. "Let's try this again at a later time."

Why did he do that? I glared at Daddy in disbelief. "Is it time, Mommy? Can I go get it?"

"We haven't cut the cake yet, sweetheart."

"We can cut the cake after he opens his present. Pleaseee?"

"Okay, Koty, you may get it."

I ran from the room. In a Super-Bat flash, I returned with the neatly wrapped package Mommy and I had purchased for today's event. I set the gift in front of our birthday boy. Surely this would make Good Ol' Al happy.

Motionless, as if frozen to his chair, Al's eyes clouded over while he gazed forward.

I inched his wrapped present closer. "Go ahead. Open it."

He flashed a glare in my direction. I swore I heard a snarl. With slow and cautious motion, Birthday Boy Al's wrinkled hands shook while he ran a finger over the edge of the bow, then tugged on the ends.

Mommy often said God gives us all plenty of opportunities to exercise patience. Well, this moment definitely counted as one. With the pace a baby bird takes to hatch from its egg, Buddy Al's crocked fingers pecked at the wrapping of his package, slowly slicing through tape.

My insides were about to burst.

Finally, he removed the paper and lifted the gift box lid.

I tried to contain myself but failed as a squeal burst loose. I slapped both hands over my mouth to stop any more sounds from popping out.

Good Ol' Al *had* to love what we bought him. I pinched my eyes shut and waited for his excited gratitude.

Nothing happened.

I peeked through one eye, then popped the other one open.

Al's bushy brows did not move as if chiseled onto his statue-like face. He stared down at the opened package. His carved-of-stone grimace settled into his bones. He lifted a single slipper from the box and held it away from his body as if it were a rattlesnake caught by the nape of its neck.

"Look, Mommy, he must be in shock. I knew he would love them." I glanced from my parents back toward Good Ol' Al. "They're the closest thing to your old pair we could find. You wear those old slippers every day, so you must love them. But they're so worn that I figured you would be thrilled to have them replaced with a brand-new pair."

I waited for a grin. Any minute now, it should appear. I just knew it would.

Good Ol' Al's thin lips drew in tight. His wild brows pinched above the bridge of his nose. "Then what? Are you going to replace me next?" The new footwear slipped from his hand, landing on the table with a thud. His eyes flashed, black as licorice, as he glared at me through narrow slits.

"I-I-But I thought you'd love these?" My bottom lip trembled. I swiped away a tear that slid down my cheek.

"What, are you dumb? Of course, I would not like these!" He picked up the one slipper and let it drop again to the table. "What were you thinking? Would *you* like it if I replaced you? Just because you grew old and worn out?"

"Okay, that's enough. You will not speak to our son that way!" Mommy sped around the table. She pulled me into her lap and wrapped her arms around me tight.

I buried my face in her safe embrace.

"Aldous, he's a child. There's no need to be so harsh. We meant no insult toward you. We were trying to honor your birthday, nothing more." Daddy's voice carried a seldomly heard, firm tone.

I poked my head out from the crook in Mommy's arm. "Just because you're hurt inside doesn't make it okay to be mean."

Mommy patted my head. "Remember, Koty, 'hurt people hurt people.' I don't believe Mr. Aldous meant to be cruel. His inner wounds are talking, not his heart."

"I don't have to take this abuse!" Aldous's sleeve caught a fork prong as he swiped his arm across the table, shoving it and the carefully undone wrapping paper, along with the opened gift box and new slippers, to the floor.

In one swift motion, Daddy sprang from his seat at the far end of the table to in front of Mommy and me. "I believe it's time for you to go." He acted as a shield from the nightmarish behavior that sat in our kitchen.

"I was going to play for you on my new keyboard the song you taught me and then ask if I could call you Grandpa." My words choked out among blubbers.

Mr. Aldous shot me a dagger-sharp glare. His chair scraped the floor and banged into the wall as he shoved it back, then stomped from our kitchen and out the side door with a certainty I never saw this old man use.

Daddy followed inches behind. The door latch clicked shut. An instant later, Daddy returned to the kitchen. He slid into the chair Mr. Aldous had sat in only moments before. Daddy leaned forward, his elbows on his knees. He propped his chin in the cup of his hands. His eyes pierced mine, then softened.

I turned toward the cake, still in the middle of the table with half-burned candles stuck in pools of blue wax. "We didn't even cut the cake. Why did Mr. Aldous act that way?"

Daddy rested his hands on my knees. "Remember when I told you that he had lived many years, and there remains much about him that we do not know?"

"Uh-huh?"

"Within all those years, a lot had to have happened, both good and bad." Puffs of warm air brushed against my ear as Mommy spoke.

Daddy sat straight up in the chair. "The other day, Aldous confided in me some of his more troublesome past. When a person does bad things, it assaults their heart. If left un-reconciled, in time, their heart shuts down, making it difficult to both give and receive love. That's one reason it's crucial to commit to whatever is needed to heal our inner wounds."

"God must get awfully sad when we do mean things like Mr. Aldous just did."

"I believe so. Even still, God loves us each far more than we will ever know. God never gives up on anyone. The only way Mr. Aldous, or any of us, can fully heal is through God and His forgiveness." Mommy's voice purred with tenderness.

"I wanted to call Mr. Aldous *Grandpa*. I never had the chance to ask his permission. Now I don't even know if I want to anymore. Are some things so terrible, they can never heal from them?"

"It often seems that way. But remember, '. . . with God all things are possible.' If we allow it, God will soften even the hardest heart." Daddy arched his back. His shoulders relaxed.

"Mr. Aldous's heart seems extra hard."

"You know, Koty. That's how diamonds are made." Mommy ran her hand over my hair.

"Huh?"

"That's right." Daddy winked at Mommy.

With a quick jerk, I turned my head from one parent to the other.

"All diamonds start as a lump of coal. After many years of being buried deep within the earth, all that pressure and burden, combined with time, convert the ugly piece of coal into a beautiful diamond."

I stared at Daddy in disbelief. "Is God turning Mr. Aldous into a diamond?"

Mommy chuckled. "You could say that. We all have a diamond hidden inside of us." She tapped me softly on the chest. "But also, each one of us carries a vial of poison. It's up to us which one we choose to let into the light for everyone to see and which one we keep buried."

"I guess today Good Ol' Al chose his vial of poison. Do you think, someday, he will take out his diamond instead and let it shine?"

"We hope so." Mommy tipped her head and gazed directly toward Daddy.

"Then I *will* be able to call him Grandpa." My sadness bubbled away.

"Let's pray for Aldous right now and ask God to help him choose to let his diamond shine."

Mommy nodded in response to Daddy's request.

"And after that, can we eat cake?"

CHAPTER

44

ALDOUS

*M*Y FEET COULDN'T MOVE FAST enough as I stormed out of that insufferable place. A rageful beat of my heart accompanied each stomp as I marched across the street toward home. How could they think up such an appalling scheme? My screen door rattled as it slammed behind me.

Oscar sensed my disgust. His eyes bulged bug-like as he scurried into the kitchen. Under normal circumstances, the crazy mutt would bounce like a rubber ball, inches from my feet, while his tail wagged so fast one would think that, at any minute, he'd take off and buzz around the room.

I kept my head low as, with far more force than necessary, I pulled shut the heavy wooden door and then bolted it.

Toenails scraped against the kitchen floor as Oscar darted under the butcher's block—his safe place whenever I displayed too much anger for his tender emotions. Disgust rose within my throat with the taste of bile. *That dang dog needs to get a backbone.*

As I turned away, my eyes caught onto my old, treasured slippers. The very same pair with which that meddlesome boy across the street had tried to replace. How could he have such gall?

Nothing had shown me more loyalty than that raggedy pair of leather. I picked up the treasured footwear and cradled them against my chest. My nose burrowed into worn-down lamb's wool as I inhaled far into my longs, the time-honored aroma of sweat mixed with leather. Oh, how familiarity brings comfort. Mariam had given me these slippers as a gift for our first Christmas together. Nothing could convince me to replace them, ever. It didn't matter how tattered they had become. Someone might as well replace me instead. "No one will separate me from my darling wife!"

Stunned, as if hit by an electrical current, the words I just spoke resonated in my ears. Mariam had been taken from me long ago, for she had removed her heart from mine many years before that dreaded day when she had passed. I could not remember exactly when it happened, somewhere after I killed off her spirit and before Lacey declared she no longer wanted to see us. "Oh, dear God, what have I done?! I've made a mess out of all our lives!"

A sharp pain shot through my right leg, alerting my conscious mind that I had dropped to my knees. For how long, I had no idea. With my slippers still clenched in my hands, my bones creaked in protest as I rose to my feet. "Dear God, how do I fix this?"

I slid my feet into the well-worn leather. My shoulders rose and fell with a breath of relief. Unaware of my legs as they moved, I fled upstairs with unbelievable ease as if a puppet connected to an invisible cord, manipulated by some far greater being.

Barely conscious of how it happened, I found myself in my bedroom, staring at Mariam's hummingbird collection. The vase I had purchased from Dakota called to my attention. I stuffed it into the hook of my arm and almost floated back down to the first floor.

I grabbed my keys off the secretary desk, where I had carelessly tossed them after returning home from that treacherous birthday dinner invite. My finger slid over the metal cutouts that matched up with a tumbler within my door. The boy had no idea what meaning lay behind that innocent gift. He and his parents tried to reach out to me, just like my beautiful wife had done countless times before her death. I had shoved Mariam and Lacey away the same as I now pushed Dakota and his family out of my life. No wonder I never enjoyed the sweet nectar of love. Every time it drew near, I threw it away. Look at all the people I have harmed.

Oscar inched back into sight cowering in the archway to the kitchen. Even this tiny, loyal mutt had tasted the bitter bile of my actions. I bent down and patted him on the head. "Sorry, dear boy. You're going to be alone a bit longer. I'm not sure when I'll return, but there's something important I need to go do."

The animal's ears perked as he tipped his head, giving the impression he understood.

Neglecting to grab a coat, I slipped through the door and locked it behind me.

A shrill grind assaulted my ears as I turned the key in the ignition, giving protest to my late-night adventure. I glanced over at the passenger's seat to where the vase sat. *The local grocery store stays open late. It will have what I want.*

I pulled into a parking space, then folded my arms across my body to keep out the chill as I fled through the nearly vacant lot.

Automatic doors escorted me inside to a much-welcomed warmth. On my right, large glass refrigerator doors provided a protective barrier for countless colorful blossoms within. I scanned the assortment and quickly found what I came for, peach-colored chrysanthemums, Mariam's favorite. Before logic settled within my tired brain, I laid down money for the flowers and then took them out to my car.

The small batch of blossoms easily slid into Mariam's new vase. Oh, how she would have loved this gift. If only she could have been here to see. I stuck my key in the ignition, pulled my car from the parking lot, then meandered down dark, winding roads toward the graveyard.

Lucky for me, only a sign affixed to the cast-iron fence warned of a sundown curfew, yet not once had I found the gates closed. I drove inside and navigated gravel pathways illuminated solely by my headlights until I found the grave marker I sought.

An unassuming headstone, cold and bare, shouted cries of loneliness. I shifted the gear shaft into park and turned the key to shut down the engine. Grabbing the vase, I slammed the door behind me. Frozen blades of grass crunched beneath the leather souls of my slipper-clad feet as they carried me to where my wife of thirty-seven years now rested.

I fell to my knees in front of the tombstone. My eyes swelled with tears as, with shaking hands, I placed the hummingbird vase filled with peach chrysanthemums beside her grave. My arthritic fingers traced the inscription—Mariam Connolly, 1953-2009, beloved wife and mother.

My heart twisted. Oh, why couldn't I have loved her while I had the chance? She gave of herself in every way, and in return, I kept my heart locked in a steel box with the key recklessly tossed aside. I had spent every day of our shared thirty-seven years shut down, unable to give or receive love. And to make things worse, I blamed sweet Mariam for all my ugly inadequacies.

I stared down at the tattered slippers that swathed my arthritic feet. That spent leather remained the only barrier to shield me from the night's bitter cold. "Sorry, my darling, but I have to make a change. My time has almost run out. God is handing me this one final chance. I must take it." I slid those same slippers, which I had treasured above all else all those years, off of my feet and laid them beside the vase, then pressed my lips on Mariam's headstone, placing a kiss.

The frost-covered ground bit its icy teeth into my bare soles. I rose and started to leave before turning back for one last look.

The corners of my frozen lips cracked as they curled into a grin. Bending over again, I pulled the chrysanthemums from the vase and divided them into two batches, then stuffed each half into the openings of my treasured slippers. Now those same slippers I had cherished above any other, I commissioned toward one last job in this most wretched life—to hold and protect my wife's favorite flowers at her gravesite. My cheeks plumped with a smile, frozen in position, while I grasped the vase and ambled, barefooted, back to my car.

DAKOTA

"*M*OMMY, THEY DON'T FIT." FULL of frustration, my foot stomped as I used every muscle to yank and tug at the sleeves of my favorite pair of cozy pajamas, yet they would not pull over my bare wrists.

"It won't make any difference. You can tug all night. Your sleeves aren't going to stretch." Mommy stood in the doorway to my bedroom, her hands filled with a load of clean towels.

I used my best pout and stared at the exposed skin above my ankles. Dump truck pictures scattered over the soft fabric. "But I love this pair. They must have shrunk in the wash."

Mommy chuckled. "No, Koty, you grew over the summer."

"I don't want to grow if that means my favorite clothes don't fit."

Mommy set the pile of freshly folded towels on my dresser. "Oh, but growing is how we develop into that special person God created us to be."

"But sometimes it's no fun to grow."

"You're right—sometimes it even hurts. I bet we can replace those pajamas with new ones you'll love just as much. Now crawl into bed so I can tuck you in." Mommy pulled back the covers and fluffed up my pillow.

I hopped onto the mattress, hoping it would bounce like a trampoline. It didn't work—another disappointment. The crinkle between Mommy's eyebrows returned. I knew that meant I better settle down, so I hunched my shoulders and slipped my feet under the blankets.

"Lay back." Mommy sat beside me.

I snuggled onto the pillow. Mommy pulled the covers up toward my chin while light glinted off the diamond on her wedding ring as her hand moved.

"Wow, did you see that twinkle like a star? Most of the time, I don't even notice your ring, but ever-so-often the light catches it. It is so pretty when it sparkles like that." I grabbed Mommy's hand.

Her arm relaxed, allowing me to twist her finger and play with light patterns as they danced off her ring. The sparkle reminded me of Mr. Aldous's party. Even *he* has a diamond hidden somewhere deep inside. "Does the chunk of charcoal grow too, as it turns into the diamond?"

"It goes through a change process, and that's what growth is. So, I guess you could say it does."

"Do you think the charcoal hurts when it grows, the same way as people do?"

Mommy snickered. "No, darling, a stone does not feel."

Struck by a brilliant idea, I sprang straight up in bed. "Maybe that's Mr. Aldous's problem. Maybe he's in too much pain."

"I'm certain you are right about that, Koty."

"So, what do we do?"

"Well, some pain is easy to fix, like . . . when you outgrow your favorite pajamas, for instance." Mommy tickled my tummy through the gap of my too-small pajama top.

I giggled and flopped against my pillow.

"All we need is a shopping trip to fix this problem to buy you a brand-new pair. Who knows, maybe we could find some Super-Bat pajamas."

I felt my cheeks plump as I grinned. "Oh boy, do you think so?!"

"It's possible, but whatever we find, I'm certain you will love them as much as you love this old pair."

"Mommy, why does growth hurt?"

"Because it's a part of the second greatest gift God gave us—the gift of free will."

I pinched my brain to help me think real hard. "What's the first greatest gift?"

"Jesus."

I knew that. I giggled. "Ooh yeah . . . so why is free will so great?"

"Because God loves us so much, He allows us to be whoever we want, even if that means we draw away from Him. Out of love, God gives us the gift of choice." Mommy's eyes sparkled like two green diamonds in a pond of clear blue water.

Again confused, my brain pinched back up. That happened a lot when Mommy had big talks with me. "What does growth pain have to do with free will?"

"We all grow, whether we want to or not, but it's our choice whether we allow that growth to break us into pieces or mold us into a sparkling diamond." Mommy wiggled her ring finger and grinned.

"Not all diamonds sparkle like yours?"

"All diamonds can sparkle. But first, they must be mined from the earth."

"They have to be found, dug out, and cleaned off?"

"Yes, similar to how we each must find and choose Jesus. But there's more to it than that. After a person mines, cleans, and polishes the diamond, someone called a diamond cutter uses a chisel and cuts facets into the gemstone. The more precision used in cutting the facets determines how brilliantly the diamond sparkles." Mommy tapped her ring. "Just like with my diamond, every person must go through unique challenges. Those hardships chisel facets into their diamond to make them sparkle."

"So every cut diamond sparkles?"

"Every diamond has the potential, whether cut or not, but not all do, and some crack under pressure. When cutting real diamonds, bits and pieces can break off, or the gem may shatter. It's not easy to chisel facets. That is part of the reason why diamonds are rare and precious."

My heart pounded in my throat. How could a loving God let people fall to pieces instead of making everyone sparkle? "Why does God make bad things happen that break us? Like when a diamond shatters—like Mr. Aldous?"

"God never makes bad things happen. God walks us through tough times and offers His strength. It's up to *us* to choose to use it or not. When we accept God's guidance and put our faith in Jesus, we emerge with another facet perfectly cut into our diamond and shine even greater than before. But if we don't allow God to lead us through, that's when our stone cracks."

"I get it! The hardship is like the chisel. And the greatest Diamond Cutter of all is God!"

"That's right. And we are the diamonds, rare and precious with facets that glisten when polished by God's brilliancy." Mommy lifted her hand and angled her ring to catch the light. "This one sparkles because it has many successfully cut facets."

"Unlike Mr. Aldous?" I gazed down at the blankets that covered me. The thought of Mr. Aldous breaking into pieces as his facets were chiseled filled my heart with sadness.

"Sometimes it appears that way." Mommy lifted my chin with her finger. "But God *never* gives up on His children—there's *always* time. However, the more breaks, the harder it is to fix."

"But God is the master at fixing things, especially people, right?"

"Absolutely."

That gave me hope. But then a new problem slam-dunked into my mind. "So, what do we do with the slippers we bought Mr. Aldous?"

"They are his birthday present, so they do belong to him. How about after school tomorrow we take them over to his house."

I gave Mommy a big smile and nodded. "Maybe that would make him happy. . . . But what if he still doesn't want them?"

Mommy drew in a deep breath. "If that happens, we'll figure something out."

"So, Dakota, are you ready for a story, or has your mom already read you one?" Daddy leaned against the doorframe with a book in hand and winked.

I sprang up, pulled my legs under my bottom, and bounced on the mattress. "I want a story."

Mommy swept back my bangs and gave me a peck on my forehead, "Enjoy your storytime." She then gathered her load of clean towels and kissed Daddy on her way out of the room.

CHAPTER

46

ALDOUS

*I*HAD NEVER FELT MORE LOST in all my ill-fated life. This entire day, I did nothing but pace across the living room rug. After several hours of Oscar's best attempts to entice me into activity, he finally gave up and laid in the corner between the rocking chair and the couch. His rounded chin rested against tiny front paws.

I had no clue what to do with myself. Everything familiar seemed to have been ripped away. I paused my pacing and gawked at my naked feet. Funny, before now, I had not noticed the ugly yellow tint of my toes. I snorted out bitter laughter. Throughout most of my adult life, those crooked appendages had remained covered by worn-out slippers— the same pair that, last night, I sacrificed to Mariam's gravesite. They outlived their purpose, just as I had outlived mine. *Face the cruel facts, Aldous.* You *are obsolete.*

A sway of the hummingbird feeder outside the window caught my attention. The shrubbery around Mariam's garden had shed most of its brilliant fall leaves. They, too, had lived beyond their purpose. Even trees release what is no longer needed or wanted. Since the beginning of time, letting go of the no-longer-useful has been a reality of life. *The sooner I accept that fact, the better.*

A deep red stain shone through the plastic base of the neglected feeder. I should have brought it in last week. All of Mariam's feathered friends would have flown south by now. How do birds adapt? Change has to be the most challenging aspect of life to adjust to. My eyes stared beyond the smudged windowpane at the deserted feeder, yet my mind wandered onto images of my beloved wife, laid to rest. My coveted slippers now held flowers at her gravesite. Without having searched, I encountered renewed purpose for the same item that, for some odd reason, I treasured above all else. *Does God also have a new purpose for me?*

Oscar lifted his furry head. His black button-like eyes darted to the right, in the direction of the door. "What is it, boy?"

The rap of knuckles sounded against the wood. Oscar darted to his feet, knocking over a pile of books as his short legs scampered toward the noise.

"Darn it, Oscar." I stooped to straighten the long-forgotten heap of children's books that Mariam had compiled. Before she passed away, she brought each item from storage, hoping to read them to her first and only grandchild. It must have torn Mariam's heart to shreds that day when Lacey informed us that we would never be honored to meet little Chloe. My wife refused to give up hope. I had ordered her with a vengeance to clean up that eyesore, but the books remained. Mariam had refused to comply—one of the few occasions she dared disobey me.

I would never understand why Mariam had remained dead set on wanting time with a snot-nosed brat that would only prove to be another energy-draining disappointment.

The knocks from whoever stood outside on my front porch persisted.

"Come in. The door is unlocked." I barely registered my own words as I picked up yet another book and placed it among the growing pile within my arms.

Oscar's excited bark blended in as background noise with the squeak from the door.

My eyes locked onto the last book I had grabbed. A picture of a large-headed beast graced its cover. *Well, that's intelligent. What kind of child's book would feature a monster? No wonder our society has so much trouble with today's kids. We scar them from the start with terrifying stories.*

"Howdy, Good Ol' Mr. Aldous. You left something important at our house yesterday. Mommy and I thought you'd like us to bring it over. So here it is."

"Fine, set it down wherever." I shot the words out in the same reflexive manner as a horse's tail would twitch at an annoying fly. Yet, my focus remained on the sharp teeth and unruly hair of the beast pictured before me. Had I become like that ugly monster?"

"What's that you've got there?" Dakota's high-pitched voice broke my trance.

"Just some old books."

"Let me see." The disruptive child snatched the item from my hands. The entire stack tumbled from my arms.

"Dakota, you have got to settle down." The firm expression on Alexandra's face softened. "I'm so sorry, Mr. Aldous. Here, let me help you."

She crouched beside me and, one by one, neatly stacked the items against the wall, similar to how Mariam originally had placed them.

"I know this book. It's a great story. Read it to me, please." Dakota shoved it under my nose.

"What? You want *me* to read *this* book?"

"You bet I do. It's great." Dakota grasped my hand with his sweaty palm and pulled me toward the couch.

"Well . . . I guess." Lost for words, I gave in to the child's pleas and sat on the couch. Dakota plopped beside me and opened the cover.

"Mommy, please bring Good Ol' Al his birthday slippers. His feet are bare."

"And cold, too, I bet." Alexandra stood before me and held out the same gift I had rejected the night before while at their house. "Here you go, Mr. Aldous."

Without thinking, I snatched the discarded items from her grip and slid them onto my feet. Soft, plump lamb's wool caressed each toe.

Dakota turned to the first page. "This is how it would be if you were my grandpa." His sky-blue eyes pierced my soul. "Instead of calling you Good Ol' Buddy Al, can I call you Grandpa?"

My head spun. I felt like someone had plucked me out of my ordinary existence, then plopped me into some unknown world. Dumbfounded, I nodded. No response fell from my tongue.

Dakota's cheeks plumped into the biggest grin I'd seen on his freckled face.

Alexandra added the final book to the pile, then sat in the rocking chair. Not knowing what else to do, I began to read the story.

My ears perked at the sound of a knock while Oscar, as usual, barked and spun on the doormat.

Trapped by both child and book, I turned to Alexandra. "Would you get that?" I flipped another page.

Dakota snuggled at my side. The entire unusual incident carried a bizarre sense like I were an outsider spying down on some stranger's affair.

Alexandra rose and went to the door while Oscar trotted at her feet.

I continued to read.

"Mr. Aldous. You have company."

I glanced up. My only daughter, whom I had neither spoken to in almost twenty years nor seen in nearly four, stepped into my home. A little girl with brunette pigtails clung to her pant leg.

"I'd like you to meet my daughter, Chloe." Lacey's facial movements mirrored that of her deceased mother. The child at her side had been an infant the last and only time I had laid eyes on her. Chloe stared with big round chestnut eyes that matched her hair, the same color as Mariam's.

"Dakota, I think it's time for us to leave." Alexandra reached out toward her son.

"But we haven't finished the story yet." Dakota turned toward me with his mouth gaped open.

"That's okay—we'll finish it another day." His mother wiggled her fingers. "Come on, Dakota."

An uncomfortable twinge inched up my spine while, instead of responding to Alexandra's wishes, the boy's eyes locked onto mine.

He relaxed his freckled chin and smiled. "I see blue specks in your eyes. They've never sparkled before. Ohhh, you must be uncovering your diamond!" Dakota closed the book and laid it beside me on the couch, then grabbed his mother's outstretched hand and hopped down. Together they strolled toward my front door.

Alexandra gazed at her son. "It looks like Mr. Aldous is getting a new beginning. New beginnings bring new opportunities, like the baby within my tummy."

Dakota gawked at his mother. His eyes widened to a size that rivaled his gaping mouth.

The twinkle in Alexandra's laugh confirmed all suspicion. "Goodbye, and nice to meet you both." She gestured toward Lacey and little Chloe and then slipped through the opened doorway with her son close in hand.

So often, the ways of God are opposite of what we humans would choose. An awkward silence sliced the air. My legs resembled unbendable tree stumps as I pulled to my feet. The floor folded away like the disappearance of years while the distance that separated Lacey and I lessened. A lifetime of memories flashed before my tired eyes. Speechless, I stood before my only child.

Lacey gazed toward her feet, reminding me of the innocent child she once was.

Chloe tugged at her mother's sleeve. "Is he your daddy?"

Lacey lifted her head. "Yes, darling, I'd like you to meet your grandfather."

I stooped to the child's eye level and stared at an identical image of Lacey at that same age.

Chloe wrapped tiny arms around my neck. She placed a wet kiss on my cheek and then pulled away and giggled. The child stretched onto the tips of her shoes and danced on the carpet, then spun toward the secretary desk and paused. Her gaze aimed toward the hummingbird vase, placed there the night before, after my trip to the graveyard.

"Oooh, that's pretty." Chloe stretched out her hand.

"Careful, Chloe. There's no need to touch."

"That's okay. I bought that for Mariam. Remember how much your mother loved hummingbirds?" As I watched the radiant child, something pierced my heart. "She would have wanted Chloe to have it." I winked at my granddaughter.

"Aahhh, thanks." Chloe cradled the vase in the hook of her arm as she traced an etched hummingbird with her finger.

Lacey choked back a swallow and breathed in deep as her slender fingers combed through strands of rich-brunette hair. "It's no use. I can't hide from you and forgive you at the same time. Chloe deserves much better. We lost our chance to reconcile with Mom now that she has passed. I didn't want to make that same mistake again." A tear ran down her cheek.

My heart pounded. I gazed into Lacey's chocolate brown eyes. Last night, God led me to release my past by placing my slippers beside Mariam's grave, and now He answers my prayers for a second chance in life as I stand before my only child. Only a God of love could create such a miracle. This time I won't let Him down.

1-13